A DEADLY GAME

They stepped out the back door, into the cool, dark summer night. Cassie knew instantly that there was something wrong. It was too dark, too cold on Lake Solaria. There were no lights on anywhere. The usual sounds of the lake—birds, radios, people—had vanished.

Nicole made her way through the darkness without faltering, leading them to the bridge. The two little girls carried their grisly burden easily; Rita Montana's body was strangely light.

"Here, Adele," said Nicole. "We'll push her in right here. Then we'll go back to the house and I'll explain everything."

My name's not Adele and I don't want to go back to the house! Cassie wanted to scream, but she could not even speak. Nicole made her drop Rita's body and shove it into the dark water.

"We're finished," Nicole said. "Let's go back and play."

Cassie screamed at last. Rita had flipped over in the water. She stared up at the girl with wide, dead eyes, pointing an accusing finger.

CLARE McNALLY

SOMEBODY COME AND PLAY

TOR HORROR

A TOM DOHERTY ASSOCIATES BOOK

SOMEBODY COME AND PLAY

Cover art by Joe DeVito

A Tor Book
Published by Tom Doherty Associates, Inc.
175 Fifth Avenue
New York, N.Y. 10010

Tor® is a registered trademark of Tom Doherty Associates, Inc.

ISBN: 0-812-52164-1

First edition: September 1987

Printed in the United States of America

0 9 8 7 6 5 4 3 2

To William P. McNally
The reason this book takes place in Ohio

Many thanks and love to:
Dorothy McNally, Denise Marcil,
Susan Geisbusch Walmsley and
Mike and Marta Pastore

PROLOGUE

LISTENING CAREFULLY FOR the sound of her school bus, Cassie Larchmont sifted through the wild flowers that grew along the lake behind her house. She chose only the prettiest ones for her teacher's bouquet, breathing in their sweet aroma as a spring breeze blew across Lake Solaria.

Her science project sat on the picnic table. The models of a butterfly's life cycle, fashioned of salt-and-flour clay, were pinned to a piece of Styrofoam. Cassie was very proud of her work, and knew it would bring her an A at the end of fifth grade.

Attracted by the smell of salt, a fluffy, black and white mutt rested his forepaws on the table. As Cassie turned around, the dog snatched a clay cocoon.

"Solo, you dumb dog!" Cassie cried. "Give that back!"

Dropping her flowers, she raced after the dog. Solo wove his way through the patches of woods, backyards, and apple groves that lined the lake. Shouting, Cassie ran past houses that were boarded up, waiting for summer residents.

"Solo!"

Lake Solaria shared its name with the Ohio town of which it was the center. The lake was kidney-shaped, half a mile across at its widest and just over a mile long from end to end. Some forty years earlier, several enterprising families had built a wooden bridge across the lake at its narrowest point. The planks had been maintained carefully over the years, replaced whenever necessary. Because the bridge was close to the water's surface, it made a wonderful place from which to dive and fish.

"Come back here!" Cassie yelled as Solo shot across the bridge.

She heard the loud honking of the school-bus horn, and looked from the bridge to her house, not knowing what to do. She couldn't be late for school, but she couldn't bring in an unfinished science project, either. Mrs. Greggs was tough, and wouldn't believe any excuses.

"Oh, baloney," she moaned, starting across the bridge. "I guess Mom'll have to drive me."

Solo was nowhere to be seen. Reaching the far end of the bridge, Cassie looked in both directions, calling to her pet. At last she spotted Solo's black and white coat, barely visible through the tall grass that grew around Lake Solaria's oldest and biggest house.

"Uh-oh," Cassie whispered, slowing to a walk.

She gazed at the Victorian mansion with wide blue eyes, feeling a little nervous as she took in the peeling gray paint and broken shutters. The house was more than a century old, built by the man who had originally owned all the property around the lake. Cassie's mother had told her many times to stay away from the place, warning her that a crazy old woman lived there. Rumor said that she had murdered her own children long ago, and that no one had ever found their bodies. Children around the lake often teased each other: "Myrtle's gonna getcha! Myrtle's gonna getcha!"

But now, Cassie had to get her model back from the dog. Carefully she approached the overgrown grass, one hand reaching toward Solo. Oblivious to her, he licked at the salty clay.

"Solo, you mutt," Cassie called softly, afraid that Myrtle might hear her. "Come on, Solo!"

This time the dog made no effort to get away from her. Sighing in exasperation, Cassie walked up to him and yanked the cocoon from his mouth. She groaned.

"Oh, gross! It's all slimy! You dumb dog!"

A door slammed.

"Who is that? Who's there?" called a quavering voice.

Cassie straightened up with a gasp, and stared as a fragile old woman walked down the back steps of the mansion. The woman shaded her eyes with a knotted, slightly tremulous hand.

"Ellen? Is that you?"

Cassie took a step back, her eyes wide with fear. She'd never seen Myrtle up close, and the woman looked just as crazy as everyone said she was. The old lady smiled, stretching out her arms.

"Oh, my sweet girl!" she cried. "You've come back to me! I knew you would! Where's your brother, Ellen? Where's Norman?"

Cassie found her legs and turned to run toward the bridge. Maybe Myrtle really was crazy! Maybe she'd kill Cassie, the way she'd killed her own children!

Cassie kept looking back over her shoulder as she ran, afraid the old woman was following her. Because she wasn't watching her step, she tumbled over a root and went crashing to the ground. Her chin smacked hard against a rock, sending dulling waves of pain into her head.

Cassie moaned, finding it impossible to stand as the grass and flowers swayed before her eyes, and she tasted blood on her lips.

"Ellen! Come to Mother, Ellen!"

Oh, golly! Myrtle's gonna kill me! Cassie thought. *I just know she's gonna kill me!*

Cassie began to cry in fear. She wanted to shout for help, but knew no one would hear her. There were only two other families living year-round on this side of the lake, and they were much too far away.

"Please, help me," Cassie mumbled. "Don't let her kill me!"

Stupid dog! Stupid science project!

Another breeze whistled over the lake, but this time it wasn't the soft wind of spring. It was icy, like winter, and it sent ribbon-thin wisps of blond hair flying into Cassie's face. She heard a soft, childish voice.

"Don't be afraid," it said. "I'll help you."

Cassie felt herself being helped to her feet. She rubbed her aching head, then turned to thank her rescuer. To her surprise, she was standing alone, just a few yards from the bridge.

"Where are you?" she called, turning to look in every direction. She was relieved to see that Myrtle was no longer following her. But who had helped her to her feet? Cassie called and called, but no one answered her.

"Weird!" she said. She sighed deeply. "Well, I better go tell Mom what happened."

Solo bounded up to her, wagging his tail.

"I'm in big trouble, you dumb mutt," Cassie said, "and it's all your fault!"

More interested now in getting home than in the mysterious person who had rescued her, Cassie ran back across the bridge.

ONE

THIRTY YEARS OF waiting was too much for Myrtle Hollenbeck to bear. Thirty years of looking out her window and watching for the return of two children who never came had finally driven the old woman to madness.

Clutching the dusty banister with a thin, gnarled hand, she walked painfully down her cellar steps. Her body didn't cast much of a shadow on the cement wall; the silhouette stretched thin like some caricature. Myrtle paused for a moment at the bottom of the stairs, her weak heart thumping. Smells that had been trapped in the unventilated room, musty odors from rain that had leaked through the casement windows, wafted toward her.

Myrtle went to a warped and peeling old chest and opened the lid. She pulled out a rope, a stuffed bear, and a doll. The doll's rubber face had dried and cracked long ago; its dress was fringed with rot. *Funny that Ellen didn't take this with her when she disappeared*, Myrtle mused.

With the rope trailing behind her like a child's pull-toy, Myrtle went back up the stairs. In the kitchen she picked up a rickety footstool, then walked out into the night. Wind stirred the surface of the lake that had been her home for three decades, carrying a chill that seemed unnatural for the end of May.

"Ellen?" she called. "Norman? Can you hear me, children?"

Myrtle knew where they were now. Voices in the night had told her they were waiting. She walked across the yard to an old oak tree, setting the stool down at the base of its thick trunk. Myrtle worked the rope into a slipknot. She hummed as she did this, a song she had sung long ago, when her children had been there. She knew they were listening and would be comforted by it.

Myrtle's bones ached from the wear of arthritis, but there was a strength in her tonight that she had never felt before. She climbed onto the stool and threw the loose end of the rope over a branch above her head, then stretched up to tie a strong knot. The action was effortless, as if someone were helping her.

Myrtle smoothed back the tendrils of gray hair that the wind had brushed into her face. She had to look perfect for her reunion with her little ones. She put the noose over her head.

"Ellen! Norman! Mommy's coming!"

The last syllable was barely out when the stool shot from beneath her feet. Her body thumped down with a jerk. Myrtle's last sight was a smiling face very close to her own.

Somebody was pushing a little girl's head under the lake. The child struggled, surfaced, and went under again. She came up one last time, blood pouring down over her eyes, coloring everything she saw a bright red. There was blood everywhere. In the water, in the sky, everywhere. . . .

"No!"

Cassie awakened with a start from her nightmare. Her fingers dug into the soft body of her handmade cloth doll. The little girl pulled it close, breathing heavily. Slowly, the dream faded, until it was no more than a vague collection of lights and colors.

After a few moments, Cassie opened her eyes and looked out at the water below her window. Lake Solaria was like a big, black hole tonight, with no moon shining on its surface. From the safety of her nest of dolls and stuffed animals, she could see Solo tracking something along the water's edge.

Cassie raised her eyes to the old Victorian house across the lake. Whenever she saw it she was reminded of that day almost a month ago, when she'd been chased by the crazy old woman who lived there. Her mother had been so angry to learn that Cassie had gone on the property that she'd grounded her for a week. Cassie hadn't told Carolyn that Myrtle had tried to catch her, fearing her mother's anger more than the old woman. Carolyn hated that house intensely, and never hesitated to say so. Trouble was, she never explained to Cassie just why she hated it.

There were few lights on in the house's many windows, but that didn't surprise Cassie. She had heard that Myrtle didn't use much of the house. Still, something about the place seemed strange tonight.

It took Cassie a moment to realize what it was. The back door was wide open, a broad banner of light shining onto the overgrown grass. What could Myrtle be doing out in the middle of the night, Cassie wondered?

Her gaze traced the path of light across the backyard. For a second, she couldn't make out what she was seeing in the glare. Was that someone standing near a tree, looking across the lake as if he could see Cassie watching? And then, there was no one standing near the tree at all. Cassie saw a shadow moving across the grass in a wide arc. When she saw what cast it, she began to scream.

Seconds later, footsteps pounded up the carpeted stairs outside her room.

"Cassie? Cassie, what's wrong?"

Cassie's door opened and her mother appeared, her auburn hair half in curlers and her robe unbelted. Carolyn hurried to take the screaming child in her arms.

"M-Mommy!" Cassie stammered. She pointed a small, shaking hand at the window.

Puzzled, Carolyn looked across the lake, and caught sight of Myrtle Hollenbeck's ravaged body hanging from a big oak tree. She gasped, turning Cassie's face away from the sight.

"Oh, my God," she whispered.

She stood up, leading Cassie from the room with an arm firmly around the child's trembling shoulders.

"I'm going to call the police," she said.

They entered Carolyn's room, just across the hall from her daughter's. Sniffling, Cassie let her mother help her into the big double bed and tuck her under a quilt. Carolyn reached for the phone on the nightstand and dialed the Lake Solaria police. When she'd told the dispatcher about Myrtle, she hung up and climbed into bed next to her daughter, holding the ten-year-old close. She could feel Cassie's body shaking.

"Why did she do that, Mommy?" Cassie asked, the blue irises of her wide eyes magnified by her tears.

"I don't know, Cassie," Carolyn answered.

She couldn't tell her daughter why Myrtle had killed herself, couldn't put her own fears into words a ten-year-old would understand. Ever since she'd been a child, living in this very house, Carolyn had had nightmares about the Hollenbeck place. Maybe it was because she'd overheard so many whispered conversations after Myrtle's children had vanished. But she had known for years that the house was a place of evil. Carolyn knew that something dark and insidious had murdered that old woman.

The doorbell rang. Holding hands, mother and daughter descended the staircase and opened the front door. Carolyn was relieved to see her good friend Susan Walken on the front steps. It was obvious by the disarray of Susan's brown curls and the fact that she still wore her bloodstained white coat that she'd dropped everything at the lab to come here. Susan threw her arms around Carolyn.

"You poor thing!" she cried, her high cheekbones flushed in excitement.

"I saw her first," Cassie interrupted, frowning up at Susan.

"That must have frightened you, Cassie," Susan said, pulling away from Carolyn to embrace the child. Cassie wrinkled her nose; Susan's jacket smelled of formaldehyde.

"I wish Paul were here," Carolyn said. Cassie's father had always been the rock she leaned on, and even six years after his death Carolyn still needed him at times.

Carolyn noticed a tall man standing behind Susan. He was studying the paneled room through wire-framed glasses, taking in the brick fireplace, the braided rug, the plaid-upholstered furniture. Old Royal Doulton statues lined the mantel.

"This is Detective Robert Landers," Susan said. "He's in charge of this case. I tagged along with him when I heard it was you who reported Myrtle's death."

Robert shook Carolyn's hand. His grip was firm, and her fingers tingled a little after he released them. His graying black hair—more gray than black—told Carolyn he was probably in his forties. His polite but tight-lipped smile and three-piece gray suit spoke of a conservative man, but then Carolyn noticed the red dogs embroidered on his tie, and guessed that he wouldn't be like the cold, stuffy investigators who had come after Paul's death.

"Susan talks about you all the time," Robert said, his voice soft and deep.

"Robert has to ask you some questions," Susan said. "It'll only take a few minutes, since we have to join the pathology team across the lake."

"Please, come in and sit down," Carolyn said.

She settled onto the couch; Cassie curled up next to her. The little girl kept her eyes on Robert, looking wary of him, all the while toying with Solo's floppy ears. Robert smiled at her in a reassuring way. At first, he couldn't see any resemblance between mother and daughter. Cassie was a pretty child, looking like sunshine with her radiantly pale skin and blond hair. Carolyn's hair was a thick, wavy auburn and the eyes that gazed worriedly at him were greenish-hazel. But then he saw their clasped hands, and noticed that they both had the same knobby fingers. And, like her mother's, Cassie's blue eyes squinted just a bit when she looked him over.

"I bet you're Cassie," Robert said. "Susan told me you were a very smart little girl. I want to make sure no more scary things happen here. Will you help me?"

Cassie's expression changed suddenly to one of keen interest. "You mean, like Nancy Drew?"

"Sort of," Robert said. "Can I ask you some questions?"

Cassie nodded.

"Did you see Mrs. Hollenbeck hang herself?"

"No," Cassie said. "I woke up from a dream and there she was."

"Was she alone?" Robert asked. "Was anyone else there?"

Cassie looked toward the picture window, thoughtful. For a few moments, the only sound in the room was the gurgling of the aquarium's filter system.

"I don't think so," she said finally. Had there

been someone there? She couldn't quite remember.

"Are you certain?"

"Robert, Cassie is a very honest girl," Susan said. "If she says no one else was there, you can believe her."

"Of course I believe her," Robert said. But he believed his instincts even more, and wrote 'Possible second party?' in his notebook.

Cassie looked up at her mother. "I'm tired, Mommy," she said, her tone weary. "I don't want to talk about this anymore."

"This is so hard on her," Carolyn said, hugging the child.

"I know," Robert replied, sighing. "And I'm sorry to put her through this. But she is a witness."

"To what?" Carolyn asked. "Some crazy old woman's suicide?"

"We can't be sure of that yet, can we?" Robert asked. "Now, Cassie, are you sure there's nothing else you can tell me?"

"I'm sure," Cassie said.

"Well, thanks," Robert told her, smiling. "You helped a great deal."

More than she realized, he thought. He had seen her slight hesitation when asked if anyone was with Myrtle. The child wasn't lying, he was certain of that. But she'd been sleeping just before she looked out the window. It was possible she had forgotten.

He turned to Carolyn.

"Mrs. Larchmont," he asked, "what can you tell me about Myrtle Hollenbeck? Do you know the name of her next of kin?"

He wrote while she talked, studying Carolyn's

face. In the years he'd been a detective, Robert had learned to read even the most subtle facial expressions, and what he saw in Carolyn Larchmont's eyes was fear. Susan had told him that she was a little on the shy side, but this seemed to go far beyond that. She had the look of someone who had been keeping a terrifying secret for years.

His heart stopped for a second. She looked, he realized suddenly, like Lynda had during her illness. Lynda's secret *had* been terrifying. She was dying of a blood disease, but it was just like her to not want to burden anyone else with her problems. Not even her husband. By the time Robert had discovered what was going on, it was too late.

He gripped his pencil tightly and focused his eyes on his notebook. He was here to do business, not remember Lynda. What had he written? "Cyril Hollenbeck." Myrtle's husband. He had left years ago, and his whereabouts were unknown.

"It all seems pretty clear to me," Susan was saying. "She certainly took her own life."

"Still, I'm going to request an autopsy," Robert said. "I want to make certain no outside forces helped that woman kill herself."

Oh, but there were outside forces, Carolyn thought.

She kept silent. Much as she loved Susan, her friend was a woman of science, and would only laugh at Carolyn's superstitions. And she certainly didn't want to voice them in front of Detective Landers, a virtual stranger.

"I hate that house," she said at last. "I hope to God they tear it down."

TWO

SOMETIME IN THE early morning, Susan gently covered Myrtle's body and stepped away from the gurney to rub her stinging, tired eyes. Myrtle had obviously been in poor health for years. That, combined with her mounting sorrow over the loss of her two children, made it clear to Susan why she had committed suicide.

Susan untied her black rubber apron and hung it on one of a series of hooks on the tiled wall. When they'd taken Myrtle down, the rope she'd used had been placed carefully in a plastic bag. Not just because it was the means of her death, but because of something extra, something odd—a thick, yellow substance clumped at the knot around the branch. Nobody had any idea what it was.

But that was for the lab people to figure out. Susan picked up the Hollenbeck file and left the morgue, walking up a cement staircase into a brightly lit hallway. In a quiet little town like Lake Solaria, there wasn't much to keep the coroner's office busy. Susan often worked by herself, blasting

15

rock music to drive away the chills that came from being alone.

Tonight, there was one office that she knew would be occupied. Robert Landers's door stood ajar. He was leaning back in his brown leather chair, studying a picture of his wife that he cradled in his large hands. When he saw Susan, he set the photo back on his desk and reached for Myrtle's file.

"You didn't have to wait," Susan said. "There's nothing here. Myrtle certainly had no help in this."

"What about the yellow stuff on the rope?" Robert asked. "Do you know what that is yet?"

"This isn't Columbus, Robert," Susan said. "We don't have a labful of researchers working the night shift. The samples I took will have to be sent out."

"Then you shouldn't jump to conclusions, should you?"

Susan put her hands on her hips, her green eyes flashing. "Last time I looked," she said, "staying up until two in the morning wasn't called 'jumping to conclusions.'"

Robert opened the file. "Sorry," he said. "But this really has me bothered."

He scanned the pages. Susan's writing was minuscule, and even with his glasses on he had to squint.

"Why?" Susan asked. "We both saw her hanging there. There aren't any bruises on her, with the exception of those around her neck. And when we went through the house, there was no sign of a struggle."

Robert pointed to something on the page. "But

look at this," he said. "You say here that Myrtle suffered from advanced arthritis for years. She had cataracts, and there were signs of malnutrition. On top of this, the woman was seventy-five years old."

"And almost half those years were spent in misery," Susan said, "waiting for those children who disappeared."

"But why now?" Robert demanded. "Why not ten years ago? Or, for that matter, ten years from now? What set her off? Who made her do this to herself?"

"What makes you so sure there was a second party involved?"

"The little girl," Robert said. "I think she was confused about what she saw."

Susan shook her head. "Robert, I think you try too hard," she said. "Cassie was tired and confused."

"But Myrtle had to have been helped," Robert insisted. "Look at how sickly she was, how weak. Tell me where a woman like that gets the strength to climb up on a stool and tie a rope around a branch overhead."

"She was determined," Susan said. "I've seen crazier things happen. When I was working in New York City, I did an autopsy on an asylum inmate who managed to bend the bars on a tenth-story window and jumped to his death. Then there was the body that came in without a head. The man's wife, who was half his size, had gotten so sick of his abuse that she found the strength to decapitate him with one slice of a butcher's knife. Impossible? The word has no meaning to me."

"Then you can't believe that my theory is impossible," Robert said. "There are just too many loose ends to write this off as a simple suicide. Give me the benefit of the doubt, Susan. Hold on to the body until I can get more information."

Susan met his pleading glance and saw how much this meant to him. "All right," she said with a sigh. "We have to try to find the next of kin anyway. She'll stay downstairs until then."

Robert smiled. "Thanks," he said. "You'll see I'm right about this."

He slid the papers back into the file, then tapped it sideways on his desktop. "Listen, there's an all-night diner we could go to," he said. "I owe you at least a cup of coffee."

Susan held up her hands. "I'll pass," she said. "The only thing I'm interested in now is sleep. Tomorrow's my day off, and Chris Geisly and I are heading to a fair in Coshocton. I need my energy for all that walking. Good night, Robert."

"Good night, Susan.

Ten minutes later, Robert was on his way home. As he entered the house, three sleek Irish setters, their cinnamon coats glistening under the track lights in his living room, scampered to greet him.

"Hello, girls," Robert said, crouching down to pet them. "You waited up for me?"

He stood and walked to the kitchen, mother dog and daughters following close behind. After refilling their food and water dishes, Robert walked down a darkened hallway to his bedroom. The ranch had seven rooms, far too many for a man alone, but Robert had no desire to give it up. The death of a loved one might make some people want to hide any reminders of that person, but Robert was comforted by the things Lynda had brought into their home.

Feeling very tired, he undressed and climbed into bed, under the wedding-ring quilt Lynda's mother had given them on their first anniversary. It still had the stain from the red wine they'd spilled on it once. Absently fingering the spot, Robert drifted off to sleep.

Dreams came rapidly. He was talking to Myrtle Hollenbeck. She stood several yards away; Lake Solaria rippled in the background. She held hands with two small children, a boy and a girl of about eight and nine.

"Do you see?" she asked: *"Everyone laughed at me, but I knew in my heart that one day my babies would return."*

The children turned to smile up at their mother. The sides of their heads were missing, smashed to bloody pulp, the brains showing pinkish-gray through mounds of swollen purple flesh.

Robert jerked himself awake, but the images of the dream refused to fade.

"No wonder you dreamed about those kids." He spoke aloud, finding comfort in the sound of his own voice. "After all those pictures you saw to-night."

He thought back over his investigation of Myrtle's house. It had been a cold place, not just because the thermostat was kept at sixty, but in its overall spirit. Robert had sensed immediately that this house hadn't known love in years.

There was nothing of Myrtle's husband in the place, no pictures, no mementos. But the children were another story. Throughout every room, there had been dozens of pictures of the two. They covered the walls, filled the tables, occupied the shelves. Closer inspection showed that many were multiple reprints. It was as if Myrtle was afraid she'd forget the children's faces if they weren't constantly in her sight.

There had been pictures, but little else. Most of the rooms were empty and obviously had been for a long time, ruling out theft as a motive for driving the woman to suicide. Robert knew there would be no easy answers to the questions whirling around in his mind. But right now, he was too exhausted to deal with them. He closed his eyes again. By the time dawn broke, he was fast asleep. This time, there were no dreams.

THREE

DURING THE NEXT few days, while Robert pursued his theory that Myrtle had been forced to hang herself, Carolyn Larchmont did her best to have the old Hollenbeck mansion torn down. She believed that it was unsafe and too great a temptation to the children on the lake. But several weeks went by, May turned into June, and the house was still standing. Carolyn's trip to City Hall had been a wasted effort, for once they heard how old the place was, there was talk that it might be considered a historic monument. Carolyn wondered why anyone would want to preserve the house. With Myrtle dead, the once-stately Victorian, was more dilapidated than ever. Its gray paint had long since peeled off in strips that hung like clawed fingers. The trimmings were either loose or vanished and the cobwebs in the windows were indistinguishable from the rotted lace curtains.

"Ugly old place," Carolyn mumbled, reaching for the paper her dot-matrix printer had just finished churning out. She quickly scanned the green-

and-white-striped sheet. Carolyn operated a small mail-order business, specializing in local crafts. She was still amazed at how city people were fascinated by the handmade, country-store items her catalogue offered. Her printout showed twenty orders for stuffed-cat doorstops alone.

"Hi, Mom!" Cassie came into the room, her blond hair pulled back in a long braid. She put her arms around Carolyn and gave her a good-morning kiss.

"Can I go to the Montanas'?" she asked. "Diane's coming in today and I want to wait for her."

"Have you done your chores?"

"I made my bed already," Cassie said, "and my dishes are in the sink. Oh, and I fed the fish right when I came downstairs."

"Okay, I'll see you at lunchtime," Carolyn said, giving her daughter a hug.

She watched Cassie go, feeling a surge of warmth run through her. Cassie was so much like her father. Carolyn looked at her lemon-ice hair and blue eyes, at the way her tongue played with her teeth, at the forward bend of her earlobes, and knew Paul was still with her, present in every cell of their daughter's body.

Carolyn closed her eyes and thought about how Paul had talked for weeks about buying Cassie a special book for her birthday. He had been so excited the day he went into town to make the purchase. But he had never brought it home, never wrapped it, never grinned to see four-year-old Cassie tearing at the paper. An armed robbery was taking place just as he walked into the store, and in a moment of panic the thief had turned and pumped a bullet into Paul's chest. He'd died instantly.

Now there was only Cassie. Nothing, Carolyn vowed, would hurt that child.

But there were things to be grateful for. At least Cassie had stopped asking questions about Myrtle's death. She was prone to nightmares, and Carolyn didn't want her dwelling on that horrible incident.

Unknown to Carolyn, Cassie hadn't stopped thinking about Myrtle. Sometimes at night, images of a face staring at her from across the lake haunted her thoughts. Had there been anyone there? She couldn't be sure. Still, those staring eyes were so vivid, so mean-looking. They were like tiger's eyes, illuminated by moonlight. Wanting to share the incident with friends and thereby lessen its severity, Cassie couldn't wait to tell Diane Montana and Lisa Westin what had happened. No one at school had believed her story, but her summer friends would!

As she walked along the water's edge, Solo bounding at her heels, Cassie heard footsteps behind her, and looked over her shoulder to see Georgie Canfield. Cassie turned her back to him and hurried toward Diane's house. She didn't like Georgie. He was the lake's troublemaker, a high-school dropout rumored to be a drug dealer.

"You little snob!" Georgie yelled. "Don'tcha wanna walk with me?"

Georgie grabbed her arm. Solo growled softly, his

big brown eyes angry behind his mop of black and white fur. Cassie's mouth dropped open, but before she could yell, Georgie said in a low voice, "I've been lookin' at you, girl. You're growing up, gettin' really pretty."

Solo barked wildly, trying to protect the little girl, and Cassie kicked the boy hard in the shins.

"You let go or I'll yell for my mother!" she cried.

Suddenly, Georgie's eyes went wide. He let go of Cassie, the pressure from his fingers leaving white stripes on her skin. Georgie pressed his hands to his temples, his eyes bulging, strange gulping noises coming from his throat.

"Oh, my God, it hurts," he choked out, emphasizing each word like some sort of robot.

Cassie shook her head in bewilderment, wondering if she should run for her mother. But suddenly Georgie breathed in hard through his nose and tilted his head back.

"Bad stuff, man," he said.

He turned and limped away, rubbing the helter-skelter mess of his brown hair. Cassie watched him for a moment, at a loss. What on earth had just happened? Well, it would give her something else to talk about when she met Diane. She turned around, and almost bumped into a little girl standing directly behind her.

"That boy is mean," the girl said, staring at Georgie's retreating figure. "He shouldn't have hurt you like that."

"Georgie's an idiot," Cassie said. "I don't like him at all." She studied the girl. "I don't know you. Are you a new summerie?"

The other girl giggled. "A what?"

"A summerie," Cassie repeated. "That's what I call folks who live on the lake just in the summer. I live here all year. My name's Cassie Larchmont."

"I'm Nicole Morgan," the new girl said.

Cassie looked over the girl's calf-length pinafore dress and black ankle boots. It was a crazy outfit to wear in June, she thought, but even so, Nicole was prettier than anyone Cassie had ever seen. Her hair fell to her waist in long brown ringlets, and was held back from her face with two silver clips. Nicole rubbed at one deep-set brown eye with a tiny finger, and Cassie gasped to see that her hands were as small as a toddler's.

"It's rude to stare," Nicole said, tucking her hands into the pockets of her apron.

"I'm sorry," Cassie said. She smiled, shuffled her feet, then laughed a bit. "I'm just so goofy when I meet new people!"

"I don't think you're goofy," Nicole said. "I think you're beautiful. I wish I had your yellow hair."

"I wish I had your long curls!" Cassie exclaimed. "Does your mom set your hair like that?"

Nicole shook her head.

"I'm going to meet my friend Diane," Cassie said. "Her family is coming today for the summer." She looked down the beach. "Look! There they are! There's the Montanas' car!"

She ran off, leaving Nicole behind. Diane leaned out through the car window and waved, her black curls fluttering in the wind. Both girls squealed in joy. Cassie stopped at the driveway's edge, watching as the Bronco pulled up to the little blue house.

"Hi, Cassie!" Diane cried, climbing out of the car. She ran to embrace her friend.

"There's time for that later," Rita Montana said, cradling a box marked "Clothes" in her arms. "Grab a bag to carry in."

"Mom, I haven't seen Cassie since last September!" Diane said, yanking a suitcase out of the truck. "Gosh, Cassie, you got taller."

"And prettier," Diane's father, Andy, said.

Cassie giggled.

"She got fatter," said Diane's younger brother. "I think she's getting ba-zooms."

"David!" Rita cried.

"Still a pest, I see," Cassie said.

The seven-year-old grinned impishly and followed his father into the house. Cassie suddenly felt a hand on her head.

"How's my other sister?" seventeen-year-old Bill asked.

"Fine," Cassie said with a shy smile.

"Help me carry something in," Diane said. "The sooner we get unpacked, the sooner we can have fun. Want to go swimming? Or maybe take out the canoe?"

"That'd be great," Cassie said.

"When's Lisa coming?" Diane asked, walking up the porch steps.

"Day after tomorrow," Cassie reported. "She called me from Toledo the other day. Her dad's got some sort of doctors' meeting he has to go to first."

Cassie had completely forgotten about the new girl, and she didn't notice Nicole standing in the distance watching them with a frown on her face.

"I'll take this little box," Diane said. She slid it out of the truck, and stumbled a little as she realized how heavy it was. "Oof! What's in this thing?"

"It says 'Utensils,'" Cassie read.

"Good, I'm getting hungry," Diane said. "Maybe after we unpack this we can eat."

She walked up the sandy driveway to the house, her body bent forward by the weight of the box. Halfway up the stairs, Diane suddenly felt a hard push at her back and stumbled forward.

Something sharp cut into her bare leg, just below her shorts. Diane screamed and rolled over onto her back, her leg stretched down the steps. Blood gushed from a long cut that ran from her hip to the middle of her thigh.

"Mrs. Montana!" Cassie cried, dropping her own box to run to her friend. "Diane, what happened?"

"I fell," Diane wailed, tears streaming down her face.

The back door burst open, and Diane's parents and brothers ran out.

"Get a washcloth, David," Andy ordered. "Bill, find the first aid kit. It's in the box marked 'Bathroom.'"

Rita was holding her daughter in her arms, staring openmouthed at the child's wound.

"Mommy, it hurts!"

Bill returned with a washcloth and the first aid kit. As Andy cleaned and dressed the wound, Diane looked at it and cried.

"Someone pushed me," she whimpered.

David looked accusingly at Cassie. She backed away, her eyes wide.

"I didn't do it!" she exclaimed.

"Of course she didn't," Andy said. "Diane, there's no one else out here. I think you just tripped."

"Maybe we should take her to the hospital," Rita said.

"*Mom!*" Diane yelled.

"It'll be okay," Andy said. "I'll get the truck ready."

"Mom, look at this," Bill said. He held up the utensils box. A gleaming blade jutted from one corner, stained with Diane's blood. Rita gasped, taking the knife from the box.

"How could that have happened?" she asked. "I packed these myself, very carefully!"

"The box must have gotten smashed during the trip here," Bill suggested.

Andy came back from the truck and took Diane from her mother. Diane rested her head on his shoulder, her sobs now silent tears. Cassie and the boys stood on the porch, watching them go. Andy promised to buy Diane a present as he helped her into her seat.

"Well, there's no point in you hanging around, Cassie," Bill said. "Diane will call you when she gets back."

"Sure," Cassie said, wondering if David really believed she had pushed Diane. "I'll see you later."

She ran down the porch steps and started home, then suddenly noticed Nicole. She realized she had neglected the new girl and felt sorry.

"I can't believe what a creep I am sometimes," she apologized. "I didn't mean to leave you flat!"

"It's all right," Nicole said. "You were so happy to see your friend."

Cassie frowned. "Poor Diane. That must have really hurt!"

"I'm sure," Nicole said. "Cassie, do you want to play with me now? Do you have any dolls?"

"I have lots of dolls," Cassie said. "I can bring some outside, and we'll have a picnic lunch."

"You're really sweet," Nicole said. "I like you. Even if the other girls fight with you, I'll always be your friend."

Cassie shook her head. "Lisa and Diane and I never fight. We're the best of friends!"

Nicole stopped short. Cassie took a few more steps before she realized the new girl wasn't beside her. Turning, she saw Nicole gazing at her with a sad look on her face.

"What's wrong?" Cassie asked.

"Could we ever be best friends?" Nicole asked. "You can't be best friends with three people."

"Why not?" Cassie said. She didn't wait for an answer. "Will you come on? It's lunchtime and I'm hungry!"

She ran ahead to her house, then turned to wait for Nicole. But, to her surprise, the child was nowhere in sight.

"Weird!" Cassie said.

She went into the house, unaware that Nicole was still watching her, hidden from view.

FOUR

CAROLYN WAS BARBECUING chicken by the light of a string of Japanese lanterns when Diane limped up to the backyard that evening. Cassie put down a tray of multicolored plastic tumblers and ran to her friend. Diane lifted up her tiered skirt to show off the butterfly bandages that crisscrossed down her thigh.

"I didn't even cry when the doctor put them on," she said proudly. "He said I was his best patient ever!"

"I'm glad it didn't hurt," Carolyn said. "Would you like to have dinner with us, Diane?"

"No, thank you," she answered. "My mom felt really sorry about what happened, so she made my favorite dinner tonight—ravioli. I'm stuffed!"

Carolyn laughed. "Ravioli sounds wonderful. I hope your mom invites us over one night this summer."

"Maybe we could all have a big picnic," Cassie said. "The Montanas and the Westins and the Larchmonts and the Morgans."

Carolyn sat down, putting the plate of chicken in

the center of the table. "Who are the Morgans?" she asked. "I haven't heard of them."

"Nicole Morgan's the newest kid on the lake this summer," Cassie said. "She's really nice."

"Is she our age?" Diane asked. "Where's she from?"

"I think she's our age," Cassie said. "And I don't know where she's from. The other side of the lake, I think."

Diane looked across the water, scanning the houses on the opposite shore, as if one of them might look different for having a new occupant. Finally, her eyes came to rest on the Hollenbeck mansion. In the dimming light, it didn't even look real, more like an image on an old black-and-white TV set. "Why's it so dark over there?" she asked, pointing at the house.

Cassie gasped. "Oh, I forgot to tell you!" she cried. "Mrs. Hollenbeck died a few weeks ago. She hanged herself, and I saw her from my window!"

"Gross!"

"Cassie," Carolyn said, "I don't think you should be talking like that."

Cassie pouted. "Okay," she said. "Anyway, Diane, now the house is empty."

"I wonder what it looks like inside?" Diane said thoughtfully.

"You can forget any ideas you're forming in that little head of yours, Diane," Carolyn said firmly. "Cassie is absolutely forbidden to go near that place."

"It's just a dumpy old mansion, Mom," Cassie said.

"I don't care," Carolyn said.

She stood up, stacking empty plates. Solo followed her to the back steps, anticipating handouts.

"I'll be working inside," Carolyn said. "You come in when you see the light go on at D'Achille's."

D'Achille's was a bar that overlooked the lake where the shoreline bent like an elbow. Old Harold D'Achille had put up a large neon sign along its side, which he turned on each night promptly at eight. Because she could easily see it from almost anywhere on the lake, the sign had become Cassie's signal that it was time to go home.

Diane leaned across the table. "How come your mom's so scared of that place?" she whispered.

"I don't know," Cassie said. "But she's always hated it. I heard her tell her friend Susan that she had nightmares about it when she was a kid. I think she keeps remembering those kids who disappeared back in the fifties."

Diane groaned, rubbing her arms. "Gives me the creeps to think about it," she said. "What do you suppose happened to them?"

"Everybody says they ran away," Cassie said. "But I think old Myrtle killed them! She was so mean and crazy!"

Diane looked across the lake again. The darkened windows made her think of black, staring, gouged-out eyes. "Did she have her eyes open?"

"I couldn't tell from so far away," Cassie said. "But it was disgusting. This detective came here and asked a lot of questions."

They heard a movement in the bushes nearby

and both looked toward the sound. A girl dressed in white jeans and a heart-print sweatshirt emerged, her light brown curls tied up with a lacy pink scarf.

"It's Lisa!" Cassie cried.

Lisa ran to her two friends, and they hugged each other amidst a chorus of giggles.

"Surprise!" Lisa squealed. "Daddy's meeting was canceled, so we came down early!"

They went back to the picnic table. Lisa hoisted herself up onto the tabletop, while Cassie and Diane straddled the benches. Lisa displayed her two sneaker-clad feet.

"Look, I've got Pembrokes," she said proudly. "They're the latest style, so Mommy just had to buy them for me. Daddy says they're too expensive, but I got them anyway."

Cassie and Diane rolled their eyes at each other, wondering if Lisa was going to spend the evening bragging about all her new summer clothes. They both wished their parents could afford the things Lisa had. Not to be outdone, Diane pulled up her skirt.

"Look at my bandages," she said. "I had an accident today."

Lisa made a disgusted face. "Gross," she said. "What happened?"

Diane told her story, watching Lisa's blue eyes grow round with fascination.

"I hate getting stitches," Lisa said. "When my neighbor's dog bit me a couple years ago, I got a hundred stitches!"

"Sure you did," Cassie said.

"It's true!"

Cassie tried to top Lisa's story. "I've got something else to tell you," she said. "Old Mrs. Hollenbeck hanged herself. And I saw it from my window! I even talked to the police myself!"

"No!"

"She did," Diane said. "Cassie's mom said so. Now that big house is empty."

Lisa looked back over her shoulder. "What a wreck," she said. "Are they going to tear it down? It's so ugly."

"I don't know," Cassie said. "My mom wishes they would."

Lisa's eyes narrowed, and she bit her lower lip thoughtfully. "Must be some interesting stuff there."

"Don't get any funny ideas, Westin," Cassie said. "We couldn't get inside, anyway."

"I can get in," a voice said.

The three girls turned to see a dark-haired child standing at the end of the table. Nicole looked at each of them, her brown eyes solemn. Her tiny hands were folded before her, resting against her pinafore.

"Who're you?" Lisa demanded.

Cassie stood up and hurried to stand at Nicole's side. "Diane, Lisa," she said, "this is Nicole Morgan. She's the new girl on the lake. We met this afternoon."

"Hi, Nicole," Diane said. "That's a pretty dress."

Nicole smiled. "Thank you," she said. "My mother made it for me."

"Really?" Lisa asked. "She's talented. My mom

can't sew a stitch, so we get all my clothes at Hoffer's."

She paused, waiting for Nicole's reaction to the name of Ohio's most exclusive chain of department stores. To her surprise, the girl said nothing. Thinking Nicole must be some country bumpkin, Lisa changed the subject. "Can you really get into the house?"

"I can," Nicole said. "I know how to get the door open."

Lisa smiled mischievously, and Diane quickly joined her.

"Oh, no way!" Cassie cried. "I'm not going to get myself grounded before the summer even starts."

"We won't get caught," Lisa said. "We'll just go in quick, take a look around, and get out."

"Count me out," Cassie said.

"Don't be a scaredy-cat," Diane teased. "Your mom won't ever know. Besides, her printer's running. A bomb could go off and she wouldn't hear it!"

Nicole took Cassie's hand. "There is something wonderful there," she said. "Something nobody knows about but me."

"What?" Lisa asked.

"You'll have to come look."

All three girls looked at Cassie.

Finally, she sighed. "Okay. But if I get in trouble, I'll hate you all forever!"

They followed Nicole along the water's edge to the old wooden bridge that connected both sides of the lake. The air seemed cooler over the water, and the wind wafted a variety of smells across the

bridge, from lilacs and roses to an array of meats
being seared on barbecues. Ducks disappeared
under the bridge, returning to the nests they'd built
in the tall grass that grew up between clumps of
rock. Cassie kept looking back over her shoulder,
expecting to see her mother's silhouette at the back
door. When they got to the other side of the bridge,
it was too late to turn back. Giggling over their
secret adventure, the girls trampled through the
knee-high grass toward the mansion. Fallen twigs
and detritus from the house itself, rotting from the
humid air and the sunlight, crunched under their
feet.

"It smells funny over here," Lisa said. "Like
something croaked."

"Maybe it's her kids," Diane suggested. "Maybe
she's got their bodies hidden in the house."

"Diane!" Cassie gasped. "Don't talk like that!
I'm already scared!"

Nicole walked up the steps to the back door.
"There's nothing to be afraid of here," she said.

The four little girls entered the darkened kitchen,
reeking with the smell of old apples and spices.
Dead plants lining the multipaned windows cast
gruesome shadows on the floor, their bent and
gnarled stems like reaching fingers.

"Something spilled in here," Lisa said. "My
Pembrokes are sticking to the floor."

"Where's the surprise?" Cassie asked, in a hurry
to get out of that creepy place.

"This way," Nicole said.

They entered a laundry room, where a basket of
unfolded clothes sat forgotten. Curious about the

square shapes that covered the walls, Lisa reached for the cord dangling from the overhead light.

"Don't do that!" Nicole cried.

Lisa's hand stopped in midair. She regarded Nicole through the shadows with defiant eyes. "I don't like the dark," she said.

"Someone on the lake might see us," Nicole insisted. "Just follow me. I know exactly where to go."

They passed through a library; moonlight illuminated dozens of picture frames. Lisa understood now what covered the walls in the laundry room. *Silly!* she thought. *Whoever heard of a picture gallery in a laundry room?*

They crossed a narrow hallway to a small door. Nicole opened it, revealing a staircase. Once all four of them were inside and the door was closed, she flicked on a light. Cassie and Diane gasped in unison. To either side of them hung countless portraits of two young children, the boy with a crew cut, the little girl with bangs curled halfway up her forehead.

"Those must be Myrtle's kids," Diane said.

"I feel like they're looking at me," Lisa complained. "Why'd she put up so many pictures?"

"She must really have loved those kids," Diane said. "Imagine losing them like that."

"I don't want to talk about it," Cassie said.

They had reached the upstairs hallway. Nicole led them through the cold, musty-smelling dark to the back of the house.

"This is it," she said, opening a door.

Cautiously, unsure of what they'd find, the other

three girls entered the room. Heavy drapes hid the window, making it safe for Nicole to turn on the light. What the dim bulb illuminated made Cassie, Diane, and Lisa gasp.

"It's like a dream room!" Lisa cried out.

Unlike the rest of the house, which was cold and dark, this was a little girl's paradise. A pink and white canopied bed sat in one corner, perfectly matching the pink rug, white furniture, and pink and white curtains. And there were toys everywhere. Beautiful dolls smiled from the shelves that lined the walls. There were stuffed animals, games, a play kitchen, a dollhouse, more toys than any of them had ever seen.

"It's like a department store!" Lisa exclaimed.

"Oh, it's amazing," Diane sighed.

"I . . . I don't think we should be here," Cassie said. "These don't belong to us."

Lisa clicked her tongue. "And who's going to play with them if we don't?" she asked.

"Cassie, look!" Diane cried. "A Lovie-Lamb doll! I've always wanted one of these, but they're *so* expensive!" She ran to pull it down from the shelf, hugging it close.

"Isn't the kitchen set adorable?" Nicole asked. She was seated on the edge of the bed now, holding a rag doll.

"There's a whole Kit-Bits Village," Lisa pointed out.

As the other girls played, Cassie went to sit beside Nicole. "How did you find this?" she asked.

"I sneaked in one night," Nicole said. "Isn't it like a dream come true? Isn't every toy you ever wanted right here?"

Cassie scanned the room. It was true—it was like waking up to the best Christmas morning ever. She picked up a doll and examined its detailed outfit. "You suppose Myrtle bought these for her kids?"

"Like she was expecting them to come home someday?" Lisa replied. She thought a moment, then said brightly, "Who cares? She's dead and they are, too. And it wouldn't be right to let these things go to waste."

Cassie put the doll down, still feeling guilty about being in the house. She got up and went to peek out the window, certain someone was watching the house. Through the crack she made in the drapes, she saw the accusing blink of D'Achille's sign.

"Oh, no!" she cried. "I'm doomed forever!" She started for the door, but Lisa grabbed her.

"We have to talk about this!" Lisa told her.

"My mom'll be looking for me!"

"Say you walked me home," Lisa said. "I'll cover for you tomorrow. Diane, Nicole, come here. Let's all join hands."

"What's this about?" Diane asked.

"A club," Lisa said solemnly. "We're forming a secret club tonight. We'll meet here in this room whenever we can. And we won't tell *anyone* about it. Swear?"

"I swear," Diane said readily.

Cassie kept looking over her shoulder at the door.

"Cassie!" Lisa said.

"I swear!" she cried.

Nicole smiled. "I swear, too," she said. "It's our secret, forever."

FIVE

CASSIE CURLED HERSELF around a big stuffed cat, burying herself under her blanket. Glad to be away from Myrtle's house, she quickly fell into a deep sleep.

She was swimming in the lake. Sunlight made tiny diamonds on the water's surface, glistening white and silver as she splashed merrily, laughing. Suddenly, the laughter was overpowered by a high-pitched scream and the silvery flecks turned to red. The water around Cassie darkened with blood. She watched, frozen, as a man shoved another little girl's head under the water.

"No, don't! Leave her . . .

". . . Alone!" Cassie's own shriek awakened her. She rolled over, knocking the toy cat to the floor. She moaned, bringing the covers up closer to her chin, as if the blankets were armor that would protect her from the terrors of the dark. She could still hear the other little girl's scream, still feel the chilly water turning blood-warm around her legs.

Solo, who had been sleeping on the rug next to her bed, jumped up and licked her hand. Needing comfort, Cassie patted her mattress, luring the mutt up to snuggle next to her. Solo scrambled onto the bed, and Cassie rested her head against his long, soft fur.

She must have had the dream because she'd disobeyed her mother by going to the Hollenbeck house, she thought.

"I don't care how many toys there were, Solo," she whispered. "I'm never going back to that creepy place again! Even if Lisa makes fun of me all summer!"

Solo thumped his tail a few times. Feeling more secure with her dog close by, Cassie closed her eyes again and was soon fast asleep.

Much to Cassie's relief, a week's worth of rain made it impossible for her friends to call another meeting. All their mothers forbade them to walk on the bridge during a storm, afraid that they might slip on the wood. The Westins' chauffeur sometimes drove Lisa around the lake so she could be with her friends. On other days, Cassie and Diane trudged through the drizzle between each other's houses, wishing they were rich enough to have a special driver, like Lisa.

One particularly bleak day when the weather was too inclement for any visitors, Carolyn made Cassie a mug of hot chocolate and sent her into the living room to read. The little girl tucked herself under a quilt that had once been her grandmother's. The fish tank motor hummed in the background as she opened a new book.

The soft tapping that sounded at the door was so

quiet that at first Cassie ignored it, thinking it was caused by the weather. But when the rapping became more insistent, she looked out the picture window to see Nicole standing on the front steps. Feeling her spirits rise despite the rain, Cassie threw the quilt aside, put her book down, and hurried to the front door.

"Hi!" she cried. "What're you doing here? It's yucky outside!"

Nicole's hair was plastered to her head and clothes, and she had her small arms wrapped around her body. She wasn't wearing a coat.

"I—I locked myself out of the house," she said, shivering. "My mother is out, and I didn't know where else to go!"

Cassie stepped back. "Come on in, Nicole. You want me to lend you a sweater? You're shaking all over."

Nicole hesitated, looking down the hall behind Cassie. She seemed nervous about something, but finally entered the house. Water dripped from her, spotting the carpet. She rubbed her chilly arms. "I'd like that," she said. "What's that funny noise back there?"

"That's my mother's computer printer," Cassie said. "She's really busy right now. We can go up to my room and play."

She led her friend up the stairs to her room, then ran to the bathroom for a towel for Nicole's hair. As Nicole admired the dolls and stuffed animals on the window seat, Cassie pulled a sweater from her closet.

"Here you go," she said. "It's gonna be a little

big, but it'll keep you warm."

Nicole finished drying her hair with the towel, dropped it on the floor and smiled. "Thank you. It's just like having a big sister to share clothes with me. Do you have any sisters or brothers?"

"Nope, just me," Cassie said. "But I always wanted a sister. How about you?"

Nicole shrugged into the sweater. The sleeves hung inches too long, and Cassie helped her to roll them up.

"There's a bunch of us," Nicole said. "But we don't get along really good. I mean, I'm not close to anyone. That's why I'm glad to meet a nice friend like you."

"I like you, too, Nicole," Cassie said.

The smaller girl's eyes brightened. "I have a great idea!" she said. "Can we pretend we're sisters? It'll be a fun game to play."

"Okay," Cassie said, smiling. "Let's pretend we're going shopping for new clothes. I've got a trunkful of neat old things that my grandmother left for me. See, my mom grew up here, and my grandparents sold the house to my parents when they got married."

She went to her closet and ducked under a row of dresses, pants, and blouses. Backing out, she lugged a small wooden trunk out into the room.

"Your grandparents don't live with you?"

"No, they're in Florida," Cassie said. She opened the trunk. "Grandma had some neat dresses and things. And there's some clothes my mother wore when she was a kid in here, too!"

Nicole pulled out a long strand of beads, her

mouth wide open in fascination. She draped the beads, around her neck, then rummaged through the old clothes for other things to wear. Giggling and admiring each other, the two girls were soon dressed in oversize blouses, circle skirts, and veiled hats.

"Oh, Nicole," Cassie said, making her voice sound grown-up. "Isn't it the most fun to shop at all these ex-cloo-sive stores?"

"It surely is," Nicole drawled. "That pink fichu is just lovely."

Cassie laughed. "Pink what?"

"Fichu," Nicole said. She pointed to the shawl that Cassie had wrapped around herself.

"Oh, this!" Cassie cried. "What a funny word— fichu. Where did you learn it?"

Before Nicole could answer, Carolyn, downstairs, called her daughter's name. Hiking up her over-long skirt, Cassie wobbled in too-large shoes to the hallway.

"What, Mom?"

"Lisa's on the phone," Carolyn said. "She says she can get a ride over here, if you want to play."

"Oh, great!" Cassie said. "Tell her to come on over!"

When she went back into her room, she was surprised to see that Nicole had taken off all the dress-up clothes, even the sweater Cassie had lent her. She stood in the center of the room with her head bowed, frowning.

"What's the matter?" Cassie asked.

"Why'd you have to invite that other girl?" Nicole asked. "We were having so much fun together, being sisters. Lisa will just spoil things!"

Cassie shook her head. "No, she won't," she said. "Lisa's fun. And we can all be sisters!"

"I don't want to be Lisa's sister!" Nicole cried. "I just want *us* to be sisters!"

"Well, I couldn't tell her not to come," Cassie said, removing her own dress-up clothes. "She's my friend, too, you know."

Nicole pouted. "I wish I was your only friend," she muttered.

"You're strange, Nicole Morgan," Cassie said. "Come on, let's go downstairs. I'll ask my mom if we can have something to eat."

She left the room, with Nicole behind her. When she reached her mother's office, she turned to ask Nicole what she'd like to eat. To her surprise, the girl was gone.

"Nicole?" she said.

Carolyn looked up from her desk. "Who are you calling, honey?"

"My friend Nicole," Cassie said. "She was right behind me, but now she's gone! I'll bet she's mad 'cause Lisa's coming over."

"You had a friend here and you didn't even introduce us?"

"You were busy, Mom," Cassie said. "Well, phooey on Nicole! If she doesn't want to play with my other friends, who needs her?"

Leaving Carolyn wondering who Nicole was, Cassie went back to the living room. She picked up her book and started reading again, waiting for Lisa's arrival.

* * *

At last the rain stopped. When Cassie woke up the next morning, the crickets were already filling the dense, moist air with song. It was a day with swimming written all over it. Grateful for the sun's appearance after so much rain, Cassie rummaged through her underwear drawer to find last year's bikini.

Cassie carried it to the bathroom, where she stepped into the panties, straightening them around her hips. Then she slipped her arms through the bra straps, reaching to hook it at the back. As if they remembered the task from a year ago, her fingers automatically went for the tightest hook. It wouldn't reach. Cassie found herself connecting it at its loosest fastener.

"Maybe David's right," she said aloud. "Maybe I *am* getting fat."

She looked worriedly at herself in the full-length mirror on the bathroom door, tossing her long hair back over her shoulders. Her torso was one line straight up and down, her legs pale and bony. No, David was a twerp. She wasn't fat at all. The bikini must have shrunk the last time it was washed.

Summoned by her mother, Cassie ran downstairs to the kitchen, where she found cereal and bananas waiting for her. Cassie poured her own orange juice, then turned her face up for Carolyn's good-morning kiss.

"Can I go swimming?" she asked, eating quickly.

"Sure," Carolyn said, "but I have to go to my warehouse this morning, so I want you out of the water before I leave."

"Okay," Cassie said. She stood up and carried

her empty bowl to the sink.

Carolyn sighed, shaking her head. "You break my heart when you wear that thing," she said.

"Why?"

"Because it makes me remember when *I* had a flat stomach," Carolyn said. "Then a certain little blond baby came along, and I haven't looked the same since."

"Lisa's mom had four babies and she doesn't have a potbelly," Cassie said.

"Cassie!"

"Well, she doesn't," Cassie insisted.

Carolyn frowned. "Dorothy Westin can afford an occasional tummy tuck."

Cassie opened the back door. "I think you're ten times prettier than Lisa's mom," she said.

Leaving Carolyn with a smile on her face, Cassie hurried off. She spotted Nicole sitting on a rock at the water's edge, skipping stones. Having forgotten all about the way Nicole had run off the day before, she hurried up to her new friend.

"Hi," she said. "Do you want to go swimming?"

"Not today," Nicole said. "The water looks cold." She looked Cassie up and down. "You aren't wearing very much."

"Just my bathing suit," Cassie said. "Why don't you put yours on? The water's really nice at this hour, you'll see."

"No, thank you," Nicole said politely.

"Well, I'm going swimming," Cassie said. "Maybe Diane's up. Come on, and we'll ring her bell."

Nicole started to protest, but Cassie was already

running toward Diane's house. The smaller girl caught up with Cassie at the back door of the small blue cottage. Cassie knocked, and David, still dressed in his pajamas, answered.

"Is Diane home?" Cassie asked.

"Where would she be?" David asked. "China? Come on in." He looked her over, his eyes stopping at her bathing suit top. "Yeah, I was right, you are getting 'em."

A bewildered look crossed Cassie's face. "You're nuts," she said. "Just send Diane out here. We'll be on the beach." She turned and hurried away, grabbing Nicole's arm.

"What did that boy mean?" Nicole asked.

"I don't know," Cassie said. "But I'm sure it was something fresh. Don't pay any attention to David. He's a pest with a capital P."

They heard the squeak of wood against wood and looked up at the house to see Diane leaning from a second-story window.

"Hi!" she called. "Be right down!"

Moments later, she was hurrying toward them. Her short black hair was still wet from her morning shower, and she wore a wraparound sundress. The three of them walked along the shore.

"Can't wait to put my shorts on," she said. "But Mom wants me to keep my bandage away from the sun."

"Does it still hurt?" Cassie asked.

"Not as much as yesterday," Diane answered. "You know what? Bill said he'd take me for a rowboat ride later this morning. Do you want to come with us?"

"That sounds like fun!" Cassie said.

Nicole looked down at the sand, kicking an empty snail shell. "I don't want to go," she said. "I don't like boats."

Cassie and Diane exchanged exasperated glances.

"How can you live on a lake and be afraid of boats?" Diane asked.

"I just am," Nicole said.

"Well, if you don't want to come, it's okay," Cassie said. "But you're sure missing out."

They had reached Cassie's yard. Solo looked up from his hiding place under the rosebushes, where he'd dug a groove in the dirt, moving the warm soil aside to expose the cooler dirt beneath. He regarded each child, his tail thumping, too lazy to move in the heat. His stare froze on Nicole, and he rose suddenly, barked a few times, and ran off.

"What's wrong with him?" Diane asked.

"Nicole's a stranger to him," Cassie said. "He didn't recognize her. Forget him. Listen, do you guys want something cold to drink? I can't believe how hot it is already."

"Sounds good to me," Diane said. "Something with lots of ice, okay?"

"Be right out," Cassie said, running up the steps and in the back door.

Alone with Nicole, Diane decided to ask her a few questions. "Do you like it here on Lake Solaria?" she began.

"It's all right," Nicole said.

Diane could tell the new girl didn't really want to talk, but she was much too interested in her to sit quietly. "How old are you, anyway, Nicole?"

"Twelve," the child answered.

She was watching the door for Cassie's return, so she didn't notice the look of surprise on Diane's face. Cassie came out bearing a tray with glasses of lemonade. She had thrown on a pink shift over her swimsuit, and she was wearing a floppy hat.

"My mom made me put this on," she said. "She's afraid I'll get sunburned in this heat."

She handed a plastic tumbler to Nicole and one to Diane. They sipped at the lemonade for a while, watching the people around the lake. Water splashed as swimmers jumped off docks, motor-boats hummed, and sailboats floated idly, waiting for any possible breeze.

"Oh, I have to go now," Nicole said abruptly after a few moments. "I think I hear my mother calling me. I have to go. I'll see you later!" She climbed from the bench and hurried away.

Diane shook her head. "That girl is *weird*," she said. "Do you know she's twelve? I wonder why she's so short?"

"I hope you didn't say anything mean to her," Cassie said, watching Nicole's retreating figure.

"Of course not," Diane said. "I'm not like Lisa. Well, listen, you want to see if Bill's ready yet?"

"Let me tell my mom I'm going," Cassie replied, gathering the tumblers and setting them on the tray. She shook her head. "Look at that. Nicole didn't even touch her lemonade."

Cassie hurried up the stairs and into the house. She found her mother packing inventory sheets into a big folder. Carolyn picked up her car keys, dangling from a photo key chain Cassie had given her the previous Christmas.

"Mom, is it okay if I go out in the Montanas' rowboat?" Cassie asked. "Bill's taking Diane out."

Carolyn tucked the folder under her arm. "Okay," she said. "But you be sure to wear a life jacket."

"I promise," Cassie said, giving Carolyn a hug. "See you later, Mom. Say hi to everyone at the warehouse!"

She went through the kitchen, grabbing a can of soda as she went.

"Hurry!" Diane said. "Bill just waved to me. I think he's getting the boat ready now."

"Great!" Cassie said.

As they hurried down the beach, to Cassie's dismay, a familiar voice called out to her. She clicked her tongue, recognizing Georgie Canfield's slurred tones. The older boy walked over to the two girls.

"Where ya goin'?" Georgie asked.

"None of your business," Cassie said. "Leave us alone, Georgie."

"Yeah, or I'll tell my brother," Diane said.

Georgie laughed. "What's that wimp gonna do to me? Hey, Cassie, you look really nice. Really pretty. Did I say I've been watchin' how pretty you're getting?"

"Georgie, you're too gross," Cassie mumbled.

Georgie pushed her. Cassie stumbled against Diane, who caught her and helped her regain her balance. Both girls looked at the older boy with wide eyes.

"Don't you *ever* call me gross, you pint-sized bitch," Georgie said. "One of these days, I'll show you just how good I am."

"You picking on kids again, Canfield?"

Cassie and Diane looked up with relief to see Bill standing nearby. He cocked his head to one side and gazed at Georgie with a challenge in his eyes.

"Just havin' some fun," Georgie said.

"Once scum, always scum," Bill said. "What does a guy like you want with a ten-year-old? Get lost, Canfield. Or I'll knock your nuts up through your teeth."

Georgie waved a skinny arm at them and turned to lumber away.

Diane put her arms around her brother. "You're the best," she said. "That boy really scared us."

"Well, just don't tell Mom what I said to him," Bill said. "Come on, now." They walked back to the dock. Diane waved to the girl who waited there, a pretty teenager with long red hair.

"Hi, Anna," she said. "This is my friend Cassie. She's coming with us."

"Hi, Cassie," Anna said with a smile. "That's a cute hat."

"Have to wear it in the sun," Cassie said, grinning.

The boat rocked gently as Bill jumped in. He made a quick check, then looked up at the girls. "Okay, it's ready," he said. "Who wants to get in first?"

"Let Anna go," Diane said. "She's your girl."

Anna shook her head, looking at Cassie. "You go ahead," she said. "I can help you from this end."

Giggling as Bill took her around the waist, Cassie jumped down into the boat. She walked carefully to a bench and sat down. Bill turned back to help Diane, but his sister backed away from him, a look of confusion on her face.

"What's that noise?" she demanded.

It was a kind of creaking, almost muffled by the swish of the water. At first, they all thought it was just the dock's wooden planking.

"I don't know, Di—" Bill began.

Diane pointed and screamed, *"Bill! Look out!"*

As Diane and Anna watched in horror, a dark line appeared at the bottom of the rowboat. It streaked like lightning from one end to the other, opening abruptly into a wide cleft that swallowed Bill and Cassie into the dark water.

A great explosion sounded in Cassie's head as the severed hull swung back and struck her. She gulped, reaching for the surface. Her hand shot through to the air above. Something tugged her, hard, down into the dark lake. She watched with growing hysteria as the light above her dimmed, feeling pressure tighten around her small body. She was going to die. . . .

Underwater, Bill heard the muffled sound of his sister screaming. He fought to regain his composure, his mind racing over the survival techniques he'd learned as a lifeguard. This close to the water's surface, it was light enough to see the pieces of the boat floating overhead. Bill swam to the surface, sputtering.

"Where's Cassie?" he sputtered.

"I can't see her!" Diane cried, panicked. "Bill, she's drowned!"

"The hell she has!" Bill cried. He dove under again, searching for the child. But the sunlight only illuminated a few inches of water. He could see nothing. He surfaced again.

"Diane, get Dad out here!" he bellowed before diving once more.

Unseen below him, Cassie was being dragged down by a piece of metal that had somehow become trapped in the folds of her sundress. Icy cold enfolded her, water pushed at her mouth and nose. She screamed silently, reaching for Bill's silhouette overhead. . . .

All this had happened in about thirty seconds. Cassie's ability to hold her breath underwater was not strong. Her lungs distended painfully, her mind went spinning as it searched for oxygen. Mentally she screamed for her mother, arms and legs flailing wildly.

Something was tugging at her. Suddenly air rushed into her lungs, as if she'd been brought to the surface. Cassie relaxed, feeling at peace. She was dead now. It was okay. She felt safe, felt good. . . .

"They want to hurt us," a voice said. "They want to tear us apart again. You must stop them!"

The voice didn't belong here, in the place of peace. This wasn't a kind voice, a godly voice. It was the devil speaking.

"Stop them," the voice croaked again.

Everything went black.

Then Cassie heard voices.

"Is she breathing?"

"Cassie, can you hear me?"

"How could she have survived so long underwater?"

Cassie slowly opened her eyes. There was a crowd gathered around her, staring down with worried and stricken faces. She blinked. "Stop them," she mumbled.

"She's delirious," Bill said, shivering in the towel his mother had wrapped around his shoulders.

"Where's her mother?" Rita demanded.

"Dad, maybe we should call Dr. Westin," Bill suggested.

"He's already on his way," Andy said. He looked at the dock, where one piece of the boat hung precariously from the rope that had tied it to the mooring. The other half had floated out into the lake's center. "How the hell did this happen?" he asked in a quiet voice that said he didn't expect any answer.

Cassie squinted up at the circle of concerned faces. She felt a blanket being laid over her, and turned her head to see Rita Montana's pity-filled eyes as the woman brushed back a spiral of Cassie's wet hair. Cassie rolled onto one side and vomited gushes of water back into the lake. At the back of the crowd, someone laughed. When Bill turned with an accusing glance, everyone regarded him soberly. His eyes rested on Georgie Canfield, but the other boy looked unusually sober.

No human had laughed. The laugh had come from another dimension, from an insidious, unseen being.

SIX

ROBERT LANDERS SAT under a tree in Buckeye Park, rereading his notes on the Hollenbeck case. His three Irish setters raced around him on the dandelion-covered grass. The remains of his lunch filled a rolled-up paper bag beside him: crumpled waxed paper and a crushed soda can. After a while, Robert dropped his notes into his lap and leaned back against the tree, rubbing his neck where perspiration had glued his collar to his skin. He was worn out looking for clues that were completely elusive. He hadn't been able to persuade his chief that this was a case worth taking on. Mike Hogan had sided with Susan, believing as she did that Myrtle had been alone in her death. Robert's investigation would have to be done on his own time.

A quick series of tones played on the beeper attached to his belt. Robert stood up, gathering his things. Kelly and her daughters followed him to his van, settling onto the gray corduroy couch. Robert reached for the mike on his dashboard and turned on his police radio to call headquarters. After hearing the message, he felt more encouraged than he had in days.

"We're going to the lake, girls," he told the dogs. "There's been another incident there—and this time, I have witnesses."

He told himself he shouldn't dare hope he'd find something that connected with Myrtle's death, but this was just too much of a coincidence. A near-drowning, the dispatcher had said—and the victim was Cassie Larchmont.

As he pulled onto Lakefront Road, he realized that most of the driveways were full. The Larchmonts' was empty, so he pulled the van in there. Glancing at the address he'd been given on the radio, he got out of the van and walked quickly to the Montanas' house. A dark-haired woman dressed in a black and white shift hurried up to him, her dark eyes rimmed red from crying.

"I'm Detective Landers," he said.

"My name is Rita Montana," the woman said in greeting. "We own the boat that was destroyed. Please follow me, Detective Landers. You can talk to my husband."

"What about the little girl?" Robert asked. "Is Cassie going to be all right?"

"I hope so," Rita said. "Her mother's taken her to the hospital. The way Carolyn was speeding, I hope they don't get killed on the way there!"

Rita led him to the dock, where she introduced him to Bill and Andy, then pointed to the remains of the boat. Robert crouched down for a better look.

"How did this happen?" he demanded.

"You tell me," Andy said.

Robert took hold of the rope and pulled the boat closer, reaching down to run a thumb along the cut. "No teeth marks," he said. "It wasn't a conventional saw."

"Who could have done such a thing?" Anna asked. "Who could be so vicious?"

Robert stood up, brushing mud from the knees of his pants. "I don't know," he said. "Maybe you should tell me what happened, right from the start."

Bill explained everything, from the moment he had climbed into the hull up to Cassie's rescue. "I feel so guilty about that," he concluded, shaking his head. "I mean, I'm a lifeguard! I should have been able to get her sooner!"

"You did the best you could," Rita said soothingly. "She couldn't have been underwater for much more than a minute."

"Do you have any idea who might have done this?" Robert asked.

"None at all," Andy said. "So far as we know, we have no enemies. How could we? We don't cause trouble, and we only come here for the summer!"

"This was no accident," Rita said. "Someone cut that boat in half, and I want you to find out who it was!"

Robert nodded, staring soberly at the center of the lake, where half the rowboat bobbed, upside down.

"Can I use your phone?" he asked after a moment. "I want a team down here to take a look at this."

"In the kitchen," Rita said. "Diane, can you show Detective Landers the phone?"

Diane, who had felt extremely helpless during all this, nodded eagerly. Robert followed her up the back steps. In the kitchen, he dialed the precinct and explained the situation, then went back outside again.

"They'll be here soon," he said. "If you need me, I'll be talking to your neighbors."

Robert hoped someone might have seen something suspicious, but after spending almost an hour checking nearly every home on this side of the lake, he began to feel discouraged. It was frustrating—no one had seen or heard a thing.

Robert walked along the lakeshore behind the houses, unaware that the very person he sought stood in front of the Larchmont house at that moment, near his van.

But if he had gone there, he would have seen only Georgie Canfield. Georgie himself was completely oblivious to the presence at his side as he reached out to touch the van's polished gray metal with nicotine-stained fingers. Grabbing hold of the ladder on the back, he hoisted himself up to look inside. He could barely make out the shadows of the sleeping dogs.

When Georgie started back down the ladder, something pressed against his back, stopping him halfway. Georgie froze, staring at his own reflection in the van window, watching as long, wormlike things slithered across his cheeks from behind his head.

He was having hallucinations. Maybe there was

something wrong with the joint he'd been smoking a little earlier. . . .

Now he heard a voice, distant yet very clear. He could feel someone's breath, icy as a winter breeze. The fingerlike things melted away.

"Listen to me, Georgie," the voice said. *"You want a van just like this one, don't you? Why don't you take it for a ride? I know where the keys are, Georgie."*

Georgie began to listen carefully, unafraid. It was tempting. He'd never been behind the wheel of anything this beautiful before. "But I can't—"

"Of course you can. No one will miss it. Climb behind the wheel, Georgie. Just climb in and see what it feels like."

Georgie looked around nervously. No one was in sight. They were all still down at the Montanas' dock. The way was clear. And if he just sat behind the wheel, what could happen?

"That's right, Georgie. What could happen?"

Georgie felt the pressure against his back disappear. He jumped down from the ladder and ran to the front of the van. He opened the door, expecting the dogs to start barking, but they lay perfectly still. That set off a warning bell in his mind, but he ignored it. Georgie climbed in and closed the door gently, looking at the van's interior. There were four bucket seats and a couch that ran across the back, all upholstered in smoky-gray corduroy. Georgie was surprised to see a small refrigerator, too. This was a class vehicle, for sure.

A voice suddenly came over the police radio,

making him jump. Georgie looked around in a panic, expecting the detective guy to show up. Maybe he should get out while it was still safe.

"Don't worry, Georgie. No one's coming. You're all alone."

"Where are you?" Georgie demanded. "What's going on here, man?"

High-pitched laughter was his only answer.

Growing anxious, Georgie reached for the handle of the door, suddenly wanting to get as far away from this place as possible.

The door was locked. He pulled up on the lock button and jiggled the door's handle, but nothing happened. Georgie climbed across the seat to the other door, but it was just as tightly sealed.

"You can't get out, Georgie. You'll never get out! You'll die in here!"

"Shit, I don't believe this!" Georgie yelled. He started pounding on the window. "Let me out of here! Hey, can't anyone hear me? Help! Help!"

But no one answered him.

He heard the laughter again, and knelt on the seat, looking into the back of the van. The dogs still slept, and he was the only person in the van.

Bad stuff. It had to be bad stuff that he'd smoked that morning. Something crazy in it—maybe angel dust.

He heard a scratching at the windshield. Georgie turned to see two small children, a boy and a girl, with their faces pressed against the glass. Hideously battered faces, pieces of skull showing through, sunken eye sockets . . .

"Nnnnnnnooooooo!"

The children beat their small palms against the glass. Georgie covered his eyes and went on screaming.

"You want out, Georgie? There's a can next to you. Open it up and you'll find a key."

The can was there, on the floor between the two front seats. Georgie hadn't noticed it before. This was a bad trip, but maybe if he played along with it, it'd be over soon. He reached down and picked up the can. . . .

At Lake Solaria's rental office, Robert was going over the list of names the caretaker had given him. Many of these people had been visiting the lake for years, and none had ever caused any trouble. There were two new names, but these were both retirement-age couples.

He was about to say something to the caretaker when his words were obliterated by an explosion so loud it made him jump. Robert ran out of the building, letting the screen door slam behind him. From the direction of the Larchmont house, he saw a towering column of red and orange flame reaching toward the sky.

Robert rushed toward Carolyn's place, stopping short when he saw the huge block of flame that sat in the Larchmont driveway. His van was on fire!

"My girls!" he screamed. "Dear God, my dogs are in there!"

Cries of dismay ran through the growing crowd.

Several neighbors had brought out fire extinguishers. Robert grabbed one, squinting against the smoke and heat as he sprayed white foam all over the back doors. As the flames subsided at the back, cooled by foam, he jumped onto the ladder, desperately working his key into the lock. The door refused to open. The dogs barked frantically, Robert picked up the empty extinguisher and pounded it against the glass, shattering the window. Now the crowd could hear the animals' hysterical yelping, the scratching of frenzied paws against metal and glass. A red head popped into view.

"Kelly!" Robert screamed.

The immense heat became too much to bear. He fell away from the van, coughing and sputtering. Andy had brought the Larchmonts' hose around, shooting a heavy spray from its nozzle. Robert took hold of it, splashing the broken window, trying to create a way for the dogs to escape. One of them had stuck her head and forelegs through the window, and was desperately trying to wriggle out. Blood appeared along her flanks as the jagged glass of the broken window cut into her.

Over the din of the flames, sirens were heard, and a hook-and-ladder rolled to a stop in front of the house. Within seconds the fire team took over. Someone yanked Robert away from the van. One woman, seeing his burned hands, hurried into her house and returned with a towel full of ice. She pressed this into his hands, but he seemed unaware of her. He struggled against the two men who restrained him, watching the dogs fight to escape the inferno.

The firefighters worked quickly, finally managing to douse the flames. The once-beautiful van was a black wreckage, its paint bubbling and its fiberglass grossly distorted. Robert felt the arms that had held him back loosen, but for a moment he couldn't move. He didn't want to see what was inside that van.

One of the firefighters, a black woman with a round face, turned with a grin. "Hey, they're okay!" she shouted. "They look fine!"

Robert shot toward the van, reaching out with shaking hands as his dogs were pulled out one by one. The youngest, Erin, collapsed at his feet, her tongue hanging out. Her side, matted with blood, heaved up and down as she panted. The other two dogs made strange choking noises.

Robert got to his knees and took Erin in his arms. Kelly and Sian pressed close to him. Robert looked up at the crowd, his eyes accusing, his teeth set in anger.

"One of you did this," he seethed. "One of you tried to kill my dogs! I'm going to find out who you are! Do you hear me? I won't sleep until I find you!"

He was interrupted by a scream, and one of the firefighters backed away from the front of the van with his hand over his mouth. Robert looked toward the group that had gathered near the door, and felt a sickening wave rush through him. Something black had fallen from the opened door, hanging half out of the van. It looked like a charred log, but the gnarled fingers made it impossible to deny the obvious. This was, or had been, human.

"Who is it?" someone asked.

Robert stood up on trembling legs, feeling as he always did when he confronted death. But he forced an authoritative tone into his voice and ordered everyone to back off. "Move aside now!" he shouted. "There's nothing here for you!"

Ira Conlon, the fire chief, put a hand on his arm. "Better get Sue Walken's team over here, fast," Ira said. "In all my years as a firefighter, I've never seen a body in that condition."

Robert nodded, staring at the blackened form until someone had the sense to throw a blanket over it.

SEVEN

LAKE SOLARIA'S SMALL police station was busier that evening than it had been in years. As phones rang continuously upstairs and people hurried back and forth, Susan worked in the lab with Larry Halen, the county coroner, who had been called in from his home thirty miles outside of town.

Susan had reached a point where she found it easier to pretend that what she was looking at just wasn't real. It could be a battered store dummy, or a prop from a movie. This thing lying on the metal table before her could be a gnarled piece of charred wood dug up after a forest fire. It was better to think that than to think it was human.

But Larry had no such qualms, having seen much worse in the past thirty years, and he touched the body with competent hands. "We have an ID?" he asked.

"A witness saw a young man named George Canfield climbing into the van just before it exploded," Susan said. "We've notified his parents."

"Still," Larry said, "for positive identification I want his dental records traced." He touched a shoulder, where an arm had once hung. The limb was now wrapped in plastic and set to one side of the gurney. "Does the bomb squad have any idea what happened?"

"They found the remains of a pipe bomb," Susan said. "The Canfield boy must have wanted to plant it in the van, but it went off before he could escape."

The door creaked open, as it had several times in the past hour. Expecting another curious onlooker, Susan didn't turn around. Then, as the newcomer reached toward the body, she recognized Robert Landers's college fraternity ring. Susan looked up at him.

"I didn't expect to see you tonight," she said. "Did you get the dogs to the vet's okay?"

As soon as he'd been able to leave the crime scene, Robert had rushed the dogs straight to the local animal hospital.

"They'll be there overnight," Robert said.

"And your van?" Susan asked. "Will your insurance cover it?"

"I haven't even called my agent yet," he said, his eyes sad. "Replacing that van is the furthest thing from my mind at the moment, considering what happened to this young man. How old was this kid?"

Susan turned to the shelf behind her and opened her folder. "Nineteen," she said.

"Nineteen," Robert whispered. "Try to figure that out—wasting your life at nineteen. Why the hell do you suppose he did this?"

Susan shrugged. "Kicks, maybe. People I talked

to said that Georgie had a reputation for being a real troublemaker. He has a record for pushing drugs. Chris Geisly arrested him once for punching out the man who runs the tobacco store in town."

Robert turned away from the corpse. Like Susan, he tried to pretend it wasn't real, but he didn't have her stomach for this sort of thing. Robert picked up the file and skimmed through it as Susan and Larry talked quietly over the body.

Georgie Canfield, age nineteen, had been the second son of Lauren and Barry Canfield. He also had two sisters, aged fifteen and sixteen. Robert tried to imagine how those youngsters would take the loss of their brother, even a brother who, judging from his record, seemed destined for such a violent ending.

But something was wrong here. The notes scribbled after the neighbors had been questioned indicated that Georgie was known to be a punk. And certainly, after his fight at the tobacco store, he would have been a notorious name among shopkeepers in downtown Lake Solaria. So who the hell would have been stupid enough to sell him the gunpowder he needed to make that pipe bomb?

"Sue, I'm going back to the lake," Robert said. "I want to ask some more questions."

"I don't see what else there is to ask," Susan said. "It's my guess that Georgie was responsible for the Montanas' boat, too. I think the case is ended, Robert."

"Not when I have questions," Robert insisted.

He left the lab, reaching into his pocket for his car keys as he ascended the staircase. Instinctively he seized the van's keys, and was out in the parking lot before he remembered that they were no longer of any use. Sighing, he searched for the pair of keys that were attached to a cardboard tab labeled "Thern Rentals." He slid into the car behind the angled steering wheel. The seat was uncomfortably hard, and his vision was impaired by a cracked windshield. Driving this bomb made him think of how long he'd saved to pay for his van, and anger began to rise in him until his knuckles turned white as he gripped the wheel.

Robert located the Canfield house, its every window brightly illuminated as neighbors came to offer condolences and help. He felt out of place here, as if somehow it were his fault the boy was dead. Maybe the Canfields were sick of talking to police. Maybe they'd tell him to go the hell away.

That seemed pretty likely when Georgie's older brother opened the door. After Robert introduced himself, Jack Canfield stared at him for a moment, a look of disdain on his face.

"I'm sorry to bother you," Robert said in a low voice, barely louder than the wind blowing over the lake. "But it was my van that was destroyed. And I don't believe your brother did it by himself."

Jack's eyes widened, and without a word he stepped back and let Robert into the house, then disappeared. A moment later, Lauren Canfield appeared, her tearstained face glistening in the hall light.

"Jack told me what you said," Lauren said. "You're the first one to believe our boy is innocent."

Robert followed her down the hall and into the kitchen. When he passed the den he saw two dark-haired teenagers holding each other close and sobbing. He felt a chill rush over him.

Barry Canfield was sitting at the kitchen table, staring with reddened eyes down into a mug of beer. He was a big man, still dressed in the gas station uniform he wore as owner of Canfield's Petrol. Robert realized now that he'd been to that same gas station many times, in the very van Georgie had set aflame.

"You want a beer?" Barry asked, not looking up.

"I can't," Robert said. "I'm on duty. But I was hoping I could ask you some questions."

Lauren, a petite woman whose waistline seemed smaller than her husband's upper arm, leaned close to Barry. "Honey, he thinks our boy is innocent."

Barry looked up.

"I—I'm afraid I didn't quite say that," Robert said, holding up both scorched hands. "But I do think he had help. That's why I need to talk to you. If there is someone else involved, I want that person caught."

"I want him strung up," Barry growled. He nodded once. "Sit down, will you? Ask your questions."

Robert settled into a yellow vinyl chair. The phone rang and Lauren answered it. Robert could tell from her end of the conversation that it was a neighbor offering condolences.

"Mr. Canfield, I know this is hard," Robert began.

"You don't know shit," Barry grumbled.

Robert sighed, then spoke. "Records show that George dropped out of high school in the eleventh grade. Before that, how did he do? Especially in science?"

"Hated it," Barry said. "Straight F's. He never studied, couldn't have cared less about school. I don't know how I got a kid like that. Look at my others, at my Jack and my girls. Popular, smart kids, each one of them. And I didn't do anything different with Georgie than with them."

"Did Georgie like to experiment with things?" Robert asked. "Did he like to build things?"

"The only things he experimented with were drugs," Barry said. "And the only thing he could build was a marijuana cigarette. Why are you asking questions like that?"

Lauren hung up the phone and came to sit beside her husband. Barry took her hand, kneading the tiny fingers in his own.

"We found a pipe bomb in the van," Robert said. "Or rather, the remains of one. I find it a little hard to believe that your son got hold of the parts himself, after hearing what people have to say about him. A reliable ammunitions dealer wouldn't sell gunpowder to a kid who was known to cause trouble."

"My Georgie was not a troublemaker!" Lauren wailed. "He was just mixed up. . . ."

"Sweetheart, the boy wasn't just mixed up," Barry said. "He was completely twisted. You could never see it because you loved him as a mother should. But even when he was a kid, when he got caught stealing the Davis kid's bike, I knew. I knew. . . ."

Barry's eyes squeezed shut, and he bowed his head. A moment later, he blinked and looked up again. His eyes were watery, but no tears fell.

"I'm sorry," he said. "It keeps hitting me. What are you thinking of, Detective?"

"I'm thinking that Georgie had help," Robert said. "Now, tell me, did he hang out with anyone? Has anyone come here who aroused your suspicions?"

Barry and Lauren looked at each other.

"Georgie kept to himself pretty much," Lauren said.

"He had no friends," Barry agreed.

"Then maybe he went somewhere," Robert suggested. "Did he ever disappear for long periods of time, when he might have been meeting with someone?"

Barry thought. "He was always on the go."

Lauren tugged at his arm. "Barry, tell him about the house."

"Georgie liked to hang around Myrtle Hollenbeck's house," he said. "I think he even used to run errands for her. I know that place is empty now, but maybe Georgie used it as a meeting place."

Robert sat back, amazed that Barry Canfield had voiced the same thoughts that were forming in the back of his own mind.

"I don't know," he said slowly. "But I mean to find out." He stood up. "Thanks for your time."

Barry walked him to the front door.

"If someone made our boy plant that bomb," Barry said, "you find him, okay? You find him, and let me have a minute alone with him."

EIGHT

CASSIE STOOD AT the picture window in the living room, her hair reflecting a strange bluish color from the aquarium light. Absently stroking the top of Solo's head, she stared out at the driveway, where the streetlight illuminated the strange, hollow black rectangle left behind by the detective's van. She had heard her mother talking on the phone about the incident, and it frightened her to think that someone had tried to kill three innocent dogs. What if one of them had been Solo?

Carolyn came up behind her daughter and put her arms around the child. "Why don't you come away from there?" she asked. "There's nothing to see, and looking out there will only keep you from pushing this out of your mind."

"I'm scared, Mommy," Cassie whispered.

Carolyn turned her around, hugging her close. "Oh, I know," she said. "But the police have caught the bad person who tried to hurt you. It's all over now, and you're safe."

"I heard something when I was under the water," Cassie said. "Like someone talking to me."

"Well, that was probably the people up on dock shouting for you," Carolyn said, leading her daughter out of the living room and toward the kitchen. "Bill, or Diane . . ."

Cassie shook her head vigorously. "No, Mommy," she said. "The voice was really clear, like someone was standing right next to me. The only thing is, I don't remember what it said."

"Cassie, you passed out underwater," Carolyn said. "Sometimes when you faint your mind plays tricks on you, sort of like a dream."

She sat Cassie at the table and set a bowl of soup in front of her. Cassie lifted her spoon, stirring the liquid absently.

"It was kinda like my bad dream," Cassie said, "the one where the little girl was drowning. Only this time, it was me."

"But you're okay," Carolyn insisted. "You're sitting here right now, eating soup—or playing with it. Cassie, please try some of that. You haven't eaten since this morning."

"I'm not very hungry," Cassie said.

Just then, there was a knock at the back door. Carolyn went to the screen door and opened it. Lisa Westin stood on the steps, her minidress swinging as she shifted her weight from one foot to the other.

"Is Cassie up?" she asked.

"Hi, Lisa," Cassie said.

Lisa hurried past Carolyn to Cassie's side. She looked her friend up and down. "You look okay," she said. "Did you really die and come back again?"

"I didn't die, Lisa," Cassie grumbled.

"Lisa, I don't think she wants to talk about it," Carolyn said.

Lisa nodded, disappointed. This was the most exciting day that had ever happened on Lake Solaria, and she wanted to know all the details. She pulled a package out from behind her back, wrapped in pink and white polka-dot paper.

"My mom said I could buy this for you, Cassie," Lisa said.

Eagerly, Cassie opened the box, and took out a little statue of a bear with a bandage around its head. "Can't bear it without you. Get well soon" was inscribed on its base.

"It's so cute," Cassie said. She half-rose to give Lisa a kiss on the cheek. "Thanks!"

"Can you come out tonight?" Lisa asked.

"I'm afraid not," Carolyn said. "I want her to rest."

Cassie frowned apologetically. "I'm really beat, Lisa," she said.

"Well, suit yourself," Lisa said. "I'll come see you tomorrow. Glad you're okay!"

Lisa left the house through the back door, shooing Solo out of the way as she crossed the yard and headed for the Montana house. David lay on his stomach through the tire swing, his toes and fingers scraping big circles in the dirt. Diane had her back to Lisa, trying to catch a firefly.

"Boo!" Lisa cried, making Diane jump.

"What's the big idea?" Diane asked, whirling around.

Lisa grinned. "Did you think it was Georgie's ghost?"

"That's gross, Westin," Diane said. "You shouldn't make jokes like that."

"Sorry," Lisa said. She looked at David, who seemed completely preoccupied by the dirt underneath his swing. "Want to go back to the house?" she asked in a low voice. "I've been dying to get to those toys all week!"

"How can I go now?" Diane asked. "My parents are watching us like hawks because of what happened to Cassie."

"It's easy," Lisa said. "Say you're coming over to my place."

"Forget it," Diane said. "I'm not allowed to cross the bridge at night. What do you care about those toys, anyway? Your parents can buy you all the toys you want."

"You're chicken," Lisa said, ignoring the comment about her wealth. "You're afraid to go to the house!"

"I am not!" Diane insisted. "And besides, what about Cassie and Nicole?"

"Cassie's too sick to come out tonight," Lisa said. "And who cares about pip-squeak Nicole? She's too weird for me."

"I think she's sweet," Diane said. She sighed. "Well, okay, I'll ask. But I'm sure my mom'll say no."

When Diane had gone into the house, Lisa went down to the dock. She found an empty film cylinder and threw it out into the lake, watching it make a tiny splash before it floated away.

"You shouldn't throw things into the water."

Lisa turned around to see Nicole at the end of the

dock, regarding her with an almost hostile expression.

"What's bugging you?" Lisa demanded, moving off the dock.

"Nothing," Nicole said. "I guess I'm just upset about Cassie. Is she okay?"

"Why don't you go to her house and ask?" Lisa said.

The Montanas' back door slammed and Diane came down the steps. "I can't believe it," she said. "My mom said yes. I guess she thinks it'll get my mind off the accident."

"Then let's go while we have the chance," Lisa said, pulling on Diane's arm.

Nicole looked at each of them. "Go?" she asked.

"Oh, hi, Nicole," Diane said. "You came just in time." She lowered her voice to a conspiratorial tone, watching David wriggle out of the tire swing. "We're going to the house," she murmured.

"Without Cassie?" Nicole said. "We're a club! We're supposed to do things together!"

"Oh, for Pete's sake," Lisa said. "Cassie can't come. So why should we be bored?"

"Shh!" Diane warned.

David was standing right behind Nicole. "It's not nice to tell secrets," he said.

"We're not telling secrets," Diane said. "Come on, Lisa and Nicole. Let's go."

They started toward the bridge.

"Where're you going?" David asked.

"To Lisa's," Diane said, lying. "Get lost, will you? Go inside and watch TV or something. I think there's a horror show on tonight—something really gross, like you like to watch."

"Oh, good!" David cried, turning to run into the house.

Lisa watched him go. "Let's get over to Myrtle's before someone else comes out here."

When they reached the bridge, Diane and Lisa walked side by side, so that Nicole had to walk behind them. She frowned at the backs of their heads, hating the rejection. Cassie wouldn't do this to her! she thought.

They reached the opposite side. The wind picked up a bit, bowing the tall grass in Myrtle's backyard at an angle and sending dried leaves swirling upward. Lisa saw someone waving to her from a nearby house, and recognized one of her neighbors. She waved back.

"Crud," she said. "Mrs. Davis will probably tell my mom she saw me here."

"So?" Diane asked. "You live on this side of the lake. What's the crime in taking a walk?"

"If we're going to the house," Nicole put in, "let's hurry. Diane, you keep a lookout while I get the door open."

Carefully, looking in all directions, they walked up to Myrtle's back door. Nicole led the way inside. In the hot sun and humidity of the past days, the plants in the cobweb-strewn kitchen window had turned even more brown and frail. Moisture had created a breeding ground for mold in the laundry room.

Lisa held her nose in disgust. "They could at least send someone in here to clean this place up. Who'd want to buy it like this?"

"They can't sell it until they find out who it belongs to," Diane said. "My dad says it's in something called rebate."

"Probate," Lisa corrected. "And I think it's in something called Gross City."

Nicole opened the doorway to the back staircase. "Never mind," she said. "Let's go upstairs."

When they reached the toy room, Lisa found an easel and paint and began to draw a picture. It depicted three little girls under an oak tree, holding hands. Nicole came up next to her.

"Where am I?" she asked.

"Oh, yeah," Lisa said absently. She sketched in another child. "Here you are—in the long dress. See? Cassie and Diane and I are wearing shorts. How come you never wear shorts?"

"I don't—"

Diane cut Nicole off, winding up a dancing doll. "We've only been together a few times. How do you know she never wears shorts, Lisa?"

"Because she's too short to wear them!"

Lisa laughed uproariously at her joke, but both Nicole and Diane remained somber.

"That wasn't very nice, Lisa," Diane said. "Ignore her, Nicole. Sometimes she's a real dipbrain."

Nicole, frowning, went to stand by Diane. "I'd like to play with that doll," she said.

Diane hesitated. The doll was beautiful, unlike any she'd ever seen. But Nicole had been hurt by Lisa's cruel remark, and it seemed that the doll would make her happy again. With a smile, Diane handed it to her.

Lisa put the paints away, then turned her attention to a dollhouse that was nearly as big as she was. It was made for a teen fashion doll and was completely furnished. Lisa worked the elevator, transporting the ponytailed doll to the top floor.

"Can you imagine an old lady buying all this stuff?" she asked. "I mean, it looks new. Didn't she think her kids would have grown up by now?"

"She was nuts," Diane said. "Say, there's a Quickstep game. Wanna play?"

The children gathered around a small table, where Diane set up the game. The die was encased in a plastic dome at the game's center, and each girl took a turn pushing it to see who went first.

"Nicole's up," Diane said.

"She is not!" Lisa said. "She had a five and I had a three!"

"You had a six, Lisa," Nicole said softly.

Lisa glowered at her. "Liar," she said. "You just want to go first!"

"Oh, who cares?" Diane asked. "Let's just play!"

"I go first," Lisa said. She reached for the dome, but suddenly yanked her hand away with a yelp. Sucking her palm, she whined, "It burned me!"

"Oh, that's silly," Diane said. She popped the dome herself. "It's not hot at all."

Tears welled in Lisa's eyes. "I'm not lying!" she cried. "Oh, go to hell, both of you! I don't need you!"

She scrambled up, knocking her chair to the floor. She ripped the picture she had painted from the easel, folded it roughly, and shoved it into her pocket, then hurried from the room.

"Lisa!" Diane cried, jumping up. "Lisa, wait up! I'm sorry!"

Lisa ignored her. As she ran out of the house, she heard someone calling after her, but kept going toward her home. Who cared if someone had seen her leave the house? Who cared if she got caught? It didn't matter, not when her own friends turned against her. And it was all because of that stupid new girl!

Lisa's older sister, Paige, was sitting with her boyfriend at the kitchen table when Lisa burst through the back door. The teenagers looked up at the little girl, but Lisa was out of the room before they could ask what was wrong. Neither of her parents noticed her as she passed the living room.

Lisa opened the door to her room and went to lie on her bed. She stared up at the ceiling, letting herself calm down. Maybe it really hadn't been her turn, maybe she'd made a mistake. But still, Diane should have stuck up for her, not for Nicole. They'd been friends a lot longer!

She stood up, opening the door to the small bathroom that connected the room she shared with Paige with her other sisters' room. Making sure both doors were locked, Lisa held her hand under the makeup mirror to see the burn mark. But there was nothing there, not even a tiny mark.

"Weird," Lisa said. "I know what I felt."

She reached into her pocket to pull out the picture she'd painted. Sitting on the closed toilet, she began to unfold it.

Instead of four little girls underneath a tree, the picture showed Myrtle Hollenbeck, hanging. Her tongue poked out between red, misshapen lips. Words had been scribbled over her head: "Die like me, Lisa!"

Lisa screamed and jumped up, dropping the picture to the floor. Myrtle's image glared up at her, red paint dripping from the cartoon mouth like blood. Lisa went on screaming. Seconds later, someone was pounding at the door.

"Lisa! Let me in!" her mother cried.

"What's wrong, baby?" her father demanded.

Lisa looked at the door in panic. She couldn't let her parents see the picture! They'd start asking too many questions! Quickly, she grabbed it, tore it to pieces, and flushed the scraps down the toilet. Then she took a deep breath and said, "I'm okay. It was just a big spider. I got rid of it."

She heard her father groan. "Lisa, you're too much," he said.

Lisa opened the door and smiled up at him. "Sorry," she said in a singsong. "But it was really ugly."

"You have to expect a few bugs in a country home, Lisa," her mother said. "Now, come on, get your sweater. We're all going to the movies."

"Really?" Lisa asked. "Great! Now I don't have to stay home and be bored!"

"We'll meet you in front of the house," her father said.

Her parents left her room and Lisa went to her closet to find a sweater. Given a moment to think, she decided Nicole must have played a trick on her. While she was playing with the dollhouse, Nicole had painted that ugly picture. Then Lisa had run from the room in such a hurry that she didn't notice it was different. Well, she'd get even with Nicole!

She heard a gurgling noise in the bathroom. Worried that the paper hadn't flushed right, she went back to investigate. A half dozen black millipedes were crawling out of the toilet.

Lisa opened her mouth to scream, but covered it quickly with a shaking hand. She didn't want to risk angering her father. Instead, she grabbed for the can of bug spray under the sink and emptied it toward the creatures, keeping her head turned away. Then she ran from the bathroom and slammed the door.

Even as she hurried to meet her family outside, the millipedes disintegrated into thin air, as if they had never existed at all.

NINE

AFTER LEAVING THE Canfields', Robert drove around to the other side of the lake, planning to investigate Myrtle Hollenbeck's house. If the bomb had been made there, he would definitely find traces of gunpowder. When he pulled into the driveway, stopping the car just short of a broken garbage bag someone must have dumped there, he noticed a little girl running away from the house. Robert yelled at her as he got out of the car, but she seemed oblivious. Well, kids were curious. The macabre had a strange fascination for them.

Using the key he'd had since Myrtle's death, Robert entered the Victorian through the front door. The big staircase loomed to his left, disappearing up into blackness. To his right was a parlor, empty except for a worn-out couch and a television on a rickety metal stand. Spiders had decorated the corners of the fireplace, and something had knocked one of the logs onto the carpeting, scattering bits of ash and wood.

Robert was convinced that the person he was seeking had been hiding in the house. Robert would wait until he came back, wait in the shadows of one of the mansion's twenty rooms until the bastard got close enough to grab. Robert wanted him. He wanted a few minutes alone with the guy before he was carted off to jail. It had been a long time since he'd thrown a good, hard punch. . . .

Something hit the floor upstairs, rolled for a moment, and then stopped. Robert looked up at the cracked ceiling, then reached under his raincoat for his gun. Obviously, he wasn't alone. Carefully, hardly breathing, he went to the stairs and crept slowly upward. He heard whispers, then running feet.

He leaped onto the top floor, aiming his gun at a shadow that moved toward the back staircase.

"Freeze!!"

The shadow stopped abruptly. Still aiming the gun, never taking his eyes from the dim figure, Robert snapped on the hall light.

He recognized Diane Montana at once. The child's eyes were huge, her mouth open.

"Oh, dear God," he moaned. He shoved the gun back in its holster. "What the hell are you doing up here? I could have shot you!" The thought of that possibility made his heart skip a beat.

"I . . . I was just playing with the toys," Diane wailed. She backed away. "Me and Nicole."

Robert looked behind her. "Nicole?" he asked. "Where is she?"

Diane turned. "Well, she came out of the room with me. I guess she ran downstairs. You aren't going to tell on me, are you? Please don't! My mother would *kill* me!"

"Well, you shouldn't be here," Robert said with a sigh, walking toward the child. "It isn't safe. You could fall in the dark." *Or Georgie's partner could get you. . . .*

Diane put her hand on the door leading to the back staircase. "I'll go straight home," she said. "Please say you won't tell on me. I won't come back here again. I promise!"

"Well, all right," Robert said. "Go on, now, go home."

Diane nodded quickly, then jerked the door open and raced down the stairs. Robert listened until he heard the back door open and close. He rubbed his eyes wearily, his stomach souring as he realized how close he had come to shooting the little girl.

A thought occurred to him. If the maniac *was* in the house somewhere, how close had those children come to being victims? He'd have to make doubly certain that none of them got back into this house. He'd insist upon twenty-four-hour surveillance, not only to keep kids out, but to watch for the person he was sure was hiding here.

Robert went through every room of the house, but there seemed to be no indication of anyone's presence. In fact, its neglected condition was like a sign that said "Nobody's Home." The place hadn't been in great shape when they'd found Myrtle, but now it had begun to smell. A slightly offensive odor hung about the place.

Whoever the lunatic was, he didn't seem to mind living in squalor. Considering what Robert had heard of Georgie, he wasn't surprised that the boy had taken up with such a lowlife. He probably found the idea of meeting in a dead woman's house fascinating.

He decided to look the place over again, top to bottom. Robert walked down the hall to the door that sat at right angles to the stairway entrance. It was narrower than the others, with a long handle for a knob. Robert pressed it downward and opened the door, revealing three triangular steps that curved around into the darkness of the attic above. He pressed a button on the exposed electric box that hung to his right, and eerie amber light washed over the ancient, wormholed beams and across the bare wooden floor. It was beastly hot up here, and he could feel sweat rising under his collar even before he reached the top step. The banister wobbled from his weight, creaking in protest.

There was nothing up here. Not a single box of old clothes, not even a cracked mirror or an ancient, forgotten mannequin. It was as if Myrtle had had no past to keep safely tucked away.

It was as if the years since her children's disappearance had never happened.

Robert walked across the floor to the window, made translucent by layers of dust and grime. Through it, he could barely make out the flashing light of the bar and grill down the lake.

The floor, though dusty, was free of any black marks that might be gunpowder. The bomb hadn't been made up here. But he had to be certain. One of the panels between the beams could lead to a secret room. Robert believed the killer might well have found such a place—old houses like this were known to have them. He could hide when the police came to investigate the house, safely concealed behind an unmarked wall.

Moving from one panel to another, Robert knocked on the wood and pushed at crevices. Nothing happened. The attic was quickly crossed off his mental checklist as he headed for the stairs.

He'd just put a hand on the old banister when the lights suddenly went out and the door below slammed shut.

"Hey!"

In his haste, running down the stairs, Robert leaned too hard on the banister, cracking it from its unstable base. He flew forward into the dark abyss, tumbling head over heels down the wooden stairs. He landed a second later, his head slamming against the closed door. Groaning, every bone aching, his head ringing, Robert managed to scramble to his feet.

He heard soft laughter.

"Who's out there?" he demanded. He jiggled the latch, but the door had been locked from the outside. Robert pressed the light switch again. Nothing happened.

"Hell," he whispered. He was inches away from the man he wanted. "Open this door!"

A distorted voice responded loudly. It was as if the person on the other side of the door were speaking through a harmonizer. "Stay away, Detective. The blood of Lake Solaria is *mine!*"

"We'll see about that," Robert mumbled, pulling his gun from his coat. He backed away a step and aimed at the latch. He fired once, then kicked the door wide open, gun still poised.

The hallway was empty.

Robert swore, then ran down the back staircase. There had been no time for the intruder to reach the front stairs. Robert's shoulders knocked a few photos from the wall as he raced to the floor below, and pictures of the Hollenbeck children smashed against the metal-edged steps.

He took a quick look into the library, then sped along the hall to the front of the house. But when he reached the front door, he realized it was locked from the inside.

In a flash, Robert turned back to the kitchen. If he lost his man, when he'd been so close . . .

The back door was wide open, revealing a night world of shadows and dark hiding places. Robert knew he'd never be able to find the S.O.B. on his own. Without thinking, he reached for Myrtle's phone. The line was dead, disconnected weeks earlier.

Robert was about to hang up when he heard something crackle in the receiver. Frowning, he slowly brought the phone back to his ear.

"Don't try to stop me, or you'll die as that boy did!"

The voice was coming over the phone wires— wires that had been unplugged from the phone jack in the wall. Robert let the receiver drop from his hand. It curled back and forth on its cord, tapping the wall.

"What's going on?" Robert said out loud, looking around. "What kind of trick is this?"

A bird that had made the oak tree its home answered him with a mocking cackle.

Robert took a deep breath. It had been a hell of a day, without a moment's rest from the time he'd gotten the report about Cassie's accident. There had been no voice over the phone. He'd imagined it. His exhausted mind was playing tricks on him.

But he hadn't imagined the locked door upstairs, or the voice on the other side of that door. His muscles ached terribly, proof that *something* had happened in the attic. Georgie hadn't been working alone. Someone *was* here, someone with a mind so clever and unfeeling that it made Robert's blood run cold.

That someone was outside, momentarily beyond Robert's reach. But he'd be back. He'd return to his hiding place, and when he came, Robert would be here waiting for him.

He wouldn't call for a backup. He'd make the creep think he'd given up and left. Robert returned his gun to its holster, then went out the back door. The yard was quiet. Nothing disturbed the overgrown grass, not even the wind.

Robert rounded the corner of the house and headed for his car. He'd drive it just far enough away to hide it, then he'd come back here on foot. And he'd wait out the night in the house.

TEN

CAROLYN COULD NOT sleep. Long after Cassie had gone to bed, she sat in her office, working on her Christmas catalogue. Illustrations and samples of copy littered her desk, marked in red with her comments and changes. When she picked up the same piece of paper for the third time in a row, Carolyn realized she was too tired to think straight.

But she wasn't tired enough to go back upstairs. Earlier, after watching a late movie, she'd taken a warm shower and climbed into bed. Cassie was curled up toward one edge, fast asleep. She'd whispered something when Carolyn's weight made the bed sag a little, but a second later she was breathing evenly. Carolyn kissed her cheek, and tried to fall asleep herself. It hadn't worked. Eventually she had gotten up again to go downstairs to her office, thinking that maybe work would help clear her mind.

Alone now in the still house, she was able to think about what had happened that day. If what Bill had told her was right, if Cassie had been underwater for such a long time, she had been only seconds away from death. It could have come so fast, just the way it had come for Georgie Canfield. Rita had called Carolyn earlier to tell her that Frank Mathis had seen the boy near Robert Landers's van just before the explosion.

Now Carolyn stood up and walked out of her office, feeling pressure around her eyes. Tears welled up, then spilled over onto her cheeks. What kind of world was this—where a good man like Paul was shot to death, where an innocent little girl could be the victim of some malicious prank?

"God, if I ever lost you, Cassie . . ." she whispered, holding onto the stairpost and looking up at her door.

She was grateful that at least the child was sleeping well. She'd been in bed for hours with no indication that she was having a nightmare. Cassie deserved a good night's sleep, after the hell she'd been through. This was not a little girl's carefree summer, Carolyn thought. Nearly drowning in a boating accident, seeing Myrtle's body hanging from the oak, having the charred remains of a neighbor pulled from the wreckage of a burned vehicle in her own driveway. Cassie had been through so much—

A thought flashed through Carolyn's mind, one that made her stagger. She sank down onto the bottom step. What if Cassie was *meant* to be in that boat? Robert Landers had seemed to think there was someone with Myrtle the night she died, someone Cassie might have seen but forgotten about. Someone who might want to silence her daughter forever. Maybe it had been Georgie, and his plans to hurt Cassie had backfired. Yes, Georgie might have been the one who tried to hurt Cassie—but Carolyn couldn't quell the nagging feeling that Cassie was still in danger. She had to make certain her daughter was completely safe, had to know beyond a doubt that the threat to her daughter had died with Georgie Canfield.

Carolyn would need help from someone. Robert Landers came to mind at once, and Carolyn went into the kitchen and pulled open a counter drawer to find her phone book. She looked up his number and dialed, not caring that it was two o'clock in the morning. She needed to talk to someone sympathetic. When his voice came on the line, Carolyn began to speak immediately, until she realized that he had continued talking. She had gotten a recording. Impatiently, she waited for the beep, then said, "This is Carolyn Larchmont. I desperately need to talk to you. Please call me as soon as you can."

Carolyn hung up, feeling terribly alone, unaware that Robert was sleeping in the Hollenbeck house across the lake.

Robert's sleep was full of ugly dreams. He was standing at the edge of the lake, watching the setters romp around Myrtle's backyard. Two children were playing with them, laughing and running. Robert reached toward the dogs, tried to call them. His voice was nonexistent.

One of the children, the little boy, turned to look at him. Norman Hollenbeck grinned broadly as Kelly leaped up to lick his broken, bloody head.

Then Myrtle was there, wagging a finger, walking toward the dogs. "Stay away from those filthy animals, children!"

Robert tried to say that his animals were not filthy, but the only sound that came from his lips was a deep tone, like the moan of an oboe.

"I'll have to wash them first," Myrtle said. "I've made a nice bath for the dogs."

She picked up Kelly as if the setter were no more than a bag of bones. Robert watched as she carried the animal to a fire that had suddenly materialized near the back door of the house.

". . . sterilize," Myrtle was saying.

Robert screamed, the sound like a thunderclap in his head. Myrtle tossed Kelly bodily onto the flames, nodding in a pleased way as she saw the red fire blend with the dog's red coat. She moved toward Erin. The children laughed and danced around the fire, their smashed faces glistening in the flames.

Robert tried desperately to move toward them, reaching forward, crying out. But the lake had suddenly swelled, and the water that grabbed his ankles was as thick as tar.

Myrtle threw Erin onto the fire. "Clean dogs," she said. "Must have clean animals for my babies. Sterilized animals."

Ellen Hollenbeck was singing a doggie song.

Sian howled, running in confused circles in search of her sister and mother.

Robert shouted, struggled, fought the dense guck that snarled his legs.

And then Lynda was there, standing inches away,

the toes of her red pumps touching the edge of the tar.

She'd been buried in her red pumps.

"You can't save them, Robert," she said. "Like you couldn't save me. You let me suffer alone, Robert."

Robert's mouth formed her name, but no sound came out. He reached for her, holding his arms out for an embrace. Lynda backed away.

"Too late, Robert. Too late. Too late. I'm dead. The dogs are dead. Myrtle's dead. You're—"

Robert jerked himself awake, his subconscious mind refusing to let him hear what was next. Lynda's voice echoed in his mind.

He was tucked inside a sleeping bag in one of the empty bedrooms, the rug beneath his head rough and musty-smelling. His heart throbbing, he pulled himself out of the sleeping bag. His legs felt as if they'd been shot with novocaine.

As if he'd tried to drag them through tar.

He hadn't meant to fall so deeply asleep. He had planned to take only a short rest, giving himself strength to fight his enemy—if his enemy ever showed up. Robert crept out of the room, down the dark hall. He had to pee something fierce. In the bathroom, he looked down at the toilet to keep from seeing the staring, photographed eyes of Ellen and Norman Hollenbeck in the faint glow from the streetlight outside. Some shrine, he thought, zipping up his pants. It's a real honor to have your picture hung over the john.

He reached to flush the toilet, but stopped himself. Water running through the pipes would alert the intruder to his presence.

Robert paused to look at his shadowy reflection, seeing the hollow, smoky eyes of a beaten man. Why had Lynda appeared to him, speaking in such mocking tones?

That wasn't Lynda, he told himself, just a dream image.

His dream self had always seen Lynda at a much younger age, long before she died. She was always happy in his dreams, laughing in a watery manner at anything he said. That was the way he wanted to remember her.

But in tonight's dream, she'd had the pale, shadowed look of the dying woman she'd been those last few weeks.

And she said he'd left her to suffer alone.

"But you never told me," Robert whispered.

You should have known, his subconscious whispered.

Oh, yes, he should have known. Dear God, he should have guessed that something was wrong. The dark circles that formed under Lynda's green eyes, the way her clothes began to sag on her body, the 1 A.M. bathroom sessions . . .

"I didn't know, damn it," Robert whispered. "Lynda, I loved you. I'm so sorry. I'm sorry I didn't see what was happening."

He'd been suspicious, but because of Lynda's otherwise cheerful demeanor he hadn't acted on his suspicions. But now he knew better. He'd learned to ask questions—like he was asking questions about Myrtle's death, about the boating incident, about the explosion. He'd learned to follow through no matter what others thought, and for this reason he was spending the night at Myrtle's house, waiting for the person he was sure had given Georgie the bomb.

Robert pushed thoughts of Lynda from his mind. His sleep, though on a hard floor and plagued with dreams, had given him new energy. Robert sensed that the energy came more from anger than from determination, but it didn't matter. He was strong enough now to face anything.

He walked back out to the hallway, moving as quietly as the old floorboards would allow. The upstairs was almost completely void of light, illuminated only by the streetlight that shone through one small window. Hearing took over where vision was almost useless, and Robert's every nerve was tensed. The maniac could be up here, hiding in the shadows. He could be down on the first floor, or sleeping in the basement. Maybe he wasn't here at all.

But he'll be back.

Robert continued slowly along the hallway, stopping at each door and listening for any unusual sound. He crept down the front staircase, with his arm rubbing the wall, his hand ready to grab for his gun.

You might be making a fool of yourself, Robert. Maybe he's not here. Maybe you're chasing a wild goose.

He ignored the thought. Everything looked the same in the living room. Even the wood chips that had spilled from the fireplace hadn't been disturbed. Robert moved through to the dining room, where the pedestal table was laden with pictures of Myrtle's children. Through the tall bay windows he could see sparkles of moonlight on the darkened lake. The houses on the opposite shore were black, with one exception.

Robert recognized the lighted home as Larchmont place. Was Cassie still up, he wondered, unable to sleep after the day's horror? Or would that be Carolyn, keeping watch over her daughter?

Maybe there was trouble over there. . . .

Robert made a quick decision. Much as he wanted to stay here, to search through every room until he ran his suspect to earth, his detective's mind ordered him to go where he might be needed. Tucking his shirt into his pants, Robert went into the kitchen and crossed to the back door. He stood for a few moments to one side of the pane of glass, watching the backyard. When he was certain that the way was clear, he opened the door and left the house.

He was heading toward the street when a shrill cry pierced his head. Robert swung around, his hand reaching for his gun at the same instant. But before he could pull it out, a dark figure leaped at him, knocking him to the ground. Teeth ripped into his cheek, nails clawed his arms.

Robert shouted, grabbing the shadowy thing by its hair. It continued screaming, a half-animal, half-human sound. And in the snarls he could almost make out words.

"Geee . . . *out*!"

Robert felt something warm trickle into his ear.

His own blood. He tried to push the thing away, rolling around the sandy driveway. Thoughts flashed through his mind in a crazy way.

It's small, lighter than me. Why can't I fight it?

It bit his shoulder. Robert yelled, throwing all his weight forward, and managed somehow to pin the wild creature to the ground. It struggled beneath him, screaming.

"Son of a bitch!" Robert cried.

It had taken a chunk out of his forearm.

He held fast to it, squinting through the darkness. He realized now that this was no wild animal, but a human! Had he caught his suspect?

"Who are you?" Robert hissed.

"You don't belong here!" a voice snarled. "Stay away and let me finish my work!"

Robert stood up, holding his captive by the front of his shirt, dragging the person up with him. The attacker felt light, almost nonexistent.

Like no one's there at all.

"Oh, God . . ."

Robert's hands opened suddenly, and an empty pile of clothes fell to the ground.

ELEVEN

ROBERT SAT ON a gurney in the emergency room of St. Martha's Hospital, watching as a young doctor with dark circles under his eyes bandaged his forearm. Robert's neck was patched with gauze, and his cheeks stung with antiseptic.

"I've put a rush on your blood tests," the intern said. "Human bites are nothing to play around with. They can be more dangerous than dog bites, in fact."

He tied off the bandage. Then he pulled a pen from the breast pocket of his white smock and jotted something down on a little pad. Ripping the sheet off, he handed it to Robert and said, "Something to keep you from getting an infection. If you have any problems, you can contact me."

"Thanks," Robert said. *I do have problems*, he thought, *but none you can help me with*.

He slid down from the table, his shoes thudding softly onto the tile floor. Watching the doctor disappear behind a green curtain, Robert rolled his sleeve down. His arm had finally stopped throbbing, but if he moved the wrong way he felt razor-sharp stings where the stitches pulled his skin.

After his assailant had escaped, Robert had chased through the woods surrounding Myrtle's property in search of him. But the creep had gotten away, and the pain of Robert's wounds was too much to ignore. He'd gone back to the scene of his attack and gathered up the clothing, careful to touch as little of it as possible. He'd found a green plastic garbage bag under Myrtle's kitchen sink, and had tied the garment inside it.

He'd figured out what must have happened. His assailant had been wearing a loose jacket or shirt, and had simply pulled out of it. It was so dark that he'd been able to slip away into the shadows before Robert realized it. But there was one consolation. This proved that there was someone else involved in the bombing of his van.

Unable to catch his suspect, Robert had walked slowly and painfully to his car, which he'd parked on a dark road that angled toward Lakefront Road. Getting in and pulling the door closed had been almost unbearably agonizing. Blood was seeping through his shirt, and his neck stung where his collar rubbed the bite on his skin. First point went to the suspect, but Robert wasn't going to give him the game.

Robert had driven himself to the emergency room and waited impatiently through all the paperwork, wanting only to get back to his own work. Now that he'd been cleared, he tucked the prescription into his hip pocket and picked up his things. He went out to his car, alone under a tall lamp in the small parking lot.

He decided to go back to headquarters, where he knew Susan would be working the night shift. The green garbage bag sat on the seat next to him. For a second, it made him think of a body bag.

Robert forced the thought aside, starting the engine. He drove a few miles down the road, then turned in where a big yellow bulb announced "Police." Both of Lake Solaria's squad cars were out, which meant that the building would be virtually empty. Robert was grateful that he wouldn't have to stop and talk to anyone. The desk sergeant looked up briefly as Robert entered and mumbled, "Hi," then went back to his crossword puzzle without questioning the bandages.

Susan, on the other hand, was all over him in a minute like a concerned mother.

"Look at you!" she cried, putting down a box of slides and hurrying over. She reached up toward his face, her fingers stopping just millimeters from the bandage. Robert was surprised to catch himself cringing a little.

"Were you in a fight?" Susan asked. "Do you want a cup of coffee? If you're off-duty, I've got some scotch tucked away in the supplies cabinet."

Robert shook his head, laying the green bag on the table. "I've got something I want you to look at," he said.

"First tell me what happened to you."

"I was attacked," Robert said, sighing deeply. "I think it was the same person who blew up my van and cut apart the Montanas' rowboat."

"Oh, Robert, that's impossible," Susan said. "Witnesses saw Georgie Canfield climbing into your van, and he was alone!"

"He was alone at the van," Robert said, "but not necessarily before. I talked to his parents, Susan. The kid was a dropout with no ambition. You tell me where he got the smarts to build a pipe bomb. And who'd sell gunpowder to a kid like that, anyway?"

"We're checking into that," Susan said. "All the sports shops, ranges, and gun shops in the area are being sent standard questionnaires."

"And they won't find anything," Robert insisted. "But I think I know the right place to look. I went back to the house after leaving my dogs at the vet's. I thought I might be able to wait it out until my suspect came back."

"You went back to the house?"

"The Hollenbeck house, of course," Robert said. "I think that's where he's hiding. I mean, where else? The place is empty now."

"Of course it's empty," Susan said. "There's no one there!"

Robert took a metal folding chair from its perch against the wall, opened it, and sat down. Susan leaned back against the counter, her arm jiggling a rack of test tubes. She pushed it back from the edge.

"If no one is there," Robert said, staring down at the floor stained with chemicals and ancient blood, "how did this happen to me?" He pointed to his face.

"I don't know," Susan said softly. "Maybe you should tell me the whole story."

Robert explained what had happened, beginning with his return to the house. "He attacked me out in the yard," he finished. He propped his elbows on his knees and wove his fingers into his hair.

"I thought I was a better cop than this," he said wearily. "I thought my reactions were quicker. Twice tonight that bastard was within my reach, and I let him get away!"

Susan reached out to lay a hand on his shoulder, then hesitated. Robert wasn't the kind of person you went around comforting in a physical way. But then again, she was.

"The hell with it," she mumbled, bending down to put her arms around him.

Robert didn't react at first; then he sat back and patted her arm.

"But I'll get him," he said. "I've got my first piece of concrete evidence. Maybe you can take a look at what's in that bag. It's an article of clothing. The guy slipped out of it when he escaped me the second time. But this proves he exists."

Susan turned toward it. "For your sake, I hope it does. I don't think the chief's going to believe you, otherwise. Meantime, Robert, have you contacted Chris Geisly? He's on patrol at the lake tonight, and he should know what happened to you."

"How could I call him?" Robert asked. "They don't provide police radios in those crates that pass for rental cars. And Myrtle's phone has been disconnected. Besides, the guy's probably far away by now."

"Maybe not," Susan said. "If he's staying at the Hollenbeck place, as you think, he's bound to return there sooner or later."

Robert's eyes widened a bit. This was the first time Susan had indicated she might be on his side.

And if he could convince her, he could make the others listen to him.

He stood up. "I'll have the dispatcher call him. Take a look at the clothes, Susan. I'll be right back." He left the room.

Susan went to the table and put on a pair of sterile gloves, wanting to disturb this evidence as little as possible. There might be a stain on the fabric, microscopic bits of gunpowder, or some other important clue.

She turned the bag upside down and dumped out the contents. For a split second, she simply stared at the pile on the table. And then a look of complete confusion crossed her face.

There was no garment in the bag at all, just a handful of shredded newspaper.

Susan looked toward the door. If it had been anyone else, she might have thought this was a joke. But Robert wasn't the joking kind, and he certainly wouldn't pull a stunt like this after what had happened to his dogs today.

Unless he was so obsessed with this case that he was imagining things.

Susan heard the sound of his returning footsteps. She quickly raked the newspapers into the bag and retied it.

"What do you think?" Robert asked as he entered the room.

Susan studied him carefully for a moment. There was no glint in his eyes, no indication that this was a trick.

"I'll have to send samples down to the lab," she said. "It looks rather ordinary, but you never know what you'll find." She pushed the bag away, touching it with only her fingertips as if it were something diseased. "Robert, when was the last time you slept?"

"I took a nap in the Hollenbeck house."

"Oh, perfect," Susan said. "I bet you slept really soundly, too."

Soundly enough to have a nightmare, Robert thought. "I was rested when I got up."

I doubt that," Susan said. "You may have had your eyes closed, but every nerve in your body was tensed for the arrival of the suspect. Robert, I bet you haven't really slept, in your own bed, since early yesterday morning."

"There's work to be done," Robert said.

"And we have people doing it," Susan pointed out. "Give it a rest tonight. Go on home."

Robert paused, looking at the bag. She was right, he thought. He needed sleep now. He prayed that that sleep would be free of nightmares.

"Good night, Susan," he said. "And thanks."

"Anything for a friend," Susan answered.

After he left, she picked up the bag. Anything, indeed, for a friend. If Mike Hogan found out about this, he'd force Robert to take a vacation. He would see, as Susan did, that Robert's fixation with the events on Lake Solaria was pushing him to the brink.

Susan stepped on the pedal at the bottom of a domed trash can and pushed the green bag down deep inside. Nobody would ever know that Robert had brought it here.

TWELVE

CASSIE FOUND HER mother with her head down on the kitchen table the next morning. Carolyn had fallen asleep waiting for Robert to call. Carolyn looked up when she heard her daughter, and Cassie's eyes widened.

"You look *terrible*. Gee, you aren't sick, are you?" Cassie asked.

"I'm just tired, baby," Carolyn said groggily. She forced herself to come awake, pushing the chair back. It felt as heavy as if it were made of stone. "I didn't sleep well last night. How do you feel?"

"Just great," Cassie said. "Can I go outside today? Please? I fed the fish and made my bed already." She mentioned her daily chores so that her mother would think everything was normal. That way, Carolyn would be more likely to let her go outside.

"Of course you can go out," Carolyn said. "So long as you feel all right. But I thought after what happened yesterday . . ."

"I'm okay, Mom," Cassie said.

Carolyn watched as Cassie helped herself to a box of cereal from the cupboard. The little girl filled her bowl with Frutti Bitz and milk and ate quickly. Much as she was grateful that Cassie had an appetite this morning, Carolyn was unnerved that her daughter seemed to show no sympathy at all toward Georgie Canfield. To Cassie, this was just like any other morning.

Cassie's blue eyes narrowed, and she looked up at her mother. "I wish I could remember what happened when I fell into the water yesterday," she said.

"Maybe you're better off not remembering," Carolyn said.

Cassie frowned. "I just have a creepy feeling that I *should* remember, like it was something really awful. I sure hope nothing bad happens when I'm playing today!"

"It's going to be a great day," Carolyn insisted, hating to hear the worry in her child's voice. "Here, give me a kiss for the morning. Go out and have a good time, and put yesterday out of your mind. If you need me, baby, I'm going to be working in my office."

Cassie kissed her mother's cheek and left the house. Solo, wagging his bushy tail, danced in circles around her as she bounded across the yard. "I'll play with you later, Solo," she said. The dog tilted his head to one side. "I'm going to Diane's house."

Nicole suddenly came up beside her. "Good morning," she said.

Cassie stopped. "What do you do, Nicole?" she asked, her voice unnaturally high. "Hide out in my bushes? You're always here!"

"If you want me to go home . . ."

"Of course I don't," Cassie said. "You're my new friend!"

Nicole's eyes brightened. "I like to hear that," she said. "What are you going to do today?"

"Oh, just hang around, I guess," Cassie said. "I can't go in the water, that's for sure. Not until my mom cools off about yesterday. We could play hopscotch with Diane and Lisa, or—I know! I've got a Chinese jump rope. I'll go and get it before we go to Diane's."

She turned back to her house, Nicole walking in double time to keep up with her. At the back door, she stopped and said, "It'll just take a minute to find it. I'll be right down!"

In her bedroom, Cassie found her Chinese jump rope in a dresser drawer. As she brought it back downstairs, she passed her mother in the kitchen. "I'll be at Diane's, Mom," she said.

"Have fun," Carolyn answered, busy fixing herself a glass of iced tea. She followed her daughter to the back door and stood there, gazing out. Cassie was skipping down the beach, swinging the jump rope like a lariat. Following the bend of the lake, she disappeared behind some apple trees in their neighbor's yard. Smiling, Carolyn started to turn away.

A child screamed.

The sound came from across the lake, from the Hollenbeck house. Carolyn turned toward the scream. A soft, tingling feeling began to creep up her back. She couldn't see anyone near the old Victorian mansion. She must have imagined it, she thought. Suddenly she was shivering despite the summer heat. From the time she'd been a little girl, the old house had made her feel nervous. As each day passed, it looked more run-down, more threatening.

Carolyn knew that the police had been in and out of the place, and she had seen Robert Landers's van parked alongside the house in the past weeks. She wondered why her driveway had been picked for the vehicle's destruction. Why not that weedy, unraked path next to the old Victorian?

"That is an unkind thought," Carolyn told herself. "Robert's van should never have been blown up at all."

She was talking out loud to herself, something she did only when she was nervous. The Hollenbeck house looked surreal through the moist, hot air.

Carolyn saw a child running through the backyard, the tall grass reaching nearly as high as the girl's shoulders. Carolyn opened the back door and took a few slow steps across the yard.

The child was gone.

Carolyn rubbed her eyes, feeling sweat on her lashes. It was hot out here. "Better get inside and do some work," she mumbled, turning back to her house.

She walked stiffly up the back stairs, her body tense, as if she expected something to jump at her. She slammed the screen door shut and went to sit at the table.

"It's just a house, Carolyn," she told herself. "Just a big empty house."

No, it's more than that. It's a place of evil. Bad

things happen there, her mind argued.

"What bad things?" Carolyn asked.

But she didn't want to know the answer to her own question. There was something tucked in the back of her mind, some memory that had to do with the place, but Carolyn would never let it surface. She only knew that she hated that old house, and just looking at it sent chills through her.

The phone rang.

"Nothing like business to ease a troubled mind," she said, walking into her office. She picked up the receiver and found herself talking to Mort, her factory foreman. While she was talking, Cassie returned to the yard with her friends. Carolyn could see them through the window, playing with Cassie's jump rope.

Outside, Cassie was listening in amazement to Diane's story.

"And he almost shot me!" Diane said. "He had the gun pointing right at me!"

"If he tells anyone about seeing you," Cassie said worriedly, "we're doomed."

Diane shook her head. "He promised he wouldn't. He seemed like a really nice guy."

"I wouldn't trust a grown-up," Nicole said.

"I would," Diane said. She gave Nicole a dirty look. "And you! What's the big idea of running off on me like that? Leaving me to take the blame?"

Nicole looked guileless. "It was so dark," she said. "I thought you were right behind me. Besides, you didn't get in trouble. You just said so."

Cassie let one end of the jump rope fall to the ground, placing her foot through the elastic loop.

She stretched it up to her shoulder. "Guess we can't have our club anymore," she said.

"Well, maybe not for a while," Diane agreed. "Not until the police are finished at that house."

"When they finish," Cassie said, "they'll take all the toys away!"

"No, they won't," Nicole said. She was staring across the lake at the house.

Diane clicked her tongue. "How do you know that?"

Nicole shrugged. "Just do. What would they want with a bunch of toys?"

"Maybe they'll give them to their kids," Cassie suggested.

"Maybe they need them as evidence," Diane said. "Or maybe they'll find some of Myrtle's relatives to inherit them. Anyway, I'm just sure our whole club is ruined." She pouted, kicking a clump of lakegrass. "I thought it was too good to last."

Nicole stomped the ground with one black boot. "It will last!" she snapped. "They won't take the toys away! They won't! They won't!"

Diane and Cassie looked at each other, amazed by such an outburst from their usually quiet friend.

Cassie touched her arm. "It's okay," she insisted. "We have other toys. And maybe the police will leave those alone. Let's not think about it. I want to play Chinese jump rope."

"I'd like to go first, please," Nicole said.

"Well, uh, sure," Diane said. Something in Nicole's tone told her that there was no room for discussion. "You go right ahead."

This was the second time in two days she'd let

the new girl have her way, first with the doll last night, now with this game. She wondered why she wanted to be so especially nice to Nicole.

Nicole smiled, her sweet self again. "Thank you," she said. "Can you sing a song?"

While Cassie and Diane chanted a jumping rhyme, Nicole stepped easily in and out of the rope that stretched between her friends' legs. When the chant was over, she stepped back.

"I'll take over your end, Cassie," she said. "It's your turn."

They switched places, and in time to another rhyme Cassie began to skip over the ropes. Then, suddenly, she stopped and let out a disgusted cry. "Oh, gross me out!"

"What's wrong?" Diane demanded.

Cassie pointed to the rope. "Look at all that squishy stuff," she said. "What is that?"

A yellowish glob, as thick as honey, dripped from the rope.

Diane paled. "I think you stepped on a slug, Cassie," she said softly.

"Ugh," Nicole groaned. "I don't want to play this game anymore."

Cassie shook her head, her yellow hair flying. "Me neither!" she said emphatically. "I'll ask my mom later to hose this off. Let's just leave it, okay?"

"Yeah, why don't we go and see if Lisa is up?" Diane suggested. "Come on, Nicole. I guess this wasn't the day for Chinese jump rope, anyway."

Nodding, the dark-haired child left the yard with Cassie and Diane.

Sometime around noon, Carolyn put her work

aside and went to call Cassie in to lunch. Though her work kept her very busy, she insisted that lunchtime be spent with her daughter. She took out the ingredients for tuna salad, one of Cassie's favorites. Thinking of the child's recent troubles, she decided she'd treat the little girl to a rare bottle of cola, something she rarely let Cassie have for fear that the caffeine would disturb her already unruly sleep.

When she opened the back door, Carolyn noticed the jump rope lying in the grass. She stared at it for a moment, confused. The jump rope had been a gift from Cassie's father, given long before she was old enough to use it, and Cassie had always cherished it. Why had she just dropped it that way? Solo was sniffing it, scratching wildly, whining.

"What is it, Solo?" Carolyn asked, crossing the yard to where the red rope was entwined through the grass. Solo looked up at her and barked.

Carolyn bent to pick up the rope, but immediately dropped it. The elastic band felt slimy, and was so cold that her hand tingled. She looked at her hand and saw a yellowish ooze streaked across her palm.

"No wonder Cassie dropped it," Carolyn told Solo. She looked the rope over, found a dry spot, and picked it up with two fingers. "What *is* this stuff?"

Carolyn carried it back to the house, deciding she would soak it in a tub of hot detergent. It was probably just a secretion from the weeds in the grass, or maybe a squished bug had gotten rubbed along it.

"Whatever it is," she said, "it's cold."

Carolyn took a basin out and set it in the sink. She laid the rope inside it, coiling it to fit, then opened a bottle of detergent and squeezed the blue liquid into the tub. A flick of her wrist sent water pouring from the faucet, and moments later steam rose from the billowing suds.

"There, now," she said. "Cassie's jump rope will be good as new in a little while."

She turned to the counter to prepare Cassie's lunch. Behind her, Solo suddenly began to jump about, whining and yelping frantically. Carolyn turned to see him gazing up at the sink, turning in circles. She was about to yell at the dog for making so much noise, but her words choked in her throat when she saw the object of his frenzy.

The sink that had been sparkling clean moments earlier was infested with worms. Fat, C-shaped blobs with red stripes wriggled over the basin's edge, dropped into the sink, stretched along the counter.

Carolyn gagged, covering her mouth with one hand. She felt her breakfast rising and tasted coffee on the back of her tongue.

One of the slimy creatures turned and seemed to be looking right at her. It opened its mouth, and Carolyn began to scream.

It had dozens of needlelike teeth. A sound gargled from its red throat. Something that sounded like . . .

Carolyn covered her ears.

"Kill—er! Kill—er!"

The slug flipped over the edge of the counter, landing on the floor with a soft squish. Carolyn screamed, fainting into blackness.

THIRTEEN

ROBERT WAS SUNK into a deep, dreamless sleep when a neighbor's barking dog jostled him awake. Momentarily disoriented, he glanced around his room, unable to remember climbing into bed that morning. His hand throbbed, and little needles of pain played over his face. Wearily, he pushed the covers aside. The mutt next door kept yapping, making him think of his own dogs. They'd been kept overnight at the vet's for observation, and Robert was due to pick them up soon.

Walking into the kitchen on aching legs, he made himself a cup of coffee. He drank it quickly, taking big gulps. The warmth ran through him, revitalizing him. By the time he was dressed to leave, he was ready to renew his private investigation.

As Robert drove toward town, he felt that yesterday had happened ten years earlier. It had already taken on the unreal, dreamlike quality of a bad memory. Yet the threadbare seat and bent steering wheel of this wreck were proof that it really had happened, and that the nightmare wasn't over.

As he turned onto Moxahala Street, the highest

point in town, he was able to look down at a section of the lake. The Hollenbeck mansion towered above the other houses, and from this distance it looked like no more than a pretty Victorian structure. A place like that would bring in a fortune in one of the bigger cities. Right now, Robert tended to agree with Carolyn Larchmont—it ought to be torn to the ground.

He stopped the car at the next corner, waiting for a boy and a girl on horseback to cross the road. As he sat there, he gazed through his open window at the old mansion. Was anyone there now? he wondered. Or had his suspect decided to move on to another hideout?

He continued driving straight along the road, rather than making the turn that would lead him to the animal hospital. He drove to the end of Lakefront Road, making his way to the Larchmont house; he wanted to ask Carolyn why she'd been up so late last night.

He parked behind her car and went to knock at the screen door. He could hear the hum of her computer, but no one came to the door. He knocked again, then called, "Hello?"

The Larchmonts' mutt came running down the hall, barking. He leaped against the screen, his claws making soft scratching noises.

"If she didn't hear the bell," Robert said, "she'll certainly hear you, boy."

The dog turned and ran back down the hall, then stopped halfway and looked over his shoulder. He barked again, sharply. Robert noticed that the dog's tail wasn't wagging, and sensed immediately that something was wrong. Calling out again, he opened the door and entered the house.

He found Carolyn lying on the kitchen floor, surrounded by shallow, soapy puddles.

"Oh, no," he said softly, kneeling beside her. He took her wrist carefully, and let out a sigh of relief at finding a strong pulse. Patting her cheek, he called, "Carolyn? Wake up, Carolyn!"

She didn't stir.

Robert got to his feet. He needed smelling salts. With Solo tagging behind him, whining in confusion, he hurried upstairs and into the bathroom, but there was no first aid kit there. He tried the hall closet next, and found a small blue case next to a box of cotton balls. He clicked it open, selected a small pink tube wrapped in gauze, and ran downstairs.

"Here you go," he said, lifting Carolyn's head. He broke the tube between his thumb and forefinger and held it under her nose.

Carolyn gasped, then coughed, knocking his hand away. She opened her eyes, and for a moment seemed to look right through him. She started brushing at herself in a frenzy, a look of complete disgust on her face. "Get them off of me!"

"Carolyn!" Robert said. "There's nothing there!"

She looked into his eyes, bewildered. "What . . . what happened?"

Robert helped her to sit up. "You'll have to tell me that," he said. "I found you lying here. You must have fainted."

Carolyn scrambled to her feet, her eyes wide. She

looked around herself. "Where are they?" she demanded.

"What?"

"Those wormy things," she said. She shuddered. "Oh, God! They were disgusting! They came crawling from that basin, dozens of them!"

Robert looked at the tub of suds, then over the counter. "Well, they're gone now," he said. He took Carolyn by the arm and led her to a seat. "Maybe you'd better tell me what happened."

Carolyn rubbed her arms. She explained how she had found Cassie's jump rope out in the yard, and how she had tried to clean it.

"Why would you want to clean a jump rope?" Robert asked.

"There was this strange stuff all over it," Carolyn said. "I guess the kids must have crushed a slug when they were playing. Ugh!"

Robert leaned forward. "What kind of stuff?" he asked. "What did it look like?"

"Well, it was yellowish," Carolyn said, wondering why he seemed so concerned, "and thick like honey, and cold. I've never seen anything like it before."

But I have, Robert thought. *On the rope Myrtle used to hang herself.* "You brought it inside and tried to clean it, then?" he pressed.

"It's in the sink," Carolyn said. "I put it in there to soak. When I turned around, Solo was barking like crazy, and these horrid worms were crawling out of it. Worms with teeth!" She rubbed her stomach. "I think I've lost my appetite for the day," she groaned. She looked at Robert. "But where do you suppose they went? How could so many of them have disappeared so quickly? And how did they—"

She stopped short, frowning. "I don't know why I'm telling you this," she said. "You're a detective, used to concrete facts. You probably think I imagined the whole thing."

"I don't think that at all," Robert insisted. "After what happened here yesterday, I'm open to believing anything."

Carolyn stood up and turned to the counter. The unopened tuna can sat waiting next to a bowl. She hooked the can under the can opener and watched it spin around. "My daughter is probably wondering why I haven't called her for lunch," she said.

"Carolyn, what do you think happened here?" Robert asked.

She dumped the tuna into the bowl and began breaking it apart with a fork, stabbing more vigorously than necessary. "I don't know," she said. "But I'll tell you something. That house has something to do with it."

"House?"

"Myrtle's house, of course," she said. She went to the refrigerator and pulled out mayonnaise and celery. Chopping the celery with abrupt strokes, she went on talking. "That house influences a lot of the things that happen around here. It gave me nightmares when I was a kid, and I'm sure it's the cause of my own little girl's bad dreams."

She struggled to open the mayonnaise jar. Robert came to her side to help her.

"Houses can't do bad things," he said.

Carolyn glanced sideways at him. "No? There's been nothing but tragedy there for years," she said. "Look at Myrtle's children disappearing, at her going crazy, at her killing herself. It's an evil place, Detective Landers." She stirred the mayonnaise into the bowl. "And I don't care if you think I'm crazy to believe that."

"I don't think you're crazy," Robert said softly.

He watched her make sandwiches, seeing her hands tremble.

"Do you want one?" she asked.

"No, thanks," Robert said. "Look, are you okay? Do you want me to finish this?"

Carolyn managed a smile. "That's all right. I have to make it just so for Cassie, just the way she likes it. I don't want her to think anything's wrong with . . ."

She slammed the knife on the counter. "Oh, damn!" she said. "I wish I could calm down! But I keep thinking of those slugs!"

"Well, I have a theory about that," Robert said, taking the knife and cutting the sandwiches into triangles. "I think the creep who set fire to my van snuck in here and dumped a box of them into the sink. Then he came back and cleared the place out while you were lying there. If I'd been a few minutes sooner . . ."

Carolyn's brows knitted. "How can that be?" she asked. "Georgie Canfield is dead."

"I don't think Georgie was alone yesterday," Robert said. "I think someone helped him. And that someone is still around, still causing trouble. I ran into him last night, as a matter of fact."

Carolyn studied his face. "I'm sorry," she said. "I was so wrapped up in myself that I didn't see you've been hurt. What happened?"

"I was at the Hollenbeck place last night," Robert said. "I went there after having a talk with the Canfields. That's why I'm here today. I noticed your light on late last night."

"I couldn't sleep," Carolyn said. "In fact, I tried to call you. Did you get my message?"

Robert shook his head. "I never listened to my answering machine," he said. "I was too busy."

"You said you ran into your suspect last night," she said. "Those cuts on your face—someone did that to you. The person you think was working with Georgie?"

"That's right," Robert said.

Carolyn looked down at the counter, sighing. "I was hoping I was wrong," she mumbled.

"What's that?"

Carolyn looked into his eyes. "I have a terrible feeling that Cassie isn't safe," she said. "Just a mother's intuition. But now you come and tell me that Georgie's death won't end the threat to my daughter. Robert, do you remember when you asked if Cassie saw someone with Myrtle that night?"

"Has she said anything about that?"

"Not much," Carolyn said, "although she did mention a couple times that she couldn't quite remember what she saw that night. What if she did see someone? And what if that person tried to kill her in the boat?"

Robert could tell by her tone that she was hoping

he'd set her mind at ease, that he'd tell her she was completely wrong. But he'd been carrying the same theory around in his mind, and he couldn't lie about it.

"I'm afraid that's a possibility," he said. "But I promise you that Cassie will be protected. I'll have patrols around this lake twenty-four hours a day. As long as she's never alone, she'll be fine."

Carolyn carried the tray of sandwiches to the table. She stared down at them for a few moments, then asked quietly, "How long is it going to take you to find him?"

"I don't know, Carolyn," Robert said.

"I'm scared."

So am I, Robert thought. He put a hand on her arm. "Don't be," he said. "I'll see that you're protected. In the meantime, I need to gather evidence. Where's the jump rope?"

Carolyn went to the sink and pulled it from the tub. Suds dripped down its red elastic. "I'm sorry," she said. "There's nothing here now. But why would you want this?"

Just then, Cassie came in the back door.

"Mommy, it's twelve-thirty," she said. "Why didn't you call me for lunch?" She saw the jump rope. "Oh, great! You cleaned it for me!"

"Say hello to Detective Landers," Carolyn said.

"Hi," Cassie said.

"Go on and wash up," Carolyn said, and Cassie hurried from the room.

"You can answer my question now, Robert," Carolyn said. "What does this rope have to do with what's been happening here?"

"That yellow substance you found on it," Robert said. "There was something similar on the rope Myrtle used to hang herself. We don't know what it is, so we sent samples to Columbus."

"What did they say?"

"They haven't gotten back to us yet," Robert answered. "I guess they didn't consider it a priority. But I'll need to ask Cassie where she had that rope. If this is a clue, it could tell us where our suspect might be."

Cassie came back in the room. "Are the dogs okay?" she asked, sitting down. "I was really worried about them."

"I'm going to pick them up at the vet's in a little while," he said. "I just stopped to talk to your mom for a minute. Can I ask you a few questions?"

Cassie's smile faded. "More questions?"

"Just about the jump rope," he said. "Your mom said there was some gucky yellow stuff on it. Do you know where it came from?"

"A bug in the grass, I guess," Cassie said, confused. "Why?"

"I'm just interested, because it sounds like something we found on the rope at Mrs. Hollenbeck's," Robert said. "Can you tell me where you were this morning?"

Cassie thought for a moment, eyeing the sandwiches. Carolyn put one in front of her. As she ate, the little girl said, "I just went to Diane's house. We hung around her yard waiting until she got ready, then we came back here."

"Who's we?"

"Diane, Nicole, and me," Cassie said.

"No one else touched the rope?"

"Uh-uh," Cassie said. She looked at her mother. "Mommy, why do I have to answer so many questions? Isn't the bad stuff over yet?"

Carolyn knelt and put her arms around her daughter, flashing Robert a warning look. "Of course it is, honey," she said. "You must have trailed the rope through something. Now, you put it out of your mind. Detective Landers will take care of everything else."

She stood up and met Robert's concerned eyes.

"It's just a routine investigation," he said. "There is nothing more for you to worry about, I promise."

FOURTEEN

AFTER ROBERT LEFT, Cassie went back to Diane's house, eager to tell her friend what the detective had said. She found Lisa there, too, sitting on the railing that surrounded the deck. Lisa was tugging at the bateau neckline of her T-shirt, griping about the heat. Cassie walked up the steps and greeted her two friends.

"The detective came back to my house today," she said. "Guess what? He was asking about that yucky stuff we found on the jump rope. He told me it sounds just like this stuff they found on Myrtle's hanging rope!"

Diane gasped. "Maybe the bad guy who did all that stuff the other day had it on his shoes! Maybe he stepped on the rope."

"What are you guys talking about?" Lisa asked.

Cassie explained how they'd been playing jump rope that morning. "After Nicole had her turn," Cassie said, "I went to jump. But there was this cold, slimy stuff all over the rope, like I'd stepped on a bug or something."

"Nicole probably did it," Lisa said. "Just like she messed up my painting last night."

128

"What about your painting?" Diane asked, leaning forward.

"She painted over the picture I had done," Lisa said. "She drew Myrtle hanging from the tree, with all this blood coming out of her mouth. And you know what else? She wrapped some bugs up in the paper so they'd crawl out when I got it home."

Diane clicked her tongue, walking over to the small metal table where her mother had set up pretzels and lemonade. She grabbed a handful of pretzels and went back to her seat. Licking the salt off one, she said. "Lisa, you tell some big fibs, but this one's a real whopper. Nicole wasn't anywhere near your picture last night. You're just pee-ohed because we caught you cheating."

Lisa's eyes widened, and she began to swing her legs beneath the railing. "It's not a lie!" she cried. "Nicole hates me! She's jealous because I have beautiful clothes and a nice house. Didn't you guys ever notice that she wears that same stupid dress every day? And how come she's never invited us to her place, huh? Maybe it's one of the dumpier bungalows, and she's ashamed!"

Cassie and Diane regarded Lisa with solemn expressions, thoughts of the jump rope momentarily forgotten as they realized Lisa had a point.

"Maybe she is," Cassie said softly. "She never talks about her family."

"But if she is poor," Diane said, "that doesn't give you the right to be cruel to her, Lisa. After all, she's the one who showed us the toy room."

"What toy room?"

All three girls turned, openmouthed, to see David climbing the back stairs. He stopped, tugging at the bill of his baseball cap, and peered into Diane's face.

"What toy room?" he demanded again.

Diane put down her glass and jumped up from her seat, hurrying toward her brother with her hand raised. She smacked him across the arm. "What do you mean by eavesdropping on us?" she cried. "How long have you been standing there?"

"I forgot my mitt!" David wailed. "You hit me! I'm gonna tell! Then you can kiss your summer good-bye! Daddy'll kill you!"

"He will not!" Diane said. "Don't you dare tell him I hit you! You deserved that!"

Cassie came to pull Diane back a little. "Diane, quiet!" she hissed. "If your mother hears . . ."

David looked from one girl to another. "You're keeping secrets from Mom," he said. "Now you're really in trouble!"

He started for the door, but Diane caught him halfway. David struggled in her grip, but she was bigger and stronger than he was.

"Okay, listen!" she hissed. "I'll tell you about the toy room."

"Diane!" Lisa gasped.

Diane shook her head at Lisa. "We don't have any other choice," she said. "Besides, David won't want to belong to our club. There's nothing in there but girl's things."

"Let me go!" David exclaimed.

"Are you gonna keep quiet?"

David nodded vigorously.

"Okay," Diane said, releasing him. "Our new friend Nicole went exploring in the Hollenbeck house one night. She found this great room full of toys. So we started a secret club. We can't tell any grown-ups about the room, or they'll take the toys away. Get it?"

David considered this. "You mean you went into that house?" he asked in disbelief. "Maybe Myrtle's ghost is still spooking the place!"

Lisa groaned. "Ghosts? David, don't tell me you still believe in stuff like that."

David glowered at her.

"It was okay, David," Diane said. "There's nothing much in the house but a bunch of pictures. But the toy room is great. Well, great for girls, anyway. There isn't anything much a boy would like, except maybe the games and paints."

"You can keep it, then," David said. "But listen, Diane, you better be nice to me from now on. 'Cause if you aren't, I'll tell Mommy that you went to that old house!"

"Get lost, David," Diane said, giving him a little push.

He swung a foot out to kick her, missing her by inches. Then he went inside the house.

"I don't think that was a smart thing to do," Cassie said worriedly.

"What else could I do?" Diane asked. "Let him scream until my mother came out?"

"Yeah, she's right," Lisa said. "But I'm worried, too, Diane. I'm sure he's going to tell one day."

Diane stared at the back door, waiting for David's return. "Not right away, though," she said. "He'll use this to blackmail me for the whole rest of the summer. The brat's going to be insufferable."

The door opened. David leaned close to his sister as he passed her. "Better be nice to me!" he said in a singsong.

"I think we're in a lot of trouble," Lisa said.

David jumped down the steps and ran to join his friends in their baseball game. Diane put her hands on the railing, watching him.

"Little brothers," she groaned. "I wish all brothers were like Bill. He's such a great guy. You know what he's doing? He's going to get a part-time job in town so he can help Daddy replace the rowboat."

"Gee, that's great," Lisa said. "But I thought you guys would never want to go out in a boat again."

Cassie shuddered. "I don't," she said. She stared out at the water. A voice came to her, very softly, almost inaudible.

"*. . . tear us apart!*"

"Let's not talk about yesterday," Lisa said. "I thought we were going to my house."

"Let me tell my mom," Diane said. "I'll be right out."

Moments later, the girls were walking toward the bridge. Carolyn Larchmont stood at the back door of her house, unable to concentrate on her work. She saw them crossing the bridge, arms gesturing animatedly, wind ruffling their hair. She saw Cassie toss her head back and knew that her daughter was laughing at something. After what had happened yesterday, there was something almost macabre in the gesture, but Carolyn wouldn't let her mind create troubles that didn't exist. She should be relieved to see Cassie in a good mood. Her daughter was just fine, and she was too much of a worrier.

She watched the girls file past Myrtle's house. Suddenly they stopped, and Lisa pointed to an upstairs window. Carolyn jerked the door open, ready to yell at Cassie, even though she knew her daughter couldn't hear her. It was dangerous to even stand near that place!

The girls started walking again, leaving the house behind. Carolyn realized her heart was palpitating and her skin was covered with gooseflesh.

"What are you afraid of?" she asked herself. "What is it about that house?"

Something bad happened there.

"But what?" she demanded. "What happened there?"

She closed her eyes, rubbing them, feeling chilled despite the day's heat. An image raced across her mind. A little boy running from something, looking back over his shoulder, a look of fear on his face. There was something small and round arcing toward his head, guided by an unseen hand—

Something hard smacked her in the arm, making her eyes snap open. Momentarily bewildered, Carolyn simply stood watching as a baseball rolled over the grass beside her and into the water.

"Hey, Mrs. Larchmont!"

Carolyn turned to see David running toward her. Her arm stung where the ball had struck her, and she reached up to rub the spot.

"Gosh, I'm sorry!" David cried. "Gary hit a fly ball, and I missed it!" He stopped, tilting his head to one side. The baseball cap shaded half his face. "Are you okay?"

Carolyn smiled. "Sure I am," she said. "You caught me off guard, that's all. I was daydreaming."

David stood beside her, watching the ball bob about four feet from the water's edge. "Well, might as well go in and get it," he said, leaning down to take off his socks and sneakers.

He had one shoelace untied when Carolyn stopped him. "I have a better idea," she said. "Why don't you run to the shed and get a rake? There's a long one in there that should just reach the ball."

"Really?" David said. "You aren't mad at me, then?"

"Of course not," Carolyn insisted, smiling. Amazing how quickly she could cover up her fears, she thought. "It was an accident. Go ahead and get the rake, but be sure you put it back where you found it. I'm going back inside now."

David went to the shed. The metal door made a grating sound as it rubbed over the rocky ground surrounding the small structure. The shed housed yard tools, a lawn mower, and sports equipment. There was a droplight hanging from an outlet in the ceiling, but enough sunlight came through the door to make turning it on unnecessary. David looked up at the row of assorted balls lining one high shelf, then over at the remains of an upright vacuum cleaner. He could see the rake in one corner, hanging from a peg.

David worked the rake loose, pushing to free it. Carrying it in both hands, he started back to the door. Just before he reached it, the door slammed shut with a loud screech. David froze, fear icing his joints. He was standing in almost total darkness.

The only light was a thin beam that seeped under the door.

Now the balls looked like decapitated heads.

Now the old vacuum was a dead body.

David hurried to the door, pushing hard to open it. It wouldn't budge.

He set down the rake and banged on the metal. The vibrations ran through the entire shed, making it reverberate like a giant cymbal.

"Let me outta here!"

It was a trick. His friends were just trying to scare him. Well, it wouldn't work!

"Gary! Mikey!" he cried. "You better open this door or I'll smash your noses in!"

He listened for the sound of his friends' giggling, but only heard the wind blowing.

"This ain't funny!"

He rattled the door, pulling and pushing at it, yelling.

"Don't be afraid, little boy." The voice was soft and thin.

"Gary?"

"I have a secret to tell you," the voice said. *"Do you want to hear it?"*

"I want outta here, whoever you are!"

"Nothing will hurt you," the voice said, closer now. *"You remember that roomful of toys your sister told you about? Well, she lied. It isn't just girl things. There are lots and lots of boy things there, too. But she's trying to keep you from enjoying them!"*

David thought about this a moment, then said, "Who is this?"

"I'm a friend, David," the voice replied. It

stretched out the word friend, making it waver a little.

"What do you want?" he demanded. "Open this stupid door or I'll break your head!"

There was a moment of laughter. *"You don't want to hurt me, David. I can show you things you've never imagined. Come to the house now, David. Come and see the wonderful toys your sister is trying to keep from you!"*

"I can't do that," David said. "I'm playing with Gary and Michael. Now, open this door, will you?"

"You'll come," the voice said confidently.

The door swung open. David ran out into the sunlight, dragging the rake at his side. He looked in every direction, then ran around the back of the shed. But no one was there.

"If you're so tough, how come you ran away?" David shouted.

No one answered.

David ran off to retrieve his ball from the water. As he did so, he looked up at the Hollenbeck place. Were there really toys inside?

"It's all a big lie," David muttered, bending to pick up the baseball as, drawn by the rake, it floated close to him. He shook the water off it and returned the rake to the shed.

Now he knew what had happened. Diane had locked him in the shed to tease him! Or maybe it had been Cassie or Lisa. They were probably hiding behind some trees nearby, laughing at him. Well, he thought as he set the rake just inside the door—he wasn't about to go back in the shed again, no way!—he wouldn't give them the satisfaction. He wouldn't go to that house!

But what if there really was a toy room? He didn't want Diane having all the fun! Now he was full of curiosity, and had lost all interest in his baseball game. David ran over to his friends and tossed them the ball, telling them his mother was calling him and he had to go.

But instead of heading home, he went toward the Hollenbeck place, anticipation making his heart pound. This was a real adventure! There was nothing at all to be afraid of, he thought. Diane just wanted him to think there was to keep him away from all the goodies.

"Nobody's cheating me out of toys," David said out loud.

He stopped at the edge of the bridge, looking back over his shoulder to make sure Gary and Mikey hadn't followed him. It wasn't that he was selfish. He'd share the toys with his friends; but first he had to make sure they really were there, because if someone was playing a trick on him he'd look pretty stupid.

He ran across the bridge, sneakers pounding the wood, and stopped again to look back when he got to the opposite side. The way was still clear. David wove his way through the overgrown grass, up to Myrtle's back door. The door opened easily.

"Police musta forgot to lock it," he mumbled, entering the kitchen.

He made a disgusted face at the smells that hit him, and covered his mouth and nose. Even though it was hot outside, the emptiness of the house made it chilly. It was dark inside, just a little light coming through the raggedy lace curtains. David made his way cautiously through the rooms, amazed at all the pictures of the Hollenbeck children.

"It's like a church," he whispered.

"I see you've come after all, David."

The little boy stopped short in the middle of the hallway. "Where are you?" he called.

There was no sound.

David shook his head impatiently, climbing up the front staircase. This was just a trick, and he knew his sister was behind it. But he'd play along, and he'd laugh with her when it was over. And if she tried to make fun of him he'd threaten to tell their parents that she'd been coming here.

All the hallway doors were closed except for one. David walked slowly toward it, expecting someone to jump out at him at any moment, his chest constricted in anticipation.

Carefully, he reached out and jerked the door open.

"Wow!" he gasped.

No one jumped him. And it wasn't a trick, after all; there really were toys in here. But it wasn't a bunch of girl stuff, like Diane had said. What a fibber! The room was filled with boyish things. David stepped inside, pausing to take in the wonderland that surrounded him. There were action figures in castles and space stations, toy cars, a table hockey game, everything he'd always wanted. There were life-size stuffed animals, and paints, and a puppet theater.

"This place is great!" David cried. "Wait'll I tell Gary and Mikey!"

He ran across the room to turn on the small projector that sat near the window. A cartoon picture bloomed on the opposite wall, and an accompanying record told the story. David left this to investigate a little parking garage, making the toy cars spin through its ramp.

"This isn't all, David."

David set his teeth. That voice again! What kind of goofy person hid all the time?

"Quit teasing me," David said. "Come on out, or I won't talk to you!"

"You have a temper, David," the voice said. *"That's a bad thing. I don't like bad boys."*

"Yeah, well, I don't like you either!"

"I want to be your friend, David. I have something nice for you. It's in the closet, David. Look in the closet."

David turned toward the closet door, but he didn't move. This was the punch line; he'd open the door and something would jump at him, maybe even Diane. Maybe she was hiding in the closet, waiting for him. She was probably angry because he'd threatened to tell on her before.

"Forget it, Diane," he said.

"Diane isn't here. Look in the closet, David. Look in the closet. Look in the closet. Look . . ."

The voice went on and on, repeating the phrase until David felt his ears burning. He didn't want to open that door. Suddenly, the room had lost its appeal, and all he wanted to do was go home.

But the voice wouldn't let go. He had to look in the closet. He had to open the door.

David jerked the door open. The closet was

empty, a black cave. He wanted to back away and run, but something pushed him from behind. He stumbled into the gaping hole.

The door slammed shut.

"You threatened to tell about this room, David. That was bad. I want to show you what happens to bad little boys."

An overhead light flicked on, a single bulb that swung on a creaking wire. David backed against the door, his mouth open, staring at the thing that was in the closet with him.

It couldn't be real. It was just a dummy with a smashed-up head. Someone had painted those greenish-gray marks on its skin, someone had strung seaweed through its hair, someone had . . .

But it was real. The horrible smell said it was real. It was a boy, about David's size, dressed in rotted khaki shorts and a torn and bloodied striped T-shirt.

It flopped forward, the bones that thrust through one hand reaching out to touch David's bare leg.

The little boy turned and pounded at the closet door, screaming in terror.

FIFTEEN

WHEN ROBERT PICKED up his dogs from the vet's, their wagging tails told him they had come through yesterday's ordeal just fine. Kelly jumped up and put her paws on his shoulders, standing nearly as tall as he was to lick his face.

After paying the bill, Robert latched three chains to the dogs' collars and led them out to the rented car. The dogs jumped into the backseat, sniffing the worn upholstery in confusion. After reassuring them, Robert started the car and headed back to the police station.

He parked in front of the precinct, then walked the dogs through the front door and down the hallway to Mike Hogan's office. He knocked, and went in. The dogs circled him, wrapping their leashes around his legs. Robert pulled them firmly to one side.

"Sit," he said. The command was obeyed immediately.

"What are they doing here?" Mike demanded.

"I just picked them up from the vet's," Robert said. "I didn't want to leave them alone today, in case there's any trouble. Especially Erin—she might go digging at those bandages."

Mike sighed, leaning his chair back. "You really are crazy," he said. "I thought you might be when you started chasing that suicide victim's nonexistent murderer. Now I'm convinced of it. What the hell is this idiotic theory you have that the Canfield boy had help?"

"I looked over the case file," Robert said, "and things didn't click. The boy's ability, for instance. He didn't seem smart enough to build a pipe bomb."

"Landers, you can get a book out of the library that'll tell you that," Mike said. "It's no big secret."

"Fine," Robert said. "Then who sold him the gunpowder? You know his reputation in this town. Who would have trusted him?"

"He didn't get it here in town," Mike said. "We talked to all the store owners who sell the stuff, and none of them have seen him lately. He went someplace else for it."

"I don't think so," Robert said. "He didn't have the money, or the means. He didn't have a car, and his father didn't seem the type who'd lend him the family's. You may think this case is closed, Mike, but I can't. I was attacked at Myrtle Hollenbeck's house last night."

"So I heard," Mike said. "What were you doing there?"

"Following up on a theory," Robert said. "Barry Canfield told me Georgie liked to hang around that place. I thought I might find some evidence of the bomb. I got more than that—I almost collared my suspect. Unfortunately, he got away, but at least I know my theory is right."

"Your theory is garbage," Mike said bluntly. "Some smart-ass kid jumped you, that's all, someone having some sick fun after what happened, 'cause you're dumb enough to look for trouble." He pointed at Robert's face. "That hurt?"

"Not much now," Robert said. "It stings a little if I move the wrong way."

"It wouldn't have happened if you'd stayed put last night," Mike said. "I want you to forget this idea, Robert. There was no other person involved. If you start poking around, you'll get people very upset. I like the peace kept around Lake Solaria, Detective. And if you disturb it, I'll have you suspended!"

Undaunted, Robert asked, "What have you learned about the boat?"

Mike shrugged. "Not a heck of a lot. The lab can't figure out how it was held together. But it almost doesn't matter now, does it? It's certain that Georgie had something to do with it, and he's already paid the price."

"Yeah, sure," Robert mumbled, standing. "I have to get my girls back home. They've had a hard night, and so have I. So long, Mike."

He left the chief's office without waiting for a dismissal. Mike said Georgie had paid a price, but Robert wouldn't rest until someone else was made to pay, too. Someone who was even more guilty than that screwed-up kid.

Cassie did not know of Robert's theory, and so she played with Solo in her backyard that evening without fear. Supper was over, and Carolyn was busy inside with her work. It was still light outside, and in almost every backyard people were enjoying picnics, games of badminton and volleyball, or evening swims.

"I wish I could go swimming again," Cassie told Solo, throwing his ball. "But Mommy's too scared now, 'cause of what happened."

Solo skidded under a hedge and caught the ball. He turned to carry it back to Cassie, but stopped halfway to her. His ears flattened out, and a low rumbling came from his throat. Half-hidden by his long fur, his eyes glistened menacingly.

"Solo, what's the matter?" Cassie demanded.

"That dog hates me, doesn't it?" Nicole had entered the yard, so quietly Cassie hadn't heard her.

"Nicole!"

"Did I startle you?" Nicole asked. "I'm sorry. I called you, but I guess you didn't hear me."

"Well, sometimes the motorboats are too loud," Cassie said. "What're you doing here?"

"I've come to play with you," Nicole said. "I want you to come to the toy room with me to-night."

Cassie looked up at the back door, afraid her mother might be standing right there in the kitchen. "I can't," she said. "My mother said I have to stay right here in the backyard."

"Your mother will be too busy to know you're gone," Nicole argued. "And you'll be back as soon as the lights go on at D'Achille's. Isn't that when you're supposed to go in?"

Cassie nodded. "But it's light out! Someone will see us!"

"No, they won't," Nicole insisted. "I know just how to sneak inside. Why, Diane and Lisa and I went in last night and no one saw us. Besides, you've only been there once. You don't even know all the great things that there are there!"

Cassie didn't want to go to the house. But then, it would be fun to see the toys again, just for a few minutes. There had been so many the other night, like a dream come true. What harm could there be? Her mother said that house was a bad place, but how could a house be bad? "Oh, I don't know . . ."

"Please," Nicole said, taking her hand. Cassie looked down at the tiny fingers in her own.

"I've got an idea," Cassie said, suddenly thinking of a way to get out of going to Myrtle's place. "Let's go to your house! I've never been there before, and I'd like to meet your family."

Nicole jerked her hand away, moving back a step. She stared down at her feet, pouting.

"What's wrong?" Cassie asked.

"I—I can't say," Nicole said.

Cassie sighed. "Nicole, why won't you ever let me meet your family? I'll bet they're really nice."

"They're not nice!" Nicole cried. "My mother and father—they're always bickering! Always fighting! I'd be so ashamed if they . . . if they . . ."

Nicole covered her face with her hands and began to cry softly. Cassie gaped at her for a few moments, not knowing what to do. Then she put her arms around the smaller girl.

"I'm sorry!" she said. "I didn't mean to upset you! I'll go to the house, if it'll make you happy!"

"Will you?"

"Sure," Cassie said. "But only until my curfew.

And only if we ask Diane and Lisa, too."

"I'd rather we played alone," Nicole said. "We don't need the others, Cassie. We can pretend we're sisters again, the way we did that day it was raining. I like to pretend you're my sister!"

"It's a club, Nicole," Cassie said. "And besides, we can cover for each other if anyone asks questions."

Nicole nodded. "You're right. Let's go to Diane's house."

"First I have to tell my mother I'm going to the Montanas'," Cassie said, "in case she looks out here. I'll be out in a minute."

Cassie hurried inside, her feelings mixed. Part of her was still wary about going into Myrtle's house, but she wanted to make Nicole happy. She thought about how unhappy Nicole's life at home must be. She couldn't imagine being so embarrassed by her parents that she'd never bring anyone home, and was grateful that her mother was so nice. With this thought, she came up behind Carolyn and hugged her tightly.

Carolyn excused herself for a moment from her phone conversation, turning to face her daughter. "Honey, I'm on long distance to California," she said. "It's very important, and I'll be on the line for quite a while."

"Just wanted to tell you I'm going to Diane's," Cassie said.

"You're not walking there alone?"

"No, Mommy," Cassie said. "Nicole's with me."
Carolyn smiled. "Fine. I'll see you at eight!"
Cassie left the house, and together she and Ni-

cole walked toward Diane's house.

"What did your mother say?" Nicole asked.

Cassie said, "She got a long-distance call just now. So, you're right—she really will be too busy!"

When they reached the Montanas', Cassie knocked at the back door, and Diane answered.

"We're going to the house," Cassie said. "Can you call Lisa and ask her to meet us there?"

"I don't know," Diane said hesitantly. "David's been missing all afternoon, and I don't think my mom's gonna let me go out."

"Tell her we're going to look for him," Cassie suggested.

"Good idea," Diane answered.

She went back inside, and returned in a few minutes wearing a sweater.

"Let's go," she said. "Lisa's gonna meet us."

Giggling, the three girls headed toward the bridge. It had been incredibly easy tonight, as if they were meant to get to the toy room with no hassles. When they reached Myrtle's backyard, they heard Lisa calling, and stopped to wait for her. Lisa frowned when she saw Nicole.

"What're you doing here?" she asked. "You've got nerve, after what you did to me!"

"Oh, Lisa, cut it out," Diane said. "Nicole didn't do a thing and you know it."

"I didn't do anything," Nicole echoed softly, reaching up to open the back door.

They walked single file up the back staircase. Each girl hurried to a particular toy when they entered the toy room.

"Look at these," Cassie said, pulling out a box of

pop-beads. "We could make some pretty neck-laces."

"I have real beads at home," Lisa boasted. "I don't need silly plastic ones."

Cassie clicked her tongue. "It's just play, Lisa," she said. "Don't be such a stuck-up."

"Don't you call me names!" Lisa retorted.

Moving around Lisa, Nicole came to sit at the little table with Cassie. Lisa put her hands on her hips.

"What's the big idea, stealing my seat?" she demanded.

"You aren't playing with the beads," Nicole answered, not looking up at her. She took a handful and began to pop them together.

"I was going to do something else!" Lisa cried. "Get up! I was here first!"

Diane, busy with a miniature vanity table across the room, grimaced at Lisa's reflection. "Oh, Westin, cut it out," she said. "You're so spoiled. You only want that seat 'cause Nicole's there."

"Nicole's the spoiled one," Lisa muttered, finally turning away from the table. "Who needs to play with her, anyway?" She came over to the vanity to see what Diane was up to. "Oh, neat!" she cried. "Real makeup! Can I try? My mom never lets me play with her stuff."

"I'll bet," Diane said. "Your mother lets you do everything. You probably have your own lipstick already!"

"I do not!" Lisa cried. She backed up a step. "Why's everyone picking on me?"

Cassie held up her beads, measuring them

around her wrist for a bracelet. "You started it, Lisa," she said. "First you make fun of what I'm doing, then you say mean things about Nicole. You always say mean things, Lisa."

Tears were welling up in Lisa's eyes. "Why don't you just say you don't want to be my friend?" she cried.

In anger, Lisa grabbed a doll and threw it across the room. It hit a shelf of toys, knocking down a large red ball, which disappeared into the open closet. All four girls stared after it.

"Who opened that door?" Diane asked softly.

"Not me," Lisa said, sniffling. "I wasn't near it."

"Me neither," Cassie said. "And I know it was shut when we walked in. At least, I think it was!"

"I didn't open it," Nicole put in.

The four girls stood up slowly, staring at the closet. Had it been closed? Or had they been too busy to notice?

"Vibrations," Lisa said, forgetting her anger.

"Huh?" said Diane.

"When I threw the doll," Lisa said, "it shook the wall and made the closet door pop open."

Cassie shook her head. "It didn't hit that wall!"

"Listen, I heard something," Diane gasped. "Oh, golly, let's get out of here. There's someone in that closet!"

But the four of them were frozen in place.

"I'm so scared," Cassie mumbled in a tiny voice.

"Well, I'm not," Lisa said. "It's a trick. Probably something Nicole set up."

"I didn't do anything!" Nicole cried. "You're just saying that 'cause you hate me!"

Ignoring Nicole, Lisa picked up her chair, aiming the small metal legs before her like a weapon. "Come out of there, whoever you are!" she demanded.

"Lisa!"

Slowly, the closet door creaked farther open. They could see nothing inside but blackness. The girls backed away a little, peering curiously, half ready to run away, half fascinated by the darkness.

And then David appeared, his hair disheveled, his face ghastly pale.

"You creep!" Diane shouted. She ran to her brother, pummeling his arm with her small fists. "What do you mean, scaring us like that? I'm telling Daddy, and you're gonna get whipped!"

Cassie noticed now that David wasn't fighting back, only staring at his sister with gray-encircled eyes. She ran to pull Diane away from him. "Stop it!" she cried.

"David, what's the matter with you?" Lisa demanded.

"He looks ill," Nicole said.

Diane stepped back and looked at her little brother. The child stared back at her with the eyes of a refugee, eyes dark with terror. Then he began to shake his head, muttering, "No, no, no, no, no . . ."

"David?" Diane asked.

Cassie put a hand on Diane's shoulder. "We better get him home," she said. "Lisa, Nicole, come help."

Cassie hooked one arm around David, while Diane took his other side. Lisa hurried to open the doors.

"What were you doing in that closet?" Diane asked.

David said nothing. He merely went on shaking his head as they walked down the stairs and out the back door.

"It's your fault for telling him about the toy room, Diane," Lisa said. "He probably got stuck in the closet and got scared, that's all."

"But we can't tell your parents that," Nicole said. "They mustn't know about the toy room, ever!"

"She's right," Lisa said. "David, you have to promise you won't tell where we were. If you do, we'll let you join our club, and you can come to the toy room with us every night!"

Abruptly, David wrenched away from Cassie and Diane and bolted toward the water, screaming, *"Nooooo!"*

"David, come back!" Diane shouted.

"Come on, Diane, we'll catch him on the bridge," Cassie said.

"Cassie, I have to go now . . ."

"Then go, Nicole!" Cassie cried. "You always have to leave!"

Without another word, Cassie and Diane raced toward the bridge, leaving Lisa and Nicole behind.

"I might as well go home now, too," Lisa said. "My mom will be looking for me." She turned and walked away.

Nicole watched her, expressionless. Then she started walking, too, following Lisa. She stopped at the edge of the Westin property, watching as Lisa opened her back door.

Something long and dark fell on Lisa's head. The little girl screamed, batting at the snake she felt twining around her neck. Her cries brought her mother running, and Lisa threw the thing to the ground just as Dorothy opened the back door.

Lisa began to retch, pointing toward the snake. It had a humanoid head, ripped from the body of a small doll.

"Lisa! Baby, what's wrong?"

"Mommy, a snake!"

Dorothy took her daughter in her arms. She peered out at the grass, but saw nothing. "Lisa, you've been out too late," she said. "The shadows are playing tricks on your eyes."

Lisa turned to point at it, but the grass was empty. "But, Mommy, it was there," she said. "It fell on my head!"

"Lisa," Dorothy said patiently, "come inside."

Lisa pulled away from her mother, taking a few steps back into the yard. She looked up and down the beach.

"I know it was you, Nicole!" she cried. "I know you did this. And you know something? I'm going to get you!" She closed her eyes and clenched her fists. "Do you hear me? I'm going to get you for this, Nicole Morgan!"

SIXTEEN

THE MEDICATION HE'D been given had pulled David down into a heavy sleep. Rita checked on him before she went to bed, pulling the covers up over his shoulders and kissing his forehead. It felt cool, and she was relieved to see that his fever had broken. An hour later, bored with the science show he'd been watching, Andy came in to look in on his son, too. David was breathing evenly, so relaxed among his stuffed animals that it seemed nothing had happened to him.

Bill came in late from a date with Anna. He'd been out all day, finishing the day by treating his girlfriend to dinner at the new Japanese steak house. Then the two teenagers had gone to see the latest Michael J. Fox film at a multiplex cinema just outside town. The crowd in the parking lot—fifty to one hundred people each for six movies—made leaving a long, drawn-out affair. It was after midnight when Bill got home, and he knew nothing about what had happened to David.

As was his habit, he ruffled his sleeping brother's hair. David usually smiled in his sleep, but this time he groaned and turned away.

"G'night, kid," Bill murmured, sliding into his own bed.

He was sound asleep when the sucking noise began underneath the floorboards. It was the gargling sound water makes when it's being pulled down a drain. David rolled over, opening his eyes. He looked over the edge of his bed at the floor, too groggy at first to understand what he was seeing.

The Montanas' bungalow was built on stilts, as were many of the summer cottages around the lake. There was a crawl space about three feet high beneath the house, carpeted with sand and occupied by forgotten pieces of driftwood, dried lake grass, and an occasional animal. There had never been a flood in Lake Solaria's history, so the raising of the houses was an almost unnecessary precaution that just made people feel better.

But now the cracks that ran the length of the floor were darkening. David watched, his eyes almost shut, one arm hanging over the edge of the bed, as water seeped up through the floor, running with the tilt of the room toward the door. Slowly, realizing through the drugged state of his brain that this was wrong, David sat up.

"Bill?"

His brother was a lump in the opposite bed, his back turned to the little boy. Bill didn't move.

"Bill, there's water all over the floor!"

No answer.

Except for sudden high-pitched, maniacal laughter.

"Who's that?" David yelled. He sat up straighter.

"It's me again, David. I wanted to make sure you understood my message this afternoon."

David began screaming, but no one came. His brother didn't move, his door didn't open to reveal concerned, protective parents. He swung his legs around to jump from the bed, and plopped his feet down knee-deep into icy water.

"Water's very scary, David. Especially when it goes over your head. It's dark and cold and it sucks your breath away."

David waded toward the door, lake grass swirling around his thighs. He could feel the bitter cold through the cotton legs of his pajamas.

"Mom! Dad!"

The water continued to rise, knocking over a desk chair, picking up toys and balls and whipping them around in circles. It was now as high as Bill's bed.

"Bill, wake up! Why don't you answer me? *Wake up!*"

The laughter sounded again. David reached the doorway, turned the knob and pulled hard.

The door began to swell, wedging so tightly into the frame that it was impossible to budge. David's palms slapped the wall before him, a solid boundary that ran the circumference of the room. The windows had vanished.

"Bill! *Bill!*"

The water was up to David's chest now. It knocked books from the desktop. Crumbled up pieces of an old comic book floated up out of the wastebasket and bobbed up and down on the dark surface. David found his strength, and began swimming toward his brother's bed.

He grabbed Bill by the shoulder, shaking him, and his brother rolled over.

But it wasn't Bill in the bed. It was the boy from the closet, the boy with the greenish-gray face, the boy with lake grass in his hair.

David screamed, his open mouth taking in a great gulp of water. And then something tugged hard at him, pulling him under. He fought, kicking in every direction, reaching desperately for the surface.

"Now you know what dying feels like. If you tell what you saw in the house today, if you spoil my plans, this is what I'll do to you!"

The voice was so clear, not at all like someone talking underwater. David had been holding his breath for more than a minute now, and his lungs felt ready to burst. He had to open his mouth, had to let go, had to suck in precious oxygen.

He gagged, hearing the echoey sound of his breath pushing water away, then felt the cold rush into his lungs.

Someone was picking him up. David's eyes snapped open, and he threw up an arm.

"It's only me, David," Bill whispered. "What're you doing on the floor?"

David looked beneath himself and saw dry, solid wood. It was a nightmare. He had had a nightmare.

"I—I don't know," he said. He coughed hard, his lungs constricting painfully.

Bill laid him back on the bed and covered him. "Want me to get Mom?"

David shook his head. "I'm okay," he said. "I guess I was walking in my sleep. 'Night, Bill."

"Dream good, kid," Bill said, returning to his own bed.

David rolled over and grabbed one of his stuffed animals, hoping desperately that he wouldn't dream at all.

The next morning when Rita came in to check on her son, David was in the throes of a coughing fit.

"You poor thing!" Rita cried, sitting on the edge of the bed. She pounded him on the back, helping him release the phlegm in his chest. When he stopped coughing, she rubbed his shoulders. "You're shivering, too. Looks like you'll be spending the day in bed, honey."

Bill, who was already up, planning to take on the early-morning trout, sat on the edge of his bed as he pulled on his socks. "I found him on the floor last night," he said. "Since when does he walk in his sleep?"

Rita frowned at David. "What happened, baby?"

David shook his head. "I don't remember," he mumbled. "I must have been dreaming."

"Do you remember how you got sick yesterday?"

David thought for a moment, staring at the door. Something about it seemed odd to him, but he couldn't think what it was. At last he spoke. "I wanted to see Mrs. Westin's horse," he said. "I followed the girls across the lake. But I tripped and fell and hit my head. I don't remember anything else."

"My angel," Rita said, kissing him. "Well, are

you up to breakfast? I'll fix you something."

"I'm not hungry, Mom," David answered, his voice weak.

His mother had believed him; she wouldn't question him further. Now the crazy person with the funny voice wouldn't get him, the way he'd gotten that boy in the closet.

Rita got up. As she made her way toward the door she picked up the metal trash can near David's desk. The picture of E.T. on the wastebasket had a dent across the nose, giving the alien a three-dimensional look.

"Trash goes out today," she said, handing it to Bill. The can sloshed as Rita moved it, and she looked down into its oval mouth. "Now, what's this?" she asked, annoyed. "How did this water get in here?"

"Beats me, Mom," Bill said.

They both looked at David, but his eyes were shut, as if in sleep. They didn't know that confused thoughts were running through his mind. He listened as the doorknob turned, followed by a loud squeaking sound.

"This door never stuck before," Rita said.

"Let me give it a yank, Mom," Bill offered. He wrapped both hands around the knob and pulled with all his strength. A dull, deep shudder ran around the room as the door gave way.

"Look at this!" Bill exclaimed.

David turned and opened his eyes.

"There's a watermark three-quarters of the way up," Bill said. "I never saw this before. It's as if the room was once flooded."

"I'll show it to your dad," Rita said. "Come on, now. Let David get some rest."

But David couldn't rest.

Because he knew now that what had happened last night was real.

SEVENTEEN

ROBERT DROVE ALONG Hillside Road, the curving street that led to the Hollenbeck mansion. Few of the neighboring houses had their porch lights on, and the beam from the rental's single working headlight was the only illumination on the dark roadway. He slowed down a bit, the tires crunching over drifts of sand that had been blown onto the roadway, and considered turning off the lights. Did his suspect recognize the car by now? Was he waiting for Robert's inevitable return?

Robert had been giving Erin medicine for her wounds, his fingers forcing a pill toward the back of her tongue, when the phone rang. Barry Canfield had called with news for him—he'd seen some children running from Myrtle's house, looking as if they were terribly frightened; he wondered if the creep who'd gotten Georgie into trouble might be there, right now.

Robert finally did cut the lights as he turned into Myrtle's driveway. After some questioning, Barry had been able to remember that one of the kids was Lisa Westin, the rich kid who lived at the far end of the lake. And he'd also remembered seeing Cassie Larchmont. Why would Cassie be in the house, Robert wondered, when her mother had expressly forbidden her to go there? And what had frightened her and her friends?

Robert turned off the engine and pocketed his keys, thinking of the night he'd almost shot Diane Montana, worrying that the children could have come face to face with a maniacal killer. He walked to the back door, opened it, and entered the kitchen.

He turned on the kitchen light, illuminating a dust-covered table and a floor dulled by footsteps. Robert imagined that more people had crossed through this kitchen in the last month than in the previous ten years.

He heard a scuttling noise and turned quickly to see a little mouse darting over the dried leaves that had fallen from the dead plants in the window. It disappeared under a cabinet.

Robert took a quick look around the kitchen, his eyes keen for any changes in scenery, any clue that someone had been here. The pantry was empty except for an economy-size bag of cereal, sacks of flour and sugar, and a few cans of vegetables. Spilled sugar that had been left for an ant's feast spoke of a neglected, forgotten house. Robert wondered if anyone would ever move in here again, bring new life to the place. But that couldn't happen until Myrtle's next of kin was found and the estate was settled.

As he moved into the laundry room, snapping on its light, he thought of the search he'd been making for Cyril Hollenbeck. He'd gone through the usual channels, checking the place where Hollenbeck had worked many years ago, talking to the lawyer who handled the divorce, questioning people on the lake who might remember the man. If he had died, it wasn't in Ohio, because there was no death certificate on file. Form letters had been sent out to dozens of retirement homes, but so far nothing had come back. Robert hoped the man wasn't out of state, in a place where he'd never be found. Cyril, Robert knew, could answer some important questions.

He pulled at a narrow door, and an ironing board popped down out of the wall. Robert knocked on the recessed area behind it, hearing a sound that was only faintly hollow. He could tell there wasn't a wide enough area behind the wall for a person to fit through. Robert left the laundry room and investigated the other rooms on the first floor, finding nothing, as he had found nothing every other time he'd been here. The place seemed to change a little each time he came, the oriental rugs looking a little more worn, the dust on the furniture a little thicker, the mantel a little dirtier—

Robert stopped, staring at the corner of the mantel. It was carved in the shape of a lion's head, a snarling mouth opened as if ready to bite. And it looked as if the stone lion *had* bitten something. There was something dripping from its frozen jaws.

Robert reached toward it, and touched the thick, cold, yellow substance. He brought some to his nose, but it had no smell. It was just like the stuff they'd found on Myrtle's rope. Excited, Robert hurried back to the kitchen and searched in the cabinets until he found an empty baby-food jar. The sight of it in an old woman's home was pathetic enough to make him pause for a moment. Then he ran back to the living room and scraped the honeylike guck from the mantel.

"I'll have this tested myself," he muttered, "not by some lab in Columbus where no one cares about this case."

If he could find out what the stuff was, he might be able to trace its source, and might thus find the person he'd been looking for. He would put the sample in his car for safekeeping.

When he turned, a child was standing in the doorway, a little boy with blood trickling down the side of his head. He stared at Robert, his lower lip pushed out a little, his blue eyes glassy.

"Who are you?" Robert demanded, taking a quick step forward.

The child said nothing. Suddenly, a strange tingling sensation ran through Robert's palm. He looked down at the jar and saw that his hand was shaking violently.

"What the . . . ?"

He looked up at the boy, who still stared at him, and suddenly couldn't find his voice. He felt as if he'd touched an exposed live wire after jumping out of a pool, the water on his skin carrying numbing currents through his body. He began to shake all over.

Robert tried to drop the jar, sensing somehow that it was the cause of this pain, but he couldn't open his hand. He looked at it, willing his fingers to open, staring at the little blue-and-silver circle that was the lid.

And then the circle began to stretch, swelling up over his fingers, drooping over his thumb like a clock in a Dali painting. The glass jar stretched and stretched and stretched . . .

This is insane! he thought.

. . . until its bottom touched the floor, hanging in a taffylike blob.

Robert looked up at the boy again, and saw that his eyes were closed. The boy turned and walked away.

And the jar exploded.

Shards of glass flew everywhere, even as Robert felt the current leave his body. He collapsed to the ground, instinctively covering his head, feeling stings in his arms and back.

Silence. Stillness.

"I can't believe this," Robert said aloud, scrambling to his feet. He ran to the hallway, shouting for the boy, looking in every direction.

"Where did you go?" he yelled. "Don't be afraid! Please, come back!"

But the house was quiet.

Robert clenched his fists. "All right, take this slow," he told himself. "It's a trick. The kid did something to you."

That child didn't change the physical shape of a glass jar!

Robert hurried back into the living room, expecting to see bits of glass sparkling in the midst of yellowish gunk.

He stared at the jar for a long time, trying to

make sense of it all, but unable to. He bent down to pick it up. It was in perfect shape, completely intact, just the way it had been when he'd found it in the kitchen. But the yellow substance was gone. There wasn't a trace of it in the room, not on the carpet, not staining the lion's head.

"I know what I saw," Robert said. "I did not imagine what happened here! That boy—I've got to find that kid and talk to him."

Robert shoved the jar into the pocket of his jacket and headed for the front door. Something caught his eye, and he turned toward one of the dozen pictures that hung on the foyer wall.

This was just impossible. He hadn't gotten a good look at the boy in the doorway, of course. He wasn't really sure what the child looked like.

"You're denying the obvious," Robert muttered, staring at the portrait of the Hollenbeck children. "You're a skeptic, just like the chief."

But he couldn't deny this. It was too clear, too real.

The child he had just seen looked exactly like Norman Hollenbeck.

EIGHTEEN

WHILE HER MOTHER prepared breakfast the next morning, Cassie stood at the back door, looking out at the yard. The smell of apples growing along the lake seeped through the screen, mixing with the aroma of frying bacon that whirled around behind her head. Her slipperless feet poked out beneath the hem of her flowered cotton robe.

"Why didn't you get dressed this morning, Cassie?" Carolyn asked, laying the bacon on paper towels.

Cassie shrugged. "Didn't feel like it."

"Why not?" Carolyn asked with concern. "You aren't sick, are you? It hasn't been that long since the accident . . ."

"It's not that, Mom," Cassie said, turning. "I keep thinking about David. What could have scared him so much?"

"Little boys have overactive imaginations," Carolyn said, feeling hypocritical as she spoke. She was terrified of that house herself, and here she was ridiculing a seven-year-old! "He was someplace where he had no business being, and he probably

166

convinced himself there was something to be afraid of."

Cassie shuffled to her chair, then sat picking at the bacon without eating it. "But you don't like that house, either," she said.

"Because it's old and dangerous," Carolyn said. "There could be loose floorboards, or pieces of the ceiling could fall."

It was an old speech, one she gave her daughter because she couldn't put her real explanation into words. She could never explain her gut feeling that the danger she sensed about the place had nothing to do with its structure.

"Well, I'm sure David will be okay," she concluded. "And I'm glad you have the sense not to play near that awful place."

Cassie took a bite of bacon, not tasting it. What would her mother do if she knew Cassie had been playing inside the house?

"So, I want you to get dressed and go out with your friends," Carolyn said.

"I can't," Cassie said. "None of my tops fit."

"What do you mean, they don't fit?" Carolyn asked. "They look fine. What about the T-shirt with the kittens on it? Or that smock top Aunt Martha gave you?"

"They cut me under the arms," Cassie complained. "David said I was getting fat. I guess he's right."

"You're just growing," Carolyn said. "I'm sure there's something you can wear." She looked across the table at her daughter, who sat pouting as she poked her eggs with a strip of bacon.

"Okay, I'll tell you what," Carolyn said, not wanting to have Cassie moping around all day. "Go upstairs and put your swimsuit on. It's so hot today, it would be mean of me not to let you go in the water."

Cassie brightened at once. "Really?" she asked. "You're gonna let me go swimming?"

"Hold it," Carolyn said, holding up both hands. "You can go in the water, but only up to your waist. No swimming for a few days yet—it's too soon after your accident. And I don't want you going in the water by yourself."

"I'll go see Diane," Cassie said, standing.

She went upstairs and found her white bikini, tossed in a forgotten lump near her window seat, and carried it into the bathroom. Cassie undressed, hanging her robe over the radiator in one corner. Then she picked up the bottom half of the suit and wriggled into it. The top was impossibly tight. Cassie pulled and pulled at the straps, finally squeezing them close enough to fasten the hooks. It pinched her chest, making it hard for her to breathe.

"I am getting fat!" she cried, looking down at the slight bulges straining to break free of the garment.

She inhaled, and the back of the bra snapped open.

"Oh, baloney!" Cassie cried. She grabbed the top, rolled it up into a ball, and ran topless down to her mother's study. Carolyn was putting her computer on-line, using a modem to connect her unit to the one at her factory.

"Mommy, my bathing suit doesn't fit anymore!"

she cried. "I *am* getting fat! David's right! I'm a fat pig!"

Carolyn turned to look at her daughter, and her eyes widened, just a quick reaction that she stopped before it turned into a stare. But Cassie had caught it. A self-conscious look passed over her face, and she crossed her arms over her chest.

"Cassie, honey, you have grown," Carolyn said. "I never noticed before, but you might be needing a bra soon."

"No!" Cassie cried. "That's dumb! Nobody I know wears a bra! And I'm not wearing one, either!"

"It's nothing to be frightened or ashamed of," Carolyn said. "You're just growing up a little faster than your friends. We'll buy you a larger size swimsuit and some bigger tops. But soon you'll have to pack away your undershirts. That's just the way it is, Cassie. It's just life."

"I still don't want one," Cassie said.

"When you're ready, Cassie," Carolyn said, "and not before. But I'll help you then, okay?"

Cassie smiled. "Okay. I'm going to put my clothes on. I guess I can't go swimming until I can get a new suit."

She gave her mother a kiss and went back upstairs. Carolyn stood in the door of her office. She wanted to reach out toward Cassie's retreating figure, wanted to grab the pretty little girl and hold her fast, so she wouldn't grow up. She wanted to keep her daughter close and safe, because she was terrified of what might happen when Cassie went out into the world on her own, unprotected. Life was full of unpleasant surprises. A man could go to a bookstore one day to buy a gift for his four-year-old and never come home again. Children could go out and play and disappear forever.

"Oh, Paul," Carolyn whispered. "What am I going to do when she's all grown up? When she doesn't need me anymore?"

She could almost hear her husband's reassuring voice, almost feel his arms around her, so warm and loving. *She's only ten,* Paul would say. *Just because she's developing physically doesn't mean she's ready to leave home tomorrow. You have years to keep her!*

Another voice came to her, a dark and gravelly voice full of evil: *If someone doesn't get her first.*

Carolyn covered her ears. Nobody was going to "get" Cassie! Her little girl would be safe.

As long as she stayed away from the Hollenbeck mansion.

Cassie came back downstairs, this time dressed in a red and blue maillot suit. She was grinning from ear to ear.

"Look, Mommy," she said. "Remember this? I wore it to that swim meet last summer, but I forgot all about it. It stretches enough so I can go swimming, after all!"

Carolyn smiled a little. "I'm glad, Cassie," she said.

Cassie ran from the house, her single blond braid flicking over the bony surface of her back. Outside, Diane and Lisa were sitting on the picnic bench.

"What took you so long?" Lisa asked. "You're usually the first one up."

"Couldn't find anything to wear," Cassie said.

"Have you seen Nicole yet?"

"That creep?" Lisa said. "Not a sign of her. She probably won't show up. I bet she knows I'm going to get her for scaring me last night."

"Oh, Lisa, you shouldn't talk that way," Cassie said. "Poor Nicole must be scared to death of you, and we're all supposed to be friends."

"She really is strange, Cassie," Diane said. "I'm not sure I like her very much."

"Well, I do," Cassie protested. She pointed to the yellow-skirted bathing suit Diane was wearing. "I see you're in your swimsuit today. Did your mom say you could go into the water?"

Diane smiled. "No, but Daddy did. And he talked Mom into it." She looked down at her thigh. "My scar doesn't look too barfo, does it?"

"You can hardly see it at all," Cassie said kindly. Actually, it was like a long, fat worm. But at least it wasn't so swollen and red anymore.

"I think—"

Cassie cut Lisa off, sensing she was going to say something mean. "Your suit is awfully pretty, Lisa," she said. "Is it new?"

"Mom bought it for me," Lisa said. She stood up, twirling to show off the suit, pink and black nylon with white net gussets at the sides. "It's the latest fashion. Speaking of new swimsuits, looks like you could use a new one, too, Cassie. Your boobs are poking out."

"They are not!"

"Cassie," Diane gasped, "you really *do* have them, just like David said. What do they feel like? Do they hurt?"

Cassie frowned, hunching her shoulders. "They

don't feel like anything," she said. "Stop talking about them. You guys are just jealous 'cause I get to wear a bra before you do!"

Lisa laughed heartily. "Jealous? Forget it! I'm going to have a model's figure, like my mom," she said. "You're the sexpot who'll need a bra!"

She started running toward the bridge, shouting, "Cassie needs a bra-a! Cassie needs a bra-a!"

"Lisa!" Cassie gasped.

Diane took one look at Cassie, who stood open-mouthed, then ran after Lisa. The little girl was shouting so loudly that other people on the lake had turned to listen. A couple of boys poked each other and laughed. Cassie watched as Diane grabbed Lisa and pushed her to the ground, shouting at her. Lisa went on laughing cruelly.

Mortified, Cassie turned and ran blindly in the other direction. She didn't stop until she came to the woods that bordered the western edge of the lake, thick growths of pine and oak that offered plenty of hiding places. Sobbing, she plunked herself down onto a mat of dead leaves.

She felt someone touch her shoulder and turned to see Nicole standing behind her.

"Where'd you come from?" Cassie asked, embarrassed.

"I saw what Lisa did to you," Nicole said, "and I followed you."

Cassie rolled onto her back. She sniffled but didn't say anything.

"Lisa is just a cruel, wicked girl," Nicole said. "And she ought to be punished for being that way. I'm going to make her sorry she hurt you, Cassie. Very sorry!"

Cassie stared up at her, suddenly frightened by the dark look in Nicole's eyes. She realized that Nicole meant to hurt Lisa.

She sat up. "She—she just doesn't think," Cassie said in a choked voice. "Lisa doesn't really mean any harm. She's just a little spoiled, that's all."

"She's evil," Nicole said. "And she'll always be evil."

"Wh-what are you thinking of doing?"

Nicole sat down next to her, taking Cassie's hand. Her own tiny one barely fit around three of Cassie's fingers. Cassie stared at it, thinking again that it was so much like a baby's hand.

"I'll just make Lisa taste a little of her own medicine," Nicole said. "I'll just make sure that she feels as embarrassed as you do, right now."

"Please, don't," Cassie said. "It's over. Lisa will say she's sorry, and we'll all be friends again. Don't make this any worse than it is!"

"Lisa can't be allowed to get away with—"

"Nicole, stop!" Cassie cried. "You're scaring me! Lisa's just a jerk sometimes. I'll be okay, really. Promise you won't do anything!"

"You really don't want me to?"

Cassie shook her head. "No, I don't. Just let it go, okay?"

"Well, all right," Nicole sighed. "But if she hurts you again, she'll be damned sorry."

Cassie stood up, pulling Nicole up with her. "Let's go back to my house. I want to wash up, and then maybe we can put up my mother's archery set."

They walked down the path that led out of the woods. The trees formed a canopy protecting them against the hot sun with thickly leaved branches. Nicole pointed at a chipmunk, and the two stopped to watch as it tried to pick up a fallen acorn. Slowly, Nicole reached toward it.

In a flash, it was in her hands.

"Wow!" Cassie gasped. "I never saw anyone do that before!"

"Isn't he cute?" Nicole said. "Do you want to pet him?"

The tiny animal chattered angrily, wriggling desperately. Cassie shook her head.

"No, you better let it go," she said.

Nicole opened her hands, and the chipmunk dropped to the ground. It raced off, disappearing into a log.

When the shadows of the trees gave way to bright sunlight, Nicole turned to Cassie and said, "I really should go home now. My mother was calling me before, but I wanted to help you first. Maybe we can get together tonight, at the house?"

"I'll see," Cassie said hesitantly. She really didn't want to go back to that place, not after the way David had acted. "There's my mother, at our back door. I've got to go, too. See you later!"

She walked away from Nicole, pulling dead leaves from her hair and drying her eyes. She stopped short of her back door when she saw the angry look in her mother's eyes.

"I thought you were going swimming," Carolyn said. "What do you mean, playing alone in the woods like that? What were you told about being alone in dark places, young lady?"

"But I wasn't alone, Mommy!" Cassie protested.

"I was with Nicole. Didn't you see her?"

"No, Cassie, I didn't," Carolyn said. "And I want to know what you were doing in those woods."

Sighing, Cassie explained what had happened. "I felt so stupid, Mommy!" she cried. "I just wanted to run and hide when Lisa said those things!"

"Lisa Westin could use a good spanking," Carolyn said. "I'm tempted to call her mother about this. That girl is terribly mean."

"Forget it, Mom, please," Cassie pleaded. "I'm sure Lisa will tell me she's sorry. If you call her mother, it will make things worse!"

"Oh, all right," Carolyn said. "But don't let me catch you alone in those woods again."

"I wasn't alone," Cassie said softly, though her mother had gone back into the house.

Cassie went inside, too, and up to the bathroom, where she washed away the dirt and debris of the woods. By the time evening came, she had put Lisa's taunting out of her mind.

NINETEEN

"YOU REALLY SHOULD tell her you're sorry," Diane said to Lisa as they took turns sharing the old tire swing behind the Montanas' bungalow. "Sometimes I can't believe how mean you are, Lisa."

"Am I gonna hear about this the rest of my life?" Lisa demanded.

"But you made fun of her!" Diane pointed out. "She probably feels stupid enough as it is. Cassie'll probably be the first girl in her class with a bra."

"That's too bad," Lisa said, grabbing the rope above the swing and pulling it to a stop.

Diane crawled out. "It's lunchtime. You want to stay?"

"Sure," Lisa said.

Rita was just hanging up the phone when they entered the kitchen.

"I asked Lisa if she could stay for lunch," Diane said. "Is that okay?"

"Fine," Rita said. "But you'll have to get your own. I'm on my way to the drugstore. That means I need you to baby-sit, Diane."

"Can we have that leftover roast beef for lunch?" Diane asked.

"Have anything you want," Rita said, taking her purse from atop a pile of magazines. "I'll be back in an hour."

When her mother had gone, Diane went to the refrigerator to take out the plate of roast beef. Lisa reached around her for the mayonnaise and the two went to the counter to make sandwiches.

"Should we make one for David?" Lisa asked.

"He doesn't seem to want to eat anything," Diane said. "It's strange, Lisa. He's been really weird ever since we found him in Myrtle's house. I wish he'd tell us what he was doing in that closet!"

"There's a mystery in that house, for sure," Lisa said. "And I want to go back there and find out what it is."

"I don't," Diane said. "That place gives me the creeps."

"We're a club, Diane," Lisa insisted. "We all go to the house together. You, me, and Cassie."

"And Nicole."

Lisa clicked her tongue, pulling the crusts off her bread. "Okay," she said. "And Nicole. Let's have a meeting tonight."

"Cassie probably won't come," Diane said. "She probably won't want to talk to you."

"I'll tell her I'm sorry, okay?" Lisa promised, annoyed. "So, will you come or won't you?"

Diane tilted her head to one side, her eyes thoughtful. "All right!" she said, giving in. "I'll meet you at Myrtle's house tonight, just after dinner."

She was about to take another bite of her sandwich when a hand came out of nowhere and knocked it away. As Diane stared openmouthed at the mess of bread and meat on the kitchen floor, David screamed, "No! No! No!"

"David, what did you do that for?" Lisa demanded.

Diane shot to her feet and slapped her brother across the face. He went on screaming, his arms rigid at his sides. "No! No! *No! No!*"

"David, you twerp!" Diane yelled. "That was my lunch. What the heck is wrong with you?"

"No house!" David screamed. He snatched up the plastic tumbler Lisa had been drinking from and threw it against the wall. Brown cola obliterated the seashell pattern of one wallpapered panel.

"David!"

David threw himself across the room, tackling his sister. Diane fought him with all her strength, but he seemed almost superhuman. This wasn't the little pip-squeak she'd defeated in so many fights.

"Lisa, get him off of me!"

Without hesitation, Lisa picked up a vase of flowers from the table and dumped the contents over David's head. Soaked through his pajamas, David crawled away from his sister and hid under the table, crying softly now.

"David, come out of there," Diane said in a soft voice.

"No house," David whimpered.

Diane looked up at Lisa, who stood with her back against the refrigerator. The empty vase was still in her hands, and flowers were scattered over the kitchen floor.

"He's afraid of the house," Diane said.

"What's there, David?" Lisa asked. "What did you see?"

David shook his head. "No house," he said again.

Diane reached under the table and laid a hand on her brother's shoulder. She was sorry that she had slapped him. He seemed so tiny and helpless now.

"Okay, no house," Diane said. "I won't ever go back to that house again. I promise."

It was a promise she didn't keep. Pressure from Lisa and the lure of all those toys brought her outside after dinner that night to meet Lisa at the end of the bridge. Together, they went to Cassie's house. Lisa had a small white box with her, and as she walked Diane could hear something liquid swishing around inside.

"What is that?" she asked. "Perfume? Bubble bath? Something to make it up to Cassie?"

"Yeah," Lisa said. "But don't say anything. I'm going to give it to her at the house."

"That's nice," Diane said.

But the gift wasn't for Cassie. It was for Nicole. After she'd left Diane that afternoon, Lisa had met Nicole halfway across the bridge. The other girl had called her names, accusing her of being a monster because she had teased Cassie. Well, Nicole would be sorry she'd said that. The thing in this box would make her sorry for everything she had done!

They reached the Larchmont house. Diane knocked at the door, Lisa on the step behind her. Cassie answered, giving Diane a friendly greeting. She wasn't as warm toward Lisa.

"Oh, hi," she said. "Come on in. Mom and I are baking apple pie."

The two girls entered the brightly lit kitchen, where the table was littered with apple peelings, sugar, and cinnamon. Three empty pie shells were lined up, waiting to be filled. Carolyn cast Lisa a disapproving look as she peeled a Granny Smith apple, but didn't say a word. She'd promised Cassie she wouldn't start anything. She filled the shells as the girls talked.

"Uh, Cassie?" Lisa said. "I want to tell you I'm sorry for what I said this afternoon. I was stupid and mean, and I won't do it again. Will you forgive me?"

Cassie smiled, throwing her arms around Lisa. "Sure!" she said. "Let's just forget it, okay? Nothing's going to stop us from being friends."

Just like that, Carolyn thought. *We adults should be so forgiving.*

"Here, now, this is ready for the oven," she said. A faint rush of hot air filled the kitchen as Carolyn opened the oven to insert the pie plate.

"So, anyway, do you want to come outside?" Diane asked. "There's tons of lightning bugs to catch."

"Can I, Mom?" Cassie pleaded. "It's a nice night, and we'll stay close. Would it be okay? There's three of us!"

"I don't know, Cassie . . ."

"Please, Mom!" Cassie begged. "We'll stay right out in the open, right along the water."

"Well, okay," Carolyn said. "But only for half an hour. It's getting too dark."

"Thanks, Mom," Cassie said.

Outside, Cassie looked back at the house to be certain her mother was no longer watching. Then she stopped and said, "You want to have a secret meeting, don't you?"

"That's the idea," Lisa said. "We can go over there right now."

"It'll have to be quick," Cassie said. "My mom said half an hour, and she meant it."

"Then let's hurry," Diane said.

Hidden by the shadows of night, the children ran across the bridge, not slowing until they reached Myrtle's backyard.

"Hello," Nicole said, appearing from behind the oak tree.

Diane gasped, and Cassie brought a hand up to her mouth.

"Damn you, Nicole!" Lisa cried. "You're always sneaking up on people!"

Nicole looked up at her, tilting her head to one side. "Aren't you glad to see me, Lisa?" she asked. "You invited me to a meeting when we met on the bridge this afternoon, remember?"

"Yeah, I'm glad you're here," Lisa said, fingering the box.

Diane pulled Cassie's arm. "We don't have much time," she said.

They went into the house and upstairs to the toy room, where each little girl chose a favorite plaything. Lisa braided the hair of a doll, all the while keeping her eyes on Nicole.

"I have to go to the bathroom," she said after a few minutes.

"Westin, you've gotta be kidding," Diane said.

"I really do!"

"Then hold it in," Cassie said. "You can't use the bathroom in this house!"

"Of course I can," Lisa said. "But I don't want to go alone. Would you come with me, Nicole?"

Nicole looked incredulous. "Me?"

"Sure, you," Lisa said. "Would you walk down the hall with me? Then I wouldn't be afraid."

"Well, all right, I guess," Nicole said, sounding unsure. Lisa had never made any effort to be nice to her before. Even Cassie and Diane exchanged surprised looks.

Lisa smiled sweetly at Nicole, picking up her box as she stood. In the hall, she turned and started walking in the opposite direction of the bathroom.

"That's the wrong way," Nicole said.

"Oh, I really don't have to go," Lisa said. "I just wanted an excuse to get out of there. I've got something I want to show you, Nicole." Anticipation of her trick made Lisa's heart pound, and it was all she could do not to break out in nervous giggles.

"What is it, Lisa?" Nicole asked with innocent curiosity.

Oh, she was so trusting! Lisa couldn't believe how easy this was going to be. She'd lure Nicole up into the attic, and while the other girl was opening the box she'd run downstairs and lock the door! Then Nicole would be left alone, with the thing Lisa had put in that box.

"I don't want the other girls to know about it," Lisa said, opening the small door at the end of the hall. "So let's go upstairs where they won't be able to hear us."

"They can't hear us out here," Nicole said.

"I want to be sure," Lisa said. "If they find out I've got something neat, they'll want some, too. And I only have enough to share with one person!"

Nicole eyed her warily. "I don't know why you're being so nice," she said. "I know you don't like me very much."

"Oh, forget that," Lisa said. "I was mean, but now I want to be friends. This is a friendship gift!"

She led Nicole up the stairs into the empty attic. They could barely see each other in the darkness.

"Then give it to me in front of the others," Nicole said, her curiosity mounting.

"It's more fun this way," Lisa said. "Come over by the window, so you can get a better look."

She handed the box to Nicole, who took it eagerly and began to pull off the tapes. Lisa backed away, ready to run down the stairs and lock the door. She was on the top step when she heard Nicole's cry of dismay.

And the sound of shattering glass.

"Lisa, how disgusting!" Nicole screamed. "How awful!"

Lisa ran back to her, the trick suddenly forgotten. She stopped short in the puddle that was growing at Nicole's feet, staring in dismay at the dissected frog that lay splattered in a pool of glass and formaldehyde. She had stolen it from her father just to scare Nicole, thinking it was the most ugly thing in the world. Its belly had been slit open, and its guts were exposed. Now, tiny intestines trailed over the wooden floor.

"You jerk!" she cried. "My father's gonna kill me!"

Nicole's eyes were full of tears. "It'll serve you

right!" she cried. "How could you play such a mean trick on me!"

Before Lisa could react, the smaller girl reached toward her feet. She scooped up the dead frog in one hand and took a shard of glass in the other. She swung the sharp glass through the air, aiming for Lisa's face. Lisa screamed, protected only by the darkness, and raced down the stairs.

"Diane! Cassie! Help me!"

Lisa ran for the safety of the toyroom, just a few feet ahead of Nicole. She pushed open the door, then recoiled in horror.

The room was empty. There was no sign of Cassie and Diane, and no toys!

Wide-eyed, covering her mouth with a shaking hand, Lisa tried to convince herself she'd opened the wrong door. But before she could move to the next one, she heard Nicole's heavy breathing right behind her. Lisa turned with a scream as Nicole slashed at her with the glass.

"You're crazy!" Lisa yelled. "Stop it! You leave me alone!"

"You hurt people, Lisa Westin," Nicole seethed. "You made Cassie cry, and you tried to frighten me! You're going to pay!"

Lisa managed to dodge around her, running at top speed for the back staircase. Where were Cassie and Diane? Had they run off? Or was this all a trick, one they were laughing at?

Slamming the door at the top of the staircase shut behind her, Lisa leaned against it for a moment to catch her breath. That was it! It was a trick! Just as she'd wanted to get even with Nicole, her friends were getting back at her for teasing Cassie! Nicole wasn't really going to cut her; the toy room hadn't really disappeared. She'd just been too frightened to think straight.

Well, the hell with them all. She didn't think this was very funny. She'd just go on home, and she wouldn't play along!

Feeling suddenly confident again, she went down the stairs and out of the house. The thought of the broken specimen jar worried her, and thoughts of the punishment she'd receive from her father began to overshadow her anger at her friends.

She heard a snorting noise, then a shuffling of leaves. To her surprise, she saw her mother's gelding sniffing at the overgrown grass. Forgetting her own problems, Lisa hurried to the horse's side.

"Major, what are you doing out of your stall?" she asked. "Mom'll have fits if she knows you're running loose! Good thing I found you!"

She mounted the horse with the ease of a child who'd been riding for years, then turned to guide him home. Suddenly, she noticed a dark, crescent-shaped mark on the horse's neck.

"Hey, wait a minute," she whispered. "You aren't one of Mom's horses after all! But who do you belong—"

"I'm not finished with you yet, Lisa!"

Nicole threw the slimy frog at Lisa with all her might. It struck the horse, startling it into a run. Screaming, Lisa pulled back hard on the horse's mane, commanding the animal to stop. Oblivious to her, it only quickened its pace. Lisa felt branches scratching at her, so concealed in the darkness that there was no time to duck out of the way.

"Whoa! Whoa!"

Something smacked hard against her forehead, and everything went black.

"Wake up now, girl."

Lisa heard a man's voice just behind her ear. Groggily, she blinked her eyes open. It was daylight. How could it be daylight?

She was still atop the horse, but she noticed through her sleepiness that a strong arm was holding her fast.

"Daddy?"

"Good, you're awake," the voice said. "No time for sleeping now, girl. There's work to be done."

Confused, Lisa turned to look behind her. When she saw the gruff, sunburned face of an unfamiliar man, she began to scream and struggle.

"Shut your mouth, girl!" the man snapped. "I won't have temper tantrums from my workers, no sir!"

Lisa went on screaming. "Daddy!! Daaaaddd-ddyyyyyy!" This was impossible!

"You ain't got no daddy!"

She was being kidnapped; Lisa was sure of it. People always tried to kidnap rich kids, to get ransom money. She had to get away!

With a cry, Lisa bent her head down and bit hard into the man's arm. Roaring, he pulled her head away by the nape of her neck. Stinging pain rushed through Lisa's head as he yanked her hair, and then her breath was jolted out painfully as she fell from the horse.

"Nnnnooooo!" Rolling to one side, Lisa looked up in horror to see the horse rearing over her head, its gleaming black hooves making patterns in the air.

There was no time to scream again before the hooves came crashing down on top of her.

Up in the toy room, Cassie suddenly noticed the time.

"We have to go now," she said. "Five minutes more and my mother'll be looking for me."

"But what about Lisa and Nicole?" Diane asked, setting a talking bear back in its place on the shelves. "Why do you suppose they're taking so long?"

Cassie shook her head. "Beats me. But I'm not going to get myself grounded because those two decided to wander around this old house. Are you coming with me or not, Diane?"

"I'm not crossing that bridge alone," Diane said. "Okay, I guess Lisa and Nicole are on their own."

Together they left the house. Diane was the first to notice a small hand sticking out from the edge of the tall grass. She stopped short, grabbing Cassie's arm and pointing.

"That's Lisa," she whispered. "I recognize her watch!"

Cassie stared at the unmoving hand, confused. Then she smiled knowingly and nodded. "She's trying to scare us," she whispered back. "Let's play along for fun, okay?"

Diane grinned, no longer afraid. Together, the two girls approached their prone friend, trying to stifle their giggles. But their mirth abruptly turned to horror when they saw Lisa's face.

She had one arm thrown up over her eyes, but they could still see the bleeding mess that had been her right cheek and temple. Diane and Cassie stared at her, for a moment too frightened to speak.

Then Diane's shaking voice cut the silence of the night. "What happened to her?"

"I—I don't know," Cassie said. "Diane, let's get out of here. I'm scared!"

"We have to tell someone," Diane said. "We have to run and tell Dr. Westin." She started to hurry away, but Cassie ran after her and swung her around, her fingernails digging into Diane's arms. She glared into her friend's eyes.

"No!" she cried. "We can't tell anyone! Not anyone!"

"But—"

"Don't you see?" Cassie said. "We weren't supposed to be here! They'll say it was our fault, that we talked Lisa into coming here with us. They'll blame us, Diane! I know they will!"

"Cassie, I'm frightened!"

Cassie sniffled. "Me, too," she said. "Diane, let's go home. We have to go home and pretend nothing happened. We were never over here, understand? Never!"

Diane threw one last look at Lisa's body, and the two friends hurried toward the bridge.

"We won't go back to that house," Diane said. "We'll never go back there again!"

"Never again," Cassie agreed.

Once they reached the bridge, they both began to

run. Both were crying openly when they got to the other side, and for a moment they hugged each other close.

"I—I have to go," Cassie said. "My half hour is up."

"Be sure to dry your tears," Diane said. "You don't want your mother asking a bunch of questions."

"But someone will ask us questions tomorrow, when they find Lisa!" Cassie realized. "What do we say?"

"Tell them Lisa got mad at us and ran home," Diane said. "We didn't see her after that."

Cassie nodded, then started to walk home. She stopped a few feet away, and turned. "Diane, what happened to Lisa? Who did that to her?"

"I—I don't know," Diane said. "But I think—I think it has something to do with that house, with what made my brother crazy."

Cassie didn't know what to say; she felt too confused and frightened to make sense of the past few minutes. Lisa was dead, all messed up and bloody. She hadn't looked real lying there.

Not real at all.

"Call me tomorrow, Cassie," Diane said, cutting into her thoughts.

Cassie waved in reply. They parted company, running home, neither one aware that Nicole had been watching them from the bridge the entire time.

TWENTY

WHEN SHE ENTERED the kitchen, Cassie went directly to the sink and turned on the cold water to splash her face. Carolyn heard the back door slam and came in, ready to berate her daughter for breaking curfew. But when she saw her daughter's bloodshot eyes, she knew Cassie had been crying, and her annoyance was immediately forgotten.

"What happened, honey?" she asked, brushing wet hair back from Cassie's red-streaked face.

"Nothing," Cassie said, a slight break in her voice.

"You were throwing water on your face to hide your tears," Carolyn said. "I know that trick, Cassie."

"No, Mommy," Cassie insisted. "I was just—I was just hot!"

"Cassie, don't lie to me," Carolyn said. "I should be annoyed that you're fifteen minutes late, but I *will* be annoyed if you lie to me about it! Now, what happened?"

Cassie was trapped. She couldn't tell her mother what had made her cry, couldn't explain the horror she had just witnessed. She wanted to throw her arms around Carolyn, to gasp out how frightened she had been to find Lisa's body lying there in the grass. Instead, she blurted out: "Oh, Mommy! Lisa and I had a fight again!"

Carolyn rolled her eyes. "Is that all?" she said. "Honestly, sometimes I wonder why that girl is your friend. All she does is upset you. What happened this time?"

Cassie hesitated, looking into her mother's eyes. What, indeed, had happened? She hadn't set that part of the story straight with Diane! Thinking quickly, she said, "We—we were going for the same lightning bug. Lisa said I was selfish and a baby because I said I saw it first. Then Diane called her a name, and before I knew it, we were all fighting!"

Carolyn took a towel from its holder on the wall and helped Cassie dry her face. "I don't understand," she said. "Lisa and Diane have been coming to this lake since you were tiny, and you never had troubles before this summer!"

"Mommy, I'm tired," Cassie said. "I don't want to talk about this anymore. Lisa will say she's sorry."

"Sure she will," Carolyn said as the two moved toward the staircase. "She always does. Lisa's a real expert at saying she's sorry."

She walked her daughter upstairs to her room and turned down the Barbie comforter on the bed as Cassie slipped into her nightgown. Cassie went to the window seat to choose a stuffed toy for that night's bedmate. As she picked up a plush lion, she looked out her window. Carolyn knew at once that she was staring at the Hollenbeck place.

"I hate that house," Cassie whispered. "I wish

someone would tear it down."

Carolyn felt a chill rush through her. She herself had spoken those same words a few weeks earlier to Robert Landers, but hearing them from a child's mouth was unnerving. Firmly, she turned Cassie away from the window and led her to her bed.

"Never mind that old place," she said. "There's no need for you to concern yourself with that house."

But I have to tell you what happened there! Lisa is dead! Cassie thought. But she merely braved a slight smile and accepted a good-night kiss. "Mommy?"

"Yes?"

"Stay with me forever, okay? Don't ever let anything bad happen to me."

Carolyn felt her chest constrict. She pulled Cassie close and rocked her for a few moments. "I will never let you be hurt!" she promised. "Never! I'll always be here for you!"

Cassie wanted to argue, to say that bad things happened every day. Like the time her father was shot to death, like Lisa being killed. She said nothing.

"Good night, baby," Carolyn said at last. "Pleasant dreams."

She left the child's room. For a long time, Cassie lay staring out at the moon, wondering if it shone on Lisa's body. But maybe it hadn't been real. Maybe Lisa was home now, laughing at the trick she'd played on her friends, washing fake blood from her forehead.

Lisa is dead, Cassie. She's dead because you all

went to that evil house!

Cassie turned on her side, clutching the stuffed lion and squeezing her eyes shut. She fell asleep quickly, but her dreams were not the pleasant ones her mother had wished for.

A little girl was drowning in the lake, splashing in water darkened red with blood. But this time, Cassie could see her face. She could see the child screaming as she struggled to free herself of the water's invisible bonds.

This time, the child was Lisa Westin.

Cassie woke up screaming, grabbing for the safety of her mother's arms as Carolyn ran into the room. It was a long time before she calmed down enough to fall into a fitful sleep, leaving Carolyn to wonder what had set off this nightmare.

On the other side of Lake Solaria, in the room he shared with his three dogs, Robert was tossing and turning in the clutches of his own nightmare. He was chasing Norman Hollenbeck through the old Victorian house, calling to him, begging him to explain his appearance the other day. Norman turned to scream something at him . . .

. . . and the scream became the sound of a ringing telephone. Kelly's bark and the nudging of cold noses at his feet woke him from his dream. Groggily, with visions of Norman still clear in his head, Robert reached for the telephone. He glanced at his clock and saw that it was past midnight. "'Lo?"

"Robert, it's Susan. Please, you have to come to the station right now. Something horrible has happened."

"What's that?" Robert asked, yawning.

"There's been another death on Lake Solaria," Susan said. "Robert, it's a child. A little girl!"

Robert sat up straight, as fully awake now as if someone had thrown ice water on him. "I'll be there in fifteen minutes."

He made it to the police station in less than ten. From his work around the lake, he recognized Dorothy and Daniel Westin immediately when he passed the chief's office. Dorothy was crying openly as Mike spoke to them, and the doctor was as pale as a sheet, twisting the end of his tie. Robert didn't report his presence to Mike, but instead went straight to the lab.

"It's the little Westin girl, isn't it?" he asked as he walked in.

"Oh, God, Robert," Susan said, putting her arms around him. He held her for a moment to comfort her. When she'd regained her composure, she backed away and indicated the gurney where Lisa's body had been placed. From the doorway, she looked like an exquisite, flawless wax doll. Robert held his ground for a moment, not wanting a closer look.

"I've never autopsied a child before," Susan said. "Robert, what monster could have done this?"

Robert had seen a lot in his years as a cop, from farmers mutilated by their own equipment to bodies burned beyond recognition in fires. But, like Susan, he had had little experience with juvenile victims. He walked toward the gurney, and felt his stomach turn over when he saw the child's battered head. "Oh, dear God," he whispered.

Susan said nothing, understanding his reaction. She went on with her work, handling Lisa as delicately as she would a precious sculpture.

She looks the way Norman Hollenbeck did, Robert thought. "Susan, do you believe in ghosts?"

He said it so softly that at first Susan wasn't sure Robert had said anything at all. She looked up at him, and saw that the color had drained from his face. "If you want to leave the room—"

Robert held up a hand. "No," he said.

"Did you just ask me something?"

"I asked if you believe in ghosts," Robert repeated.

Susan sighed, reaching for a pair of calipers. "I believe there's something evil out there," she said. "No sane force killed this child."

Robert touched Lisa's arm, and drew his finger quickly away when he realized how cold it was. "When did she come in?"

"Half an hour ago," Susan said. "When she didn't come home at the expected time, her father went looking for her. I don't know the details, but I do know he found her behind Myrtle Hollenbeck's house, in the grass."

She took samples of blood from the wound and smeared them over slides. Robert watched her in silence. The only sound in the room was a low, even-pitched humming from the giant clock on the tiled wall behind him. It began to mesmerize him, to lull him into almost believing this was just another nightmare.

He began to tell Susan what was on his mind.

"Susan, I have to tell you something," he said.

"Please, don't ridicule me or say I've been working too hard. I know what I saw the other night, and I know it has something to do with this child's death."

"Maybe you should talk to Mike."

"He wouldn't believe me," Robert insisted. He went on to tell Susan what had happened at the old house that afternoon, leaving nothing out in his desperation to share the story, ending with the appearance of Norman Hollenbeck.

"His head was bashed in, Susan," he said. "Just like this little girl's!"

"Robert, please," Susan said. She sighed. "I only wish I had been able to examine her at the scene of the crime. Moving a body after death can alter some test results."

"Her father found her near the Hollenbeck house?"

Susan looked up at him. "They live nearby," she said.

"Everything bad on that lake is connected to that place," Robert said. "Carolyn Larchmont said there was evil there, and I'm beginning to believe her. Whatever's going on at that house, I think it's something beyond what we can deal with!"

Susan slapped down the instrument she was holding. Resting both hands on the edge of the gurney, she looked over the small body at Robert. "Right now, the only thing *I* have to deal with is explaining to those nice people upstairs what killed their daughter," she said, angered by Robert's sudden unprofessional outburst. "Ghosts! You'd better keep your mouth shut, Robert, because if

Mike hears you talking like this, you'll lose your gold shield. Now, please. I called you down here for support, not to hear talk of ghosts!"

She went back to her work, her hands moving with quick, jerky gestures as she examined Lisa's body. Robert watched her in silence, regretting that he'd mentioned his vision of Norman Hollenbeck. He should have realized that Susan was a woman of science, one who needed concrete evidence to prove everything. He was as alone in his beliefs as he'd been a day earlier.

Susan spoke into her microphone. "The curved appearance of the contusions on the right side of the victim's face closely matches the shape of a horseshoe," she said. "The initial opinion of this pathologist is that the child was trampled to death by a horse."

"A horse?" Robert asked.

"It looks that way," Susan said, switching off the mike. "Of course, I have more tests to do. Meanwhile, I'm sending out photos of the wounds to be blown up for more detailed analysis, but I can see shavings of metal very clearly in the blood samples I put under the microscope. So you see, Robert, no ghosts. My major question is, was the horse running free, or did it have a rider?"

"Your major question is whether or not this was murder," Robert said softly.

"Right," Susan answered. She covered Lisa's body, and Robert felt his muscles relax for the first time since he'd entered the precinct. Under that sheet, the little body no longer seemed to exist. "Robert, there's nothing more I can do until the county coroner gets here. But I have to take this report upstairs to Mike. Do you want to come with me?"

"Not now," Robert said. "I have some thinking to do."

"Then I'll see you later," Susan said, taking off her apron. She washed her hands clean of Lisa's blood, picked up her folder, and headed for the door. "Thank you for coming down here. I'm sorry I snapped at you."

"It's okay," Robert said.

He stood by the covered body for a long time after Susan had left the room. Another death on Lake Solaria. The old house had claimed another victim, but no one seemed to see the connection.

"I'll find it, Lisa," Robert whispered to the child who couldn't hear him.

TWENTY-ONE

CASSIE WOKE UP late the next day to the sound of her mother's rattling printer and the smell of coffee. In the light of early morning it seemed that everything that had happened was just one more terrifying dream. She got out of bed and padded over to the window seat, looking out at the lake below. Everything seemed so normal.

Then she noticed a bright yellow something fluttering amidst the grass in Myrtle's yard. Cassie studied it for a moment, and realized with growing sickness that it was a ribbon, a police marker entwined through stakes that had been placed around the area where Lisa's body had been.

Everything that had happened last night was real. Lisa was dead.

Cassie wanted her mother. She left her room, and as she descended the staircase she heard Carolyn's office phone ringing. She listened to her mother's end of the conversation, hearing worry in her tone.

"Oh, my God," Carolyn was saying. "How could that have happened? We just saw her last night!"

Carolyn noticed Cassie standing in the doorway.

"Rita, Cassie's up," she said. "I'll call you later."

She hung up and opened her arms to Cassie. Without hesitation, the little girl ran to embrace her.

"Cassie, I have some terrible news," she said. "I don't know how to tell you this."

But I already know, Mommy. Lisa is dead. Cassie said nothing.

"Lisa didn't go home last night," Carolyn said, as an unpleasant feeling of déjà vu washed over her, and the words of six years ago echoed in her mind: *Your daddy isn't coming home, Cassie.* "She—she was found behind Mrs. Hollenbeck's house," Carolyn went on. "I'm afraid something bad happened to her. She's dead, Cassie."

"Oh, Mommy," Cassie whispered, hugging her more tightly.

Carolyn frowned. She had expected screams and tears from her daughter, even denials, but not this calm reaction! It just wasn't like Cassie. But then, ever since the accident, Cassie hadn't really been herself.

"Honey, do you understand what I just said to you?"

She heard the soft brushing of Cassie's hair against her shirt as her daughter nodded.

"Lisa's dead," Cassie repeated. She pulled away and looked up at her mother. "What happened to her, Mommy? What killed her?"

"We—we don't know," Carolyn said. "Maybe it was just an accident."

"Are the police gonna come?"

"I suppose so," Carolyn said. "They might want to ask you some questions."

Cassie backed away. "That detective guy didn't believe me," she said. "He thought I saw someone with Myrtle."

"You were just confused," Carolyn said. "Robert knows now that you were telling the truth."

"But maybe I wasn't!" Cassie said. "Sometimes, in my mind, I can see pictures of Mrs. Hollenbeck, and there's always someone with her. I can't see his face, but he's there. Mommy, someone bad killed Mrs. Hollenbeck, and he killed Lisa, too! And he tried to kill David!"

Cassie's voice had risen to a frenzied tone. Before Carolyn could take her into her arms for comfort, she had turned and run from the house, Solo close behind.

The lake was strangely quiet today, as if everyone was sharing in the Westins' mourning. There were no motorboats running, no water-skiers or swimmers. The lake seemed as dead as on a deep winter's day.

As dead as Lisa Westin.

"No!" Cassie cried out, her knees buckling. She covered her ears and rocked back and forth in a kneeling position. "No! Lisa isn't dead!"

Solo barked at her, trying to poke his nose at her tearstained face. Angrily, she shooed him away. The dog sped toward the bridge, where he stopped to look back over his shoulder at her. He wagged his tail, expecting Cassie to chase him, then whimpered a little when he realized she wasn't moving. Understanding finally that there would be no game, he crept down to the water's edge for a drink.

Cassie stretched out on the grass and sand, burying her face in her arms and sobbing until her mother came out to get her.

"Come back inside, honey," Carolyn said.

Without protest, Cassie stood up and walked home with her mother.

As Carolyn had predicted, Robert Landers knocked at their front door early that afternoon.

"Hello, Cassie," he said in greeting, smiling a little.

Cassie stared up at him, waiflike in a smock dress that seemed too tight on her. Her blue eyes were unusually hard, as if she'd prepared herself to face an ordeal as stoically as possible. She said nothing.

"I've been talking to everyone around the lake today," Robert went on, following Carolyn and her daughter into the living room. He stopped at the fish tank, trying to find some way to ease the tension. "But you know, none of them have beautiful tropical fish like you do. That blue and green one there, what's it called?"

"Duffy," Cassie said softly.

Robert laughed a little.

"I think he wants to know what kind of fish Duffy is," Carolyn said.

Cassie turned away from the tank without answering and plunked herself down on the couch. Carolyn sat beside her, putting an arm around the child.

"All right," Robert said gently. "This is hard, Cassie, I know. So we'll do it fast. I'm going to ask you some questions, and you tell me whatever you know."

"I don't know anything," Cassie growled.

Carolyn kissed the side of her head. "Cassie, it's okay," she reassured her daughter.

Robert opened his note pad. "I spoke to the Montanas just a short while ago," he said. "Diane says you and she were playing with Lisa last night. Can you tell me what time she left you?"

"I don't remember," Cassie said.

Carolyn shifted a little. "You went outside about eight o'clock," she said. "And your curfew was for eight-thirty. Can you figure it out from there?"

"I guess she left about twenty-five after, then," Cassie said, looking down at her hands.

"Why did she leave, Cassie?" Robert asked.

"We—we had a fight," Cassie said.

"Go ahead, honey," Carolyn urged. "You can tell Robert what happened."

Cassie repeated her story about the lightning bug. Robert scribbled it down, amazed at what he was hearing. Diane had given him a completely different story, saying that Lisa had made fun of Cassie because of her eight-thirty curfew.

"That's exactly what happened?" he asked when she finished. He didn't want to think Cassie was lying to him. Maybe she was confused, like she had been after Myrtle's death.

"Just like that," Cassie said. "Lisa ran home, and I didn't see her after that."

"Okay," Robert said. He looked back through his notes. "Diane says a little girl named Nicole was with you. She was with you the day of the boating accident, too, but I was never able to find out where she lives. Can you tell me, Cassie?"

Cassie shook her head. "She never told me."

Robert, sensing he'd get no more information here, closed his notebook and stood up. "Cassie, thank you for answering my questions," he said. "I'm sorry that every time I come over here it's on police business, because I really like you and your mommy."

Carolyn smiled a little.

"Are you gonna find the man who murdered Lisa?" Cassie asked. "Are you gonna kill him so he doesn't come back and hurt any more people?"

"Cassie, we don't know that Lisa was murdered," Robert said.

She was! I know she was! Cassie thought wildly.

"I don't understand," Carolyn said.

"Susan looked her over last night," Robert said. "It seems she might have been trampled by a horse."

"But there wasn't any—" Cassie cut herself off, just short of saying that there hadn't been any horse near Myrtle's house. Both adults turned to look at her. "I mean, there wasn't any light," Cassie finished. "Why . . . why would a horse be outside at night?"

"We're trying to figure that out," Robert said. "Dorothy Westin swears her stables were locked and none of the horses were out. The Westins are the only family on that side of the lake that owns horses, and I doubt an animal came over the bridge by itself from this bank."

"Then you aren't sure about the horse?" Carolyn asked.

"Until we get all the test results back," Robert said, "we can't be sure about anything."

He started out of the room. Carolyn got up to follow him, leaving Cassie playing with a tassle on one of the throw pillows. Quietly, unheard by the little girl, Carolyn spoke to Robert at the front door.

"It's that house again," she said. "Lisa was found near that house. Please, Robert, do something before the evil there hurts some other innocent child!"

"I'm working around the clock," Robert said.

He left the Larchmont place and walked down Lakefront Road toward the next house. Hearing soft scuffing noises behind him, he turned to see the Larchmonts' dog a few dozen yards away. The dog scampered over the sandy grass, furiously shaking the white ball he had in his mouth. The ball looked strange, misshapen, as if it had been partially deflated. Thinking nothing of it, Robert continued walking.

Behind him, he heard Carolyn's front door open, and then her voice calling Solo. He glanced over his shoulder again, and saw the dog racing home.

And then he turned completely around, amazed at what the dog held clamped in its jaws.

Robert raced back to Carolyn's house, his hand reaching toward the dog. "Hold it!" he cried. "What's that he has?"

Carolyn came out on the front steps and closed the door behind her, staring. "Oh, God, Robert," she breathed, "don't let Cassie see that thing!"

Solo's forequarters were pressed to the ground. He eyed the humans, knowing that they planned to take his new prize away. His teeth tightened around the white bone of a child's small skull.

"Solo, drop it!" Carolyn ordered.

The dog growled.

"Solo!"

The dog understood the warning tone in his mistress's voice, and let the hideous thing go. It rolled onto its side, exposing a huge, gaping hole in its curves.

Carolyn gasped. Images of a little boy running from Myrtle's house filled her mind, followed by a huge splash of blood that seemed to come from nowhere. She swayed, and Robert moved quickly to catch her.

"It's one of the Hollenbeck children," she whispered. "It has to be!"

"Get me something to put it in," Robert said. "I have to take it down to the station."

Glad to get away from the thing, Carolyn hurried into the house. Cassie had plunked herself in front of the TV, something she never did on a sunny day like this. She seemed completely unaware of her mother. Carolyn went into the kitchen, retrieved a bag from underneath the sink, and went outside again.

"Here's a grocery sack," Carolyn said.

Robert took the bag and carefully placed the skull in it. It was wet, and there were bits of lake grass and sand stuck to its surface.

"I know they dragged the lake after those children vanished," he said. "But they never found this."

"Where . . . where do you suppose the rest of the remains are?"

"I'll have to send a search team over," Robert

said. "With any luck, the dog will show us exactly where he dug this up."

He rolled the top of the bag shut. Now it looked as innocent as a sack of milk and eggs. "I'll call you when I can, Carolyn," Robert said, and headed for his car.

He sped toward the station, his mind racing. This child had died because of a blow to the head, had died so long ago that there was no longer any flesh on the bones, nothing to hold the lower half of the jaw to the upper skull. The lichen that had fastened itself inside the eye sockets had probably been there for years.

"Thirty years," Robert said out loud, turning into the station.

He went downstairs to the lab, where Susan was getting ready to leave. She'd stayed long past her shift, and looked completely wiped out. Robert knew she would be in no mood for what he had to tell her, but her haggard appearance didn't stop him. He started toward her, holding out the bag.

"More newspaper?" Susan asked, her sarcasm sharpened by exhaustion.

Robert frowned, and she realized he had no idea what she was talking about. Before he could say a word, she turned to the counter behind her and picked up an envelope.

"It's from the state labs in Columbus," she said. "Seems you aren't the only one who believes in ghosts. You remember that yellow substance we sent there?"

Robert let the sack fall to his side for the moment. "The report said it was something organic," he said.

"Sure it was." Susan nodded. "They didn't really know. Well, this guy named John Carvellina knew, but he wasn't sure if he should risk his reputation by writing to tell us. He finally did, and here's his letter. You know what he says that stuff is?"

"What?"

"Ectoplasm!"

Robert shook his head. "I don't recognize the word."

"It's something a ghost leaves behind," Susan said. "Frankly, I'm in no mood for this. I haven't slept in eighteen hours, and I'm really not receptive to the idea of spooks. I just want to go home and fall into bed."

Robert put the sack on an empty gurney. "You can't do that just yet," he said.

Susan glared at him, but she opened the bag. The dark circles under her eyes seemed to disappear as she removed the contents, and a new burst of energy ran through her. "Where on earth . . . ?"

"Carolyn's dog dug it up," Robert said. "It's one of the Hollenbeck children."

"Well, we can't be sure of that."

"Who the hell else could it be?" Robert demanded. "Those are the only children ever reported missing on the lake, and now we've found one of them!"

He took Susan by the wrist, a little too firmly. "And I want you to look at something, Susan," he said. "Look at that hole in its skull. How did I tell you Norman Hollenbeck appeared to me the other night?"

Susan swallowed hard, running her finger around

the jagged edge of a wound that had never healed. "You said," she answered slowly, "you said the whole side of his face had been smashed."

"How could I have known that, Susan?" Robert said. "No one's seen this thing before! You explain to me how I knew just the way Norman died!"

"We . . . we don't know it's Norman," Susan argued weakly.

"Maybe it's Ellen Hollenbeck, then!" Robert cried. "A little skull like that—seems the right age, doesn't it? What difference does it make? All I know is that *I told you something yesterday that I couldn't possibly have known!*"

Susan closed her eyes, visions of Lisa Westin's corpse coming into focus. It would be months before Lisa's flesh was gone, but no doubt her little skull would look exactly like this one. She had died in the same way.

"Whoever killed the Hollenbeck children is back again," she said. She opened her eyes and looked at Robert. "We have to tell Mike about this."

"I know," Robert said. "But I wanted to show it to you first, to see if you agreed with my theory."

Together, they went upstairs to Mike's office. The chief was on the telephone, but he hung up as soon as Robert deposited the skull on his desk blotter.

"What the hell is that?"

"I was doing work around the lake," Robert said: "Carolyn Larchmont's dog dug this up somewhere along the banks, and I think it's one of the Hollenbeck kids."

Mike whistled softly. "Jesus," he said. "They spent weeks dragging the water when those kids disappeared, but they never found anything."

"Apparently," Susan said, "the murderer buried them near the water."

Mike picked up the skull. It felt slimy, and had a strange, watery smell. "How come this never surfaced?"

"It's possible the bones were buried very deep," Susan said. "But as the water shifted over the years, the pieces must have begun to work toward the surface. I imagine we'll find bits and pieces of the skeletons over the next weeks."

Mike handed the skull back to Susan. "Have it sent down to Columbus for dating," he said. "And see if you can find out who the Hollenbecks' dentist was. There might be records for a positive identification."

"Will do," Susan said.

Robert touched her arm to stop her from leaving. "Chief, don't you think it's strange that this happens to show up during a summer when we've had so much trouble on the lake?" he asked.

"Coincidence," Mike said. "Like Sue told us, the shifting of the lake dug up these bones. Don't tell me you think their discovery is connected to what's been happening over there?"

"It goes back to my original theory that the Hollenbeck house has something to do with it," Robert said.

Mike shook his head. "I think it's pretty strange for a murderer to lie dormant for several decades, then suddenly reappear. No, I don't think this is connected at all."

His phone rang again, and he picked up the receiver. "Yes, Mr. Mayor," he said. He signaled

Robert and Susan to leave the room.

"He's a stubborn S.O.B., isn't he?" Susan said when they were out in the hall."

"Mike just doesn't want trouble stirred up," Robert said. "But if trouble's going to solve this, it's just what I'm going to cause." He took Susan by the elbow. "I want you to do something with me. It's a farfetched possibility, but I think I know a way we can prove my theory once and for all."

"About ghosts?"

"There's no other explanation!"

"Oh, Robert," Susan sighed. "What do you want to do?"

"I want to rent a video camera," Robert said. "I want to go through every room in that house, and if we're lucky we'll catch something on tape. Please, Susan, it would help if you'd come along."

Susan looked down at the skull. "I have to send this out, Robert."

"This can't wait!"

For a moment, Susan gazed into his imploring eyes. Then she said, "On one condition."

"Name it."

"If you don't find anything on that film," she said, "we chalk the 'vision' you had of Norman up to exhaustion, and you swear you'll never mention ghosts again."

Robert nodded. "You have my word."

"Then let's go," Susan said. "My joints all feel like taffy and I don't know how long they'll hold up."

She returned the skull to her lab, hiding it in a cabinet so the chief wouldn't know she hadn't sent it out immediately. "I'm ready," she said.

TWENTY-TWO

SUSAN VOLUNTEERED THE use of her car for the trip, refusing to sit in Robert's rented rattletrap. They drove into town in silence, each anticipating what they'd find at the house. Susan was certain the film would show nothing at all. Robert was caught between hope and fear that he would find something. He wanted to be wrong. He wanted to believe that he was dealing with a mortal suspect. But mortal suspects don't conjure up images of long-missing children and melting glass jars.

They stopped at a video store on Moxahala Street to rent a camcorder. It was late afternoon when they arrived at Myrtle's house, and the sky had taken on a soft, misty quality. Robert looked down the driveway at the lake. He wondered if people ever thought, as they enjoyed Lake Solaria's beauty, that somehow this all could be taken from them.

"Are you ready?" Susan asked, opening the front door. "I think we should have the camera rolling from the moment we enter. We'll go through every room on this level, then up the back staircase to the second floor. We'll end by coming down the front staircase and going out this door again."

Robert removed the camera from its case and hoisted it onto his shoulder. Twisting the lens and the microphone into position, he switched the camcorder to "Play/Record." A red light indicated that it was working.

He followed Susan into the foyer, aiming the camera in all directions, taking in the portraits of Myrtle's children, the watermarked, flowered wallpaper, the entrance to the living room. There was nothing here now, no sign of the ectoplasm he'd seen the previous day. The place was as cold as ice, but with a strangely innocent feeling in the air.

They went through the entire first floor, then up the back staircase. Trying to lighten the situation, Susan pretended to be a tour guide.

"And here on our right and left we have the Hollenbeck picture gallery," she said. "In fact, we have a gallery throughout the whole house, folks. Next, we'll see the actual rocking chair where Myrtle wasted away her days."

Robert didn't smile.

"Let's hit the attic first," she said, opening the small doorway.

The detective felt something tighten in his chest, a fear that warned him not to go up into the darkness. But he had to go, had to film every inch of this house.

"Maybe we won't find a ghost," he said. "But maybe, by analyzing this film, I'll be able to see something I couldn't find on my own."

They went up the steps.

"Do you smell that?" Susan asked. "Formaldehyde."

She crossed the attic, attracted by sparkling lights on the floor. The sunshine that had managed to seep through the filthy window bounced off fragments of glass.

"This wasn't here before," Robert said. Balancing the camcorder, he bent and picked up a shard of glass, using a handkerchief to keep his fingerprints off the shiny surface. "You can take it back to the lab for examination."

"But you don't think it's worth my effort," Susan said. "You don't think we'll find anything, because ghosts don't leave prints."

Robert stood up again, the camera still filming. The air up here was thick, almost choking in its heat. He wondered what had been contained in the now broken jar.

"I'm finished here," he said. "Let's go downstairs." He was grateful to go back down again.

Susan wouldn't admit it, but the place made her a little nervous, too, and she welcomed the sight of the hallway. "Just the bedrooms left," she said.

They filmed each of the bedrooms. Halfway down the hall, Susan noticed that one of the doors was slightly ajar. She pointed this out to Robert, who looked around from behind the eyepiece of the camcorder.

"That wasn't open when I was here the other night," he said. "I'm sure of it."

"Well, let's take a look," Susan said.

She pushed open the door and entered a bedroom, empty except for a worn blue rug and a single bureau. Susan walked to the curtainless window and looked down at the backyard, at the very tree where Myrtle had been found hanging a few weeks earlier. Susan rested her finger on the frame, feeling soft dust beneath their tips, listening to the hum of the camcorder in the background.

A spider scurried out from behind the gossamer tent it had built in one corner of the window. Susan jumped back.

"Well, this place certainly has the *feel* of a haunted house," she said.

"You're making fun of me," Robert said.

"Can you blame me?" Susan asked. "Come on, Robert! Other than some spilled formaldehyde and broken glass, there's nothing here!"

"Open the closet door," the detective ordered.

With a sigh and a shake of her head, Susan reached for the closet door. She pulled it open slowly, wondering why she was wasting her time here. They'd been through nearly every room and hadn't found a—

The door jerked out of her hand, slamming back against the wall with such force that the doorknob cracked a hole through the plaster.

"Why'd you do that?" Robert demanded.

"Robert, I didn't—"

There was no time to say more. A huge gust of wind blasted out of the dark closet, a wind so fierce that it knocked Susan clear across the room. She screamed, tumbling to the floor, raising her arms to shield her face against the impossible heat. Robert let the camera fall on its strap, staring open-mouthed as a brilliant white cloud swirled around the room. It lifted the bureau and threw it against a far wall, smashing wood and plaster.

"Susan, get up!" Robert shouted. He reached out to help her, one arm cradling the camcorder, hair blowing back from his face.

"What is this?" Susan yelled back, scrambling to her feet.

Holding hands, the two made their way to the door, through what seemed like an indoor tornado. It pushed the skin of their faces tight onto their skulls, wrapped their clothes firmly against their bodies, made breathing nearly impossible.

Squinting, Robert reached for the doorknob, trying to wrench it open as he held fast to the camera.

Suddenly the instrument flew from his arm, as easily as a scrap of paper picked up by a hurricane. As Susan and Robert watched in amazement, it catapulted across the room and crashed through the window.

Susan screamed again.

And then everything was silent.

Breathing heavily, Susan leaned back against the wall, staring at the shattered glass. Robert still had his hand clenched on the doorknob, which now opened easily. He was too stunned to move. In spite of the things that had happened here before, in spite of his conviction that something was very wrong, he hadn't expected anything like this.

Susan swallowed hard and managed to speak. "Robert, will you please explain what the hell just happened here?"

The detective shook his head. "I don't know."

He looked at her. "But I'm right. You can see I'm right, can't you?"

"Sure," Susan said with a slow nod. "Robert, let's get out of this place."

"We—we have to find the camera," Robert said.

The two of them hurried from the room, down the back stairs and out of the house. Robert half expected a crowd to have gathered, summoned by the breaking glass, but no one was around.

"Find the broken window," Robert said, "and that'll lead us to the camera."

They scanned the back of the house, studying the grimy windows, which had taken on a dull, purplish sheen in the afternoon sun. Outside the house, pursuing the constructive task of finding the camcorder, both of them began to relax. Robert heard glass crunch under his feet. He stepped back and pointed.

"Up there. So the camera must be nearby."

"Here it is," Susan called, triumphantly raising the camera. She made a disgusted face, and held it out at arm's length. "Look at this thing! What happened to it?"

In spite of the impossible thing that had just happened in the house, neither was prepared for the appalling condition of the camcorder.

Susan handed it to Robert. "It looks like we pulled it from an explosion," she said.

"I think we did," Robert answered.

There was little to suggest the original shape of the instrument. It was now a blob of black and gray, the lens twisted down like an elephant's trunk. The red indicator light was cracked in half and the microphone cover had been completely burned off. The shoulder rest was stretched like marshmallow that had been left to melt in the sun.

"Whatever did that," Robert said, "is the same thing that killed Myrtle Hollenbeck."

"If only we had proof," Susan sighed. "Now that the camera has been destroyed, no one will believe what happened in there."

Robert stared down at the mess of plastic in his hands, frustrated to realize she was right. He'd come so close, again, to proving his theories! "Wait a minute," he said.

"What's wrong?"

"Do you have a tool kit in your car?" Robert asked. "A screwdriver, or something we can jimmy the door open with?"

Susan took a closer look at the camera. "Oh, Robert, the tape!" she cried. "Maybe the tape is okay!"

"I hope so," Robert said.

They went back to the car, where Susan opened the glove compartment and fished through it until she found a metal nail file. Robert used it to crack away the melted plastic. He pulled out the tape, perfectly intact.

"Let's find a VCR," he said.

Susan started the car. As she drove, she tried to convince herself that this was all an illusion, some kind of trick. But the scientist in her could not deny the obvious, and she was finally convinced that Robert's theories had substance.

"Whatever happens," she said, "I'm behind you now. I'll help in any way I can."

"I appreciate that," Robert said. "I'm tired of

working alone. So, do you know where we can find a VCR?"

"I know the library has one," Susan said. "I just hope some kid isn't watching a movie on it."

"I have my badge with me," Robert said. "We'll call this police business."

There was no one using the library's single VCR when they arrived, but Robert's badge did get them fast service. A plump woman with blond braids across the top of her head showed them how to use the thing, then left them alone in the room.

Robert rewound the tape, then hit the "Play" button. He and Susan watched the film intently. Just as they'd filmed, all the rooms were innocent of any extraordinary beings.

"Fast-forward it," Susan suggested. "Let's get upstairs, right before we entered the bedroom."

Robert hit the "Forward/Search" button. Susan's image skitted up the stairs, into the attic and out again, down the hall. Robert stopped the film just as she was reaching for the doorknob of the bedroom.

"I hope we got that thing on film," Robert said.

But they hadn't. What they saw on the film was not at all what Robert had seen through the camera lens. Susan shook her head in confusion, leaning forward as if a closer look would reveal some answer to the impossible.

"Look at the toys!" she cried.

Instead of the empty bedroom, they were viewing images of a beautiful child's room. There was a ruffled bed, shelves of dolls, stacks of games; every toy a little girl could dream of sat in that room.

A room neither adult had laid eyes on.

TWENTY-THREE

CASSIE SPENT MOST of the day indoors. The bright sunshine, glistening water, and sweet-smelling flowers around the lake all seemed wrong, and Cassie didn't want any part of them. Things were supposed to look sad when someone died. In the movies, death scenes were always played with rainy backgrounds.

A few people had called Carolyn to talk to her, but other than Robert Landers no one had shown much interest in Cassie. She wondered how her other friends were taking the news. Especially Diane, who had found the body along with her. And Nicole—where on earth had Nicole been last night?

Cassie sat in her window seat, holding one of her dolls close and rocking it. She didn't realize that this was a comforting thing she had done before. After her father had died, she'd spent hours rocking back and forth, staring off into space.

Today, however, she was looking across the lake at the big house. She could see police there now. They'd been back to the house several times that day, taking pictures and writing notes. And a while earlier, she had seen Susan and Robert coming from the house. They'd spent some time looking around in the grass, then left the grounds carrying a strange-looking black thing.

Cassie noticed one of the policemen pointing toward an upstairs window. Her eyes followed the imaginary line indicated by his finger, and saw the shattered glass. She untucked the leg that she'd been sitting on and repositioned herself, kneeling on the window seat for a better look. How had that window gotten broken, she wondered? Had it happened when Susan was there?

"Cassie!"

Her mother was calling her. Sighing, wishing she could watch the house some more, she put her doll aside and started to leave her room. She heard her name again.

"Cassie, come out and play!"

It wasn't her mother. Maybe Diane was in the yard below, waiting for her? She went back to her window and looked down, searching the grass around the apple tree. There was no one there.

"Who's calling me?" Cassie said out loud.

She opened her window and lifted the screen, leaning out a little bit. Unable to see anyone, Cassie pulled herself back into her room, let the screen down, and closed the window. Then she went downstairs. She could hear her mother on the phone, arguing with someone. Light from the floor lamp in the office broke up around her mother's hands, casting weird, animated silhouettes on the wall opposite the door.

"Haven't those people suffered enough?" Carolyn was saying. "No, I don't know anything. And my daughter most assuredly doesn't want to talk about it, either! Please, don't bother us!"

Cassie came into the office as Carolyn was hanging up the phone.

"Reporters," Carolyn said with disgust. "It isn't enough that a child has died, but they have to look for the most gory, horrible copy they can come up with."

Her words started an image forming in Cassie's mind, an image of Lisa's shattered head. Cassie quickly changed the subject to drive it away. "I'm going outside," she said. "Just sitting around in here makes me really sad, 'cause all I do is think of Lisa."

As she left the house, Solo ran up to her, carrying something white in his mouth, wagging his tail.

"I don't want to play fetch," Cassie said. "I'm busy."

Solo dropped his prize at her feet.

"What's this?" Cassie said, picking it up. "A bone? Where'd you get this thing from, someone's trash? Gross, Solo! Take it and bury it, will you?"

She flung the bone away with all her might, unaware that it had been buried in the lake for thirty years. Not understanding the irritated tone in the little girl's voice, Solo ran after it.

"Cassie! Come and play! Come to the house!"

"Who is that?" Cassie yelled.

Only the whistles of birds answered her. She looked across the water at Myrtle's house, but couldn't tell if anyone was there. Could Nicole be calling her? She did live on that side of the lake.

"Come to the house, Cassie." The voice was quieter now, no louder than the wind.

"Cut it out," Cassie said, annoyed. She turned in a complete circle. "Quit teasing me!"

"Come to the house, Cassie. Come to the house. Come to the house. Come to the house. Come to the—"

"I don't want to go there!" Cassie screamed. "Not ever! Never again!"

She covered her ears and ran back into the safety of her own house, slamming the back door shut tight so that she couldn't hear the voice that beckoned her across the lake.

At the Lake Solaria precinct house, Robert was anxiously awaiting the right time to show his new evidence to Mike Hogan. The chief had been busy all day, dodging reporters and making statements. Robert paced the hall outside his office, turning hopefully each time the door opened only to be pushed aside by someone who believed he or she had more urgent business.

"What're you hanging around for?"

Robert looked over his shoulder to see Chris Geisly, Susan's boyfriend. He was a few inches shorter than Robert, but his slight build concealed the strength of a fifth-degree kung fu black belt. His light brown hair was scattered around the rim of his blue cap like straw on a scarecrow. Chris was smiling, and Robert knew the question was meant as a friendly greeting.

"I'm waiting for a minute with the chief," Robert said.

"You and a lot of others," Chris said. "It's been a devil of a night here."

Robert nodded, thinking that the statement made more sense than Chris realized. He saw Mike's door open again. "Talk to you later," he said, hurrying into the chief's office.

Mike was leaning as far back as his chair would go, his legs stretched out before him and hidden beneath his desk. He looked somewhat annoyed at Robert's presence.

"I've been through hell today," he said. "Talked to more people in the last few hours than I have in the past year. I'm gonna tell you straight out, Landers, I'm in no mood."

Armed with the videotape, Robert was undaunted. "I have a report to make," he said.

"File it," Mike answered.

"I don't want to put this in writing just yet," Robert said. He saw Mike roll his eyes, and held up a hand. "Please, this is important. It's not one of my—what you call my 'crazy theories.' It's solid evidence that something strange is going on at that house." He laid the videotape on Mike's desk.

The chief made no move to take it. "What's that?"

"A film of the Hollenbeck house," Robert said. "Susan and I made it this afternoon. You have a VCR at home, don't you? Take it with you tonight and look at it."

Mike's chair clunked forward. "You filmed the house?" he said. "What the hell for?"

"To see what my eyes couldn't see on their own," Robert said. "And I was successful. Mike, Susan and I went through every inch of that place and found nothing. But when we played the tape back, there was a room on it that neither of us had seen. It was set up like some kid's room and there were more toys in there than I've ever seen in my life. You figure out how something that doesn't exist could show up on film."

"I don't know if I want to look at this at all," Mike said.

"You won't be wasting your time," Robert promised.

Mike groaned. "I must be out of my mind, but I'll watch it at home tonight."

Robert thanked him, and turned to leave the office. Now everything would be going his way, and no one would make fun of his theories about the house. He'd have the backup he needed to trap his suspect once and for all.

Right now, though, he was tired and hungry. Tonight he would rest, so he would be strengthened for the work he had to do in the morning. He'd go back to the house, this time accompanied by a team Mike assigned to him, and he'd find out what force had destroyed the camcorder and altered the tape.

As he drove home, he listened to a local radio station. After just a few minutes news of Lisa's death came on the air. The reporter speculated, as Susan had reported, that the child had been trampled by a horse. Robert was grateful for Susan's work, though he didn't agree with her answer. At least it gave the public an explanation they could accept. Murder by unnatural forces was beyond anyone's understanding.

Deciding on spaghetti for dinner, Robert filled a pot with water and set it on the stove to boil. He poured a jar of sauce into another pan, placing it on a back burner. While he waited for his dinner to cook, he played with the dogs for a few minutes. Erin's bandages had been removed, and blackish scars, evidence of the fire, streaked through her cinnamon-red coat. Robert took the dog's head in his hands and kneaded her ears.

"I'm working on it, girl," he said, "I'm working on finding the bastard who did this to you."

The buzzer on the oven went off. Robert strained the spaghetti, drowned it in sauce, and carried the plate into the living room. He switched on the news, catching the tail end of the weather report. The meteorologist's map faded away to a picture of Lake Solaria. Robert pushed Kelly's nose away from his plate as he leaned forward to pick up the channel changer. He knew what this story would be about, and he'd had enough of it for one day.

When he'd finished eating, Kelly's whining prompted him to gather up three leashes to take the dogs for a walk. It was dark out now, a cool and quiet night. Robert lived on a street where the curbs were still made of brick that had been laid down decades earlier, each one stamped "Zanesville Pottery." The street lamps were of wrought iron, and many of the houses, including his own, had the kind of white picket fence everyone equates with a peaceful, middle-American existence. These were the things that had attracted Lynda to the town in the first place, made her willing to leave her native Toledo to join Robert on his first real job as a detective. He'd served as a rookie in Toledo, where he'd worked hard to earn his gold shield. When jobs were offered, it was a toss-up for him between Columbus and Lake Solaria. All Lynda had to hear was that the crime rate in Lake Solaria was almost nonexistent, and things were settled. "This isn't the town we moved into, Lynda," Robert whispered, stopping as the dogs found a trash can to sniff. "Things aren't so peaceful on Lake Solaria now."

But it really was a beautiful place, and Lynda had adored it so. She'd wanted to raise children here, but her illness had wiped out any hopes of that. Robert started walking again, turning the dogs back up the other side of the street, imagining Lynda walking at his side. She'd reassure him that everything would work out, and she'd make him feel strong.

She wouldn't be the accusing Lynda he'd dreamed of that night in Myrtle's house.

Finally, Robert crossed the street again and pushed through the gate into his yard. The phone was ringing when he entered the house, but he took the time to unleash the dogs before lifting it off the hook.

"Took you long enough," he heard Mike say.

"Chief?"

"Yeah, it's the chief," Mike said. "I got curious about this film of yours, and since it was my dinner hour anyway I took it home to look at it."

"What did you find?"

"I found out that everything I said about you is

true," Mike snapped. "You're crazy. I don't want to see you around the precinct, Landers, and especially not around Lake Solaria! You're on indefinite leave of absence."

Robert sat down, his shoulders feeling suddenly heavy. "I don't understand," he said. "Didn't you look at the tape?"

"Yeah, I looked at it," Mike answered. "And you know what I found? Nothing! There's nothing on that tape but a bunch of stupid kids' cartoons!"

"But Susan was with me!" Robert protested. "She saw it all, too!"

"I called her earlier," Mike said, "and she told me the tape must have been switched. But that's impossible, since it never left my hands. Only reason I don't suspend her, too, is that we need all the lab help we can get these days!"

"Chief—"

"I don't want to hear another word," Mike snapped. "You're crazy, Landers. Really sick!"

Robert set the receiver down in the middle of Mike's ravings and buried his head in his arms as a wave of painful, all-consuming defeat washed over him.

TWENTY-FOUR

CASSIE'S SLEEP WAS torn apart by nightmares, visions of a drowning child with Lisa Westin's face. She woke up screaming twice, so shaken the second time that Carolyn took her into her own bed. She held her daughter tightly the whole night, unable to sleep herself as she felt the child's body trembling in her arms.

The next morning, Rita Montana called to say that Lisa's wake would take place that evening. It would only be for one night, and the casket would remain closed. The entire Montana family would attend, and Rita wondered if Cassie and Carolyn wanted to join them.

"I'm not sure Cassie should go," Carolyn said. "It's been so hard for her." She looked across the kitchen at her daughter, an ashen-faced waif with lackluster hair who was absently stirring a bowl of cereal. "What about Diane? How's she taking this?"

"She's been very edgy," Rita said. "Diane was always a bit short-tempered, but these days everything you say to her sets her off. Of course, we understand what's happening, that it's her reaction to this horror. At least she *is* reacting. David still hasn't said a word, except to scream." There was a slight choking noise over the line, and Carolyn guessed her neighbor was crying. "He was at that house, too. It could have been my son."

Carolyn wanted to say something reassuring, that the police were working hard to find the responsible party. But she knew that whatever words she might speak would be untrue, and that the truth would be too hard to believe. Rita would never understand that it was the house that had killed Lisa, not some maniac lurking around Lake Solaria.

"Cassie's calling me," she said, making an excuse to get off the phone. "I'll talk to you tonight, Rita."

"I wasn't calling you," Cassie said dully as her mother hung up the phone.

"I know," Carolyn said. "Honey, Mrs. Montana says that Lisa's wake is going to be tonight. Do you want to go? If you don't, I'll understand."

Cassie pushed her still-full cereal bowl away, spilling milk on the table. "Why do they call it a wake?" she asked. "Nobody wakes up after they're dead."

Carolyn couldn't help a slight smile at the innocent remark, but before she could answer Cassie was talking again.

"I'll go," she said softly. "I want to say good-bye to Lisa." *Because I ran away from her the other night and didn't say good-bye then,* she added silently.

"Fine," Carolyn said. "We'll just stop by the

funeral home for a moment, to pay our respects."

She picked up a sponge and started to clean the table. "Cassie, I have an idea," she said. "The roses are so pretty these days, and it would be nice to bring a bouquet tonight. Can you get my shears from the shed and cut a few?"

Cassie pushed her chair back and stood up. "I guess so," she said, though she didn't see the point of giving flowers to someone who would never see them.

When she went outside, everything seemed to be normal on the lake. The sound of a motorboat engine filled the air, competing with someone's loud radio and the chattering of countless birds. Cassie could see one of her neighbors preparing a rowboat for a trip on the lake. She opened the toolshed and went inside to find the rose clippers. As she was turning to leave, her arm accidentally brushed against the rake, sending it crashing to the cement floor. The reverberation of the metal tines took on the sound of words: *"Come . . . come . . . come . . . come to the . . . come to the house."*

Cassie kicked the rake across the floor, watching it crash against an old vacuum cleaner.

"Cassie . . . Cassie . . . come to the house, Cassie!"

"Shut up," Cassie growled, holding the clippers like a weapon. "I'm not gonna listen to you."

She went to the rosebushes that lined the side of her house and started randomly assaulting Mount Shasta, American Beauty, and Peace roses.

"Come to the house, Cassie!"

"No!"

Someone tapped her on the shoulder. Dropping the roses, she whirled, pointing the clippers. Nicole stepped back from her, wide-eyed.

"What are you doing!" she cried.

"Oh, Nicole," Cassie said, relaxing visibly. She let the clippers fall to her side. "You startled me."

"I can see that," Nicole said. "I heard you yell, 'No!' Who were you talking to?"

Cassie bent down to gather up the roses, careful not to touch the thorns. "Come over here and sit on the picnic bench," she said. "You can help me pull off thorns." She handed half the roses to Nicole and led her to the bench.

"So, who were you talking to?" Nicole pressed, pinching off thorns and laying them in the apron of her long dress.

"I don't know," Cassie said. 'I keep hearing someone calling me from across the lake. Someone's trying to get me to go back to that house, but I won't!"

"The house won't hurt you, Cassie," Nicole said.

"But someone's hiding there," Cassie said. "I know it. The person who made David crazy and killed Lisa."

"God killed Lisa," Nicole said. "He punished her for her wicked, cruel ways."

Cassie let out a cry as a thorn stabbed her. Poking her thumb into her mouth to suck on the injury, she made a face at Nicole. "That's sick," she said, talking around her thumb. "Lisa was weird, but she wasn't wicked. She didn't deserve to die! How can you talk that way?"

"It isn't up to us to decide who deserves to die," Nicole said. "The Lord chooses our destinies himself. Sometimes, one's ending is long in coming and peaceful. But some deaths are deservedly violent, as Lisa's was."

Cassie stood up. "You give me back my roses," she said. "I don't want to talk to you when you say such dumb things."

"But I'm right," Nicole said. "And in time, you'll understand how right I am."

Cassie gathered the roses in her arms and hurried into the house without saying good-bye. Nicole was talking crazy, and that frightened Cassie.

Nicole smiled slightly, gazing after Cassie, but it was not the shy smile Cassie found so cute. This smile was full of malevolence, shades darker than should be possible for a child of twelve. Cassie was frightened now, Nicole knew, but soon she would welcome Nicole's presence at all times, without question. Soon, Nicole would be her only friend.

The little girl in the old-fashioned dress stood up from the picnic bench, crushing thorns in her palm without feeling them. She walked along the water's edge toward the Montanas' house, where she climbed into the tire swing and waited patiently for Diane to come out. The time had come, she realized, to rid herself of her last enemy.

Nearly half an hour later, Diane came out onto the deck, dressed in a halter top and shorts. Nicole painted a smile across her face as she approached Diane.

"Good morning," she said.

Diane turned to her. "Hello," she said. "I'm surprised to see you."

"Why?"

"Well, my mother won't let me wander away from our property," Diane said. "She's afraid something will happen. And I think Cassie's sticking around her house. I'm surprised that your mom let you cross the bridge."

Nicole climbed up the steps and settled into the chaise longue, smoothing her long skirt. "My mother doesn't care what I do," she said. "Besides, there's nothing to be afraid of. Didn't you hear? Lisa was trampled by one of her mother's horses."

"That's what everyone says," Diane answered. "But my mother says Mrs. Westin swears the horses were locked up that night. So if it was a horse, maybe someone was riding it and killed Lisa on purpose."

Nicole smiled a bit, wind blowing her brown curls back from her face. In the morning sunlight, Diane noticed how very pale she was, almost sickly.

"What are you thinking about?" Nicole asked.

"Nothing," Diane insisted.

"You've been staring at me," Nicole accused. "I don't like that."

"I didn't mean to!" Diane cried.

Nicole stood up. "Do you want to play with me?" she asked. "There aren't any police at the house right now, so we can sneak in and play with the toys."

"Are you crazy?" Diane asked. "I'm never going back to that place again!"

"Yes, you are," Nicole said, her voice quietly confident.

"Forget it," Diane said.

"You will come to the house, Diane," Nicole said. "It's our last chance to enjoy those nice things. In fact, I bet we could sneak a few out and hide them. I want you to help me do that, Diane."

Diane turned away from her, looking out over the water. Something about Nicole gave her the creeps this morning.

"Come to the house, Diane," Nicole said.

Diane shook her head vigorously. Nicole came up behind her, her breath like the icy winds of December.

"Come to the house, Diane," she whispered in her ear. "Come to the house. No one will see you. I promise. No one will know."

"My . . . mother . . ." Diane's voice faded.

"Your mother won't know," Nicole insisted. "Come to the house. Come and play, Diane."

Diane found herself nodding. She heard Nicole's footsteps descend the wooden stairs, but instead of running into the safety of her house, she let go of the railing and followed the smaller girl.

They passed a few people on the way to the bridge, then one or two crossing it, but no one seemed to notice the two little girls. Diane recognized one of the Canfield girls, but Georgie's sister didn't greet her. It was as if no one saw her.

When they reached Myrtle's property, she noticed the yellow ribbon surrounding the place where Lisa had been the other night. There was a sign: Police Area. Keep Out.

In silence, she followed Nicole into the house and up to the toy room.

It was strangely cold in here today, unlike the times she had come here with the others. But Diane sensed that it was because she felt guilty this time. She had wanted to come up here for all the previous meetings, but she didn't want to be here today.

"Let's not stop to play," Nicole said. "There's a big bag here, and we can fill it with as many toys as possible. When they do sell this house, no one will miss them."

"It feels like stealing," Diane objected.

"When things don't belong to anyone anymore," Nicole insisted, "you can take all that you want." She went to the canopied bed and picked up a huge canvas sack. Loosening the drawstring, she turned and surveyed the room, evidently to decide which toys to take.

"Where'd you get that?" Diane asked.

"I found it in the laundry room," Nicole said. "Here, I'd like to take these puzzles, and these two dancing dolls." She put the toys into the bag. "Come on, Diane, pick something."

Diane just stood in the middle of the room, unsure what to do.

"Well, I know what I want," Nicole went on. "This bear that talks and this doll with all the pretty clothes. And some paints . . . and this Kit-Bits Village . . ."

She continued filling the bag. "Diane, it's okay," she encouraged. "Pick something out!"

"Well," Diane said, hesitating, "I guess it'd be okay to take one thing. They're probably just gonna give it all away, anyway."

"That's right," Nicole agreed.

Diane looked around the room, finally choosing the Lovie-Lamb doll that sat in a wooden doll-size high chair. She had always wanted one of these, but her mother and father couldn't afford to buy one. Now, she'd have one of her own. She held it close, smelling the new vinyl of its head.

"This is what I want," she said. "Just this."

"Okay," Nicole said. "Put it in the bag."

Diane took a step back. "No!" she cried. "It'll get all messed up. You've got pastels in there loose that might ruin her pretty christening gown."

"That's stupid," Nicole sneered. "And you can't carry her out. Someone might notice."

"Oh, and no one's going to see you dragging that big bag."

"No one will," Nicole said confidently.

"Well, she's too good a doll to stuff in there," Diane said. "I just want to hold her for a while."

"Suit yourself," Nicole said.

Diane went to the bed and climbed up onto it, cradling the doll in her arms. She sat playing with the lace that frosted its long white gown, humming a lullabye. What could she do with the doll, she wondered? She could never bring it home. Wherever Nicole planned to hide the toys, she'd have to put Lovie-Lamb there, too.

"She's crying too loud," Nicole said.

"Who is?"

"Don't be silly," Nicole snapped. "You can hear her! Your baby is crying too loud, and I want you to shut her up!"

"You're nuts," Diane grumbled, tired of Nicole's weird games. She slid off the bed. "I'm going now," she said. "I know you're gonna get caught stealing those toys, and I'm not gonna be here when you do."

Nicole lunged for the door, slamming it shut. "You aren't going anywhere until you silence that brat of yours!" she cried. "I will not tolerate such noise!"

"Oh, shut up!" Diane yelled. "Quit being so idiotic! Dolls don't cry and you know it!"

"She *is* crying!" Nicole screamed. "She's crying, and I'm going to silence her!"

Nicole reached toward a pile of wooden blocks that lay scattered over a low table. Before Diane realized what she was doing, the smaller girl lifted the block and brought it plunging down. With a scream, Diane dropped the doll and leaped out of the way, thinking the blow was meant for her. Instead, it landed hard on the side of the doll's head, denting the vinyl.

"Shut up!" Nicole screamed. "Shut up! Shut up!"

Again and again, she struck the doll, crushing its head; one of the glass eyes popped out. Horrified, Diane managed to find her legs. She ran from the room and stumbled down the back staircase. Nicole was crazy! Lisa had always claimed she was, but until now Diane hadn't believed her.

"Diane! Diane Montana, don't you dare run away from me!"

Diane didn't stop. She heard Nicole's voice screaming angrily, and with each call, ice seemed to form in her joints, slowing her. Something bad was going to happen to her. She just knew it! Nicole was going to hurt her!

"Diane!"

She reached the bridge, panting loudly; her house was so close. Diane tried to rush toward it, but suddenly Nicole had her by the arm. Nicole swung Diane around, pushing her hard against the railing of the bridge.

"It's your turn," Nicole hissed. "Your turn to die!"

Diane tried to wrench away from her, but Nicole's strength and speed seemed inhuman. Suddenly Diane found herself falling over the side of the bridge. She screamed, taking in a great mouthful of water as she hit the lake's surface.

Something was tugging her under, dragging her down. She was going to die. She was going to die. She was going to die just like Lisa, like Georgie, like Myrtle. She was going to . . .

Silver-streaked blackness enveloped her, cutting off the voice in her terrified mind.

TWENTY-FIVE

ROBERT HAD SPENT much of the night trying to understand what had happened to the videotape. There just hadn't been any opportunity for someone to tamper with it! He fell asleep with these thoughts in his mind, his brain working too hard to leave room for nightmares.

He knew the only thing he could do now was to go back to the house alone, to fight whatever lived there on his own. There was no one to help him, and he didn't want to involve Susan further in his investigation. He had almost cost her her job already.

As if summoned by his thoughts, the phone rang, and Susan's voice came over the wire.

"I figured you'd still be asleep," Robert said.

"I'm too wired to sleep anymore," Susan said. "Robert, I wish I'd been better at sticking up for you. But the chief caught me half-asleep and I wasn't thinking straight. And by the time I was, I couldn't convince him that we weren't lying!"

Robert sighed wearily. "I don't know how much more I can do right now," he said. "I can't go near that house for a few days. Mike's surely going to have the investigation team watching out for me."

"But there is something you can do," Susan said. "Robert, there's been news on the Hollenbeck case. Chris called me a little while ago. All those letters you sent out in search of Cyril Hollenbeck paid off. We've found him!"

Robert stood up, excitement rushing through him. He leaned against the screen door and watched the dogs romping around the backyard. "When did that come in?" he asked. "Why wasn't I told about it?"

"I guess the chief doesn't plan to tell you anything for a while," Susan said. "Fortunately, Chris knew how much it meant to you. Hollenbeck's in a home in Zanesville. If he's got any news for us, this could be the break we've been looking for."

"I hope so," Robert said. He found a pencil and an old envelope to write on, and took down Cyril's address as Susan dictated it. "I'll call you when I get back."

As he hung up, Robert looked at the clock. It was eleven now; if he left right away, he'd be in Zanesville by one o'clock. Opening the back door, he called the dogs into the house. Robert filled their food dishes and water bowls, then bent to give each cinnamon-colored head a massage.

"See you later, girls," he said.

Walking across his lawn, Robert stopped a few feet from the rental car and shook his head. Hell, it was a long drive to Zanesville, and he wasn't about to go in that crate. Checking his wallet for his credit card, he decided he'd take it to the small airport near Mansfield and trade it for a newer model.

The sense of defeat he'd had the night before was

completely gone now, and as he drove he felt that everything was going to fall into place this afternoon. If anyone could answer his questions, it would be Cyril Hollenbeck. Robert headed down Moxahala Street to the route that would take him out to Highway 71.

Half an hour later, he saw the green sign indicating the exit ramp for Mansfield. The airport was a quiet one, and it didn't take any time at all to switch cars. The old rental had lacked air conditioning, so the first thing Robert did after climbing behind the wheel of the new car was to turn the system on high. The soft whirring of the fans, combined with the humming of the motor, helped him to relax. He was so full of thoughts about his coming meeting with Cyril that he hardly noticed the scenery passing by, old factories, giant tracts of farmland, and small towns fitting together like pieces of a puzzle.

Within an hour, he was driving through Columbus. Passing the brick and stone buildings of the university, he eventually crossed Broad and Main Streets and turned east on Highway 70. Though the road was crowded, he made good time, and signs for Zanesville began to appear after a short while. Exiting the highway, he stopped at an Exxon station to get his bearings. A thin man in a clean gray jumpsuit came out to greet him.

"Fill it up, premium," Robert said, getting out of the car. "Do you have a local map?"

"Right inside on the counter," the attendant said. "Help yourself."

Robert pushed through the glass door of the

station office. There was a pretty teeenage girl at the register, surrounded by car deodorizers, cigarettes, and candy. She smiled at Robert, and her voice had a thick drawl when she spoke.

"Can I help ya?"

"I'm looking for the Dryden Rest Home," Robert said, opening a map across the counter.

The girl leaned forward, her long blond hair spilling onto the map. For a moment, Robert was reminded of Cassie Larchmont—or what Cassie might look like in about seven years.

"It's right there," the girl said. "See? You hang a left onto the Y Bridge, then drive straight along Pine Street, and you'll find it." Robert refolded the map. "Thanks a lot," he said.

After paying for the gas, he continued on his way, once again wondering what Cyril would be like. Minutes later, he was driving past a big stone wall that had been etched with the name "Herbert Dryden Rest Home."

The virtually empty parking lot told him that visiting hours had not yet begun. When he walked through the double glass doors, he was greeted by a round-faced, dark-haired woman named Lelia Marson, according to her name tag.

"Good morning," he said. "I'm here to see Cyril Hollenbeck."

Lelia eyed him with a stern expression. "Visiting hours begin at three," she said.

"This isn't a social call," Robert said, taking out his badge. He didn't like flashing the thing around like some braggart, but there were times he was grateful for its golden authority. "I'm Detective

Robert Landers, from Lake Solaria. I sent a letter here in search of Mr. Hollenbeck."

Still frowning, Lelia picked up a phone receiver. "Let me refer you to our supervisor," she said to Robert, then spoke quietly into the phone. Moments later a man of about Robert's age appeared.

"Good afternoon, Detective," he said, holding out a hand to shake Robert's. "I'm Dr. Orton. We received your letter a few days ago, but you can imagine how important it is for us to check up on these things."

"Of course," Robert agreed, following the doctor down the institutional green hall into his office.

"Your letter really surprised us," Orton said. "You see, Mr. Hollenbeck has been with us for eight years now, and never once has anyone contacted him. He told us he had no family to speak of, so when we learned that his wife had recently passed away, we were all quite amazed."

"The Hollenbecks were divorced many years ago," Robert explained, taking a seat in an oxblood leather chair. "But since there is an estate to settle, and since Cyril is apparently Myrtle's only surviving kin, it was our duty to find him." He refrained from mentioning his real reason for wanting to see the old man. Talk of a murder investigation might prompt the doctor to say Cyril couldn't handle it.

"Just what sort of property is involved?" Orton inquired. "Is it worth driving Mr. Hollenbeck so far to see it?"

"There's a large house on a lake," Robert said, "and some furnishings and jewelry." He started to mention the roomful of toys, but stopped himself.

"The location of the property makes it quite valuable," he continued. "In fact, there's talk of turning it into a historical monument because of its age. But it does belong to Mr. Hollenbeck, and it's his choice what to do with it."

"We told Cyril about his wife," Dr. Orton said. "The old man seemed somewhat indifferent, but I guess after all these years she was practically a stranger to him. I have a feeling he won't be too receptive to you."

"It's still important that I talk to him," Robert said. "Please, may I see him now?"

The doctor stood up. "Come on upstairs with me."

Robert had conjured up various images of Cyril Hollenbeck over the past weeks. The thought of his being alone for so many years after the loss of his children had caused the detective to believe he'd find a sickly, bitter old man. He waited curiously as Dr. Orton opened a door.

"Mr. Hollenbeck," Dr. Orton said in a slightly louder tone than before. "You have a visitor. He's here to discuss your wife's estate."

"Whatever I left with Myrtle is no concern of mine now," said a wheelchair-bound man who sat facing a tall window.

Robert took a step into the room. "Mr. Hollenbeck, I'm Detective Robert Landers," he introduced himself. "I need to talk to you about more than your wife's estate. It's vitally important to an investigation that's taking place on the lake right now."

A squeaking noise filled the room as Cyril swung

his chair around. Robert was surprised at the old man's appearance. His hair was still thick and neatly combed, he wore a tailored beige sports jacket and perfectly creased tan pants, and his face was rimmed with a trim white beard. Cyril's blue eyes were as clear as those of a man half his age.

"Investigation?" Cyril said. "Had enough of investigations thirty years ago, and they didn't bring my kids back to me."

"I'm sorry, Mr. Hollenbeck," Robert said quietly, imagining that even three decades couldn't erase the memory of beloved ones. Lynda's face appeared briefly in his mind.

"We'd like some privacy, Dr. Orton," Cyril said.

"I'll be making rounds," Dr. Orton said, nodding at Robert before he left the room.

Cyril watched the door, his knobby fingers opening and closing over the armrests of his chair. "Now that we're alone," he said, "you tell me what this investigation is about. I don't imagine you tried this hard to find me just to tell me I've got an old house and some sticks of furniture coming to me."

"The house must be worth something," Robert said.

"And what would I do with the money if I sold it?" Cyril said. "Damned stroke I had a few years back put me in this home and made my legs good for nothin'. As far as the house is concerned, I'll sign anything I have to, and you can just donate the contents to charity. Maybe someone will find more happiness in that place than we ever did."

Robert sat down in a dark green vinyl lounger, leaning forward to fold his hands between his knees as he spoke. "Could you tell me exactly what happened back then?"

"It's been a long time," Cyril said, lifting one hand to examine his fingers. "Don't know how much I remember. Why?"

"Mr. Hollenbeck, some . . . some things have happened recently," Robert said. "Some people have died on the lake."

"So?" It wasn't an uncaring question. Cyril simply couldn't see what he had to do with it.

"One of them was a little girl," Robert went on. "Her body was found behind your old house, and it looks as if she was trampled by a horse. But I have good reason to believe that the house had something to do with it."

Cyril sighed, leaning back a bit. "You have more than good reason," he said. "That house is full of black spirits, of a force so hateful it destroys anything that comes near it."

He paused, indicating a pitcher that sat on the table. "That's just water," he said, "but one of the volunteers brought it in right 'fore you came. Good and cold, if you want some."

"Not right now, thanks," Robert said, eager to hear Cyril's story.

"Fine," Cyril said. "But I'll just pour myself a cup. I'll need it, 'cause I'm gonna be talkin' for a while."

Cyril wheeled over to the table, and after pouring himself a drink he turned to face Robert again. He began his story by telling how he and Myrtle had moved into the house just after he'd gotten a job in a cash-register factory a few miles outside Lake Solaria. The kids were then eight and ten years old, and the family considered themselves lucky to have found such a nice place to live.

"Then things started happenin'," Cyril went on. "My daughter started talkin' about a little playmate that no one else could see. Myrtle kept insisting she heard crying in the night, even though I knew it was no more than owls. Kids who came to visit my two would never come back again, sayin' the house was too scary. I couldn't figure it out, but by the time I realized something *was* happening, it was too late to do anything."

"The children disappeared," Robert said.

Cyril nodded. "Went outside one day to swim in the lake," he said, "and we never saw them again. Of course, we called the police, and searched every square inch for two miles around the area. Radio reports filled the airwaves for weeks afterward, and the few people who had TV sets in those days saw pictures of my little ones. But no one ever saw them again. I don't know what happened to them, but there's one thing that's kept me goin' all these years. Not knowing lets me believe they're alive somewhere, thinkin' about me and wonderin' where I am."

An image of a tiny, battered skull came to Robert's mind, but he forced it away. He decided there was no use in telling this old man what had really happened to his children.

"You know how these things are," Cyril continued. "People do all they can to help for a few weeks, and then they start wonderin' what's the use. The investigation eventually dwindled down to a few pages in some tucked-away file cabinet. I kept trying to tell myself that it was over, that it was time to start puttin' my life back together. But Myrtle couldn't do the same. She started to take matters into her own hands."

He turned to look out the window again. The drooping branches of a weeping willow wavered in the breeze, their stooped posture seeming to reflect the old man's sadness.

"Normal methods hadn't found the children," Cyril said, "so Myrtle started relying on the supernatural. She called in mediums, clairvoyants, all those types of people who claim they can see what others can't. I can remember coming downstairs one night to find her sitting in front of the fireplace with a Ouija board on her lap. I don't know where she got the darn thing from—we were good Christians, and I wouldn't allow such a tool of evil in my house. I told her as much, but it was as if she couldn't hear me. She was talking to someone, and when I listened I heard her whispering the names 'Norman' and 'Ellen.'"

"By that time, about two years after the children vanished," Cyril explained, "Myrtle no longer believed they were alive. But she knew they'd come back to her—or so she said. She just had to contact them, to let them know she was waiting."

Robert shook his head, at a loss for words.

"You don't know what it's like to watch someone you love deteriorate," Cyril said, his clothes suddenly looking a little less pressed, his hair a little less trim than before.

Yes, I do, Robert thought. *I watched Lynda fade*

away and I couldn't do a thing about it.

"I tried to help Myrtle," Cyril said, as if echoing Robert's thoughts, "but it was no use. I just couldn't take it anymore, Detective. For my own sanity, I had to leave her, though I still loved her deeply. Funny, though—much as I feel warmth for my children after all these years, Myrtle has become no more than a faded memory. Like the first girl you ever dated. You never forget her, but you'd never recognize her in a crowd."

He swung away from the window again.

"That's what happened to the Hollenbecks," he said, "at least until I left. Couldn't tell you what Myrtle's been doing all these years. I'm just surprised her end was so late in coming."

Robert decided it was time to press on with his own investigation. "Cyril," he said, feeling he was familiar enough with the old man now to use his first name, "could you answer some questions for me? Do you have any other relatives, anyone who might have visited Myrtle recently?"

"Myrtle was an only child," Cyril said. "I had two brothers, but they've both died in the past ten years. Anyone else who might have called himself family broke away from that claim years ago. Myrtle wasn't an easy person to be with, and I imagine she alienated herself from more than her husband and her neighbors. No, even though I don't know much about her now, I believe she was alone when she died."

"That's one of the reasons I'm here," Robert said. "I'm not so certain. I won't go into the details, but I believe someone helped her kill herself. And I think that same person murdered a teenage boy and a little girl."

He used the word "person" for lack of a better definition of the thing he was seeking now. Cyril's talk of Myrtle's fascination with the macabre didn't surprise him, but it didn't give him any answers.

"Can you think back again to the days before the children vanished?" Robert said. "You told me that some strange things happened. Is there anything else you can recall?"

Cyril looked down at his lap, shaking his head. Then he lifted his head.

"Yes, come to think of it," he said. "I do remember. You know, that house was too big even for four of us. We used to close off several rooms to save heating bills. The kids liked to explore in them, and we didn't see the harm since they were empty. Great imaginations in those kids. You know what they told me? They kept insisting there was a room upstairs just filled with all kinds of toys!"

Robert felt his heart jump. "A roomful of toys?" he echoed.

"'Course, there was no such thing," Cyril said. "But I remember it because Ellen was so insistent. Ran crying when I said she was just making believe. She said her little friend would believe her— that little friend no one else could see."

"What was her little friend's name?"

Cyril thought for a long time, rubbing a knuckle along his lower lip.

"Nicole," he said at last. "The child's name was Nicole Morgan."

TWENTY-SIX

AM I DEAD now?

The thought was like a scream in Diane's mind, and when she opened her eyes it was to see misty balls of light floating above her. She knew that she had to be in heaven now, for she could hear angels singing.

God . . .

Her arm lifted. She felt as if she wasn't doing it herself, but was being maneuvered like a puppet. Then she heard voices from far away.

"She moved!" someone cried. "Did you see her arm move?"

The luminous globes started to solidify.

"Diane, baby," someone was saying, "can you see me?"

Now the singing of the angels resolved itself into the sound of a woman crying. Her mother. Diane could hear her mother crying.

"Mommy," she whispered.

Her vision cleared, revealing a dozen concerned faces where the light globes had been. Diane was suddenly aware of the wetwood smell of the bridge, of the song of gulls. She was alive.

"The ambulance is here," she heard a man say.

Diane called her mother again, her throat burning.

"Shh," Rita soothed her, laying a warm hand against her daughter's wet cheek.

Diane closed her eyes and listened to the other conversation above her.

"What exactly happened?" someone asked.

"I'm not sure," Bill replied. "I was fishing off our end of the bridge when suddenly I saw Diane running from Myrtle's house. It was as if someone was chasing her, but there wasn't anyone there. Next thing I knew, she fell over the railing."

"Thank God you were able to rescue her before she was under too long!" a woman said.

Diane heard sirens now. She opened her eyes again, but felt so dizzy looking up at everyone that she quickly closed them. A few moments later, she felt herself being lifted by strong arms.

Rita and Bill stood up as Diane was placed on a stretcher and carried to the ambulance.

"You stay here with David," Rita said. "Your father will meet us at the hospital."

Twenty minutes later, Andy Montana made his way into the emergency room. Rita was waiting outside a curtained-off area while a doctor examined their child. She put her arms around her husband.

"Who hates our children so much?" she demanded brokenly. "Who could want to hurt them?"

"When Mrs. Fogle called me," Andy said, "I

thought she said Diane had fallen from the bridge."

"Bill says it looked as if someone was chasing her," Rita said. "She was running from Myrtle's house. Oh, Andy! What if it was the monster who killed Lisa Westin?"

Andy looked toward the green and blue flowered curtain, wanting to push it aside and see what was going on.

"Rita," he said, keeping his voice calm, "we don't know that someone did kill Lisa. The talk is that she was trampled by a horse."

"Someone could have been riding it!" Rita insisted. "And what was it that terrified David so much that he won't even talk to us? It's the same person responsible for Diane being in there now!"

The curtain opened at that moment, and the doctor beckoned them in.

"Your daughter is lucky," he said. "I understand her brother saved her life. If no one had seen her fall into the water . . ." He stopped, the pause indicating a possibility too frightening to think about.

"She's going to be okay?" Andy asked hopefully.

"Physically, yes," the doctor replied.

Andy and Rita looked at each other.

"What do you mean, physically?" Andy demanded. "You don't think . . ." He almost choked on the words. "Brain damage?"

"That depends," the doctor said, "on how long she was denied oxygen. We want to keep her here overnight for tests."

Rita walked over to the gurney where her daughter lay, tears welling in her eyes again. Biting her lower lip, she took the child's small hand and kissed it. Diane opened her eyes a little and mumbled something.

"She's trying to talk, Andy," Rita said.

Andy came closer and leaned down over her daughter.

"Can you tell us who was chasing you?" Rita asked. "What scared you, Diane?"

"Ni—Nic . . ." Diane began to cough.

"She needs to rest," the doctor said.

"And we need to know who tried to hurt her!" Rita snapped.

"Rita, please," Andy soothed.

Diane turned toward her mother, her eyes a little wider now. "Nicole," she croaked. "Nicole tried to . . . to . . ."

"To what?" Rita pressed.

"Tried to hurt me," Diane said, before collapsing into a coughing fit.

"I'm going to have to ask you to leave," the doctor said, signaling to a nurse.

Rita was about to say something, but Andy led her firmly away. Looking over her shoulder, she said, "Did you hear that? She said Nicole tried to hurt her! Well, I'm going to have a long talk with Nicole's mother!"

"I think she's delirious," Andy said. "Why would she be so frightened of another little girl? Look, Rita, I'm going to stay here and fill out whatever forms they need for Diane's treatment. Why don't you go on home and pack an overnight bag for her? And while you're at it, stop at Hoffer's. You know Diane's always wanted a Lovie-Lamb doll, and I think it would cheer her up."

Rita frowned at her husband, knowing he was changing the subject. Why couldn't he believe the obvious? Nicole Morgan had put their baby in the hospital, and when Rita got through with her, she'd never scare another child again!

"Go on, Rita," Andy said, more gently now.

"I'll send Bill back," Rita said.

When she got back to the house, she didn't tell her teenage son what Diane had said. She had realized on her way home that it might not be a good idea to call up Nicole's mother making accusations. If the child was strange enough to have chased Diane off a bridge, nearly killing her, there was no telling what kind of nut her mother might be.

"I need someone else's help," Rita said out loud, alone in the kitchen after Bill had left with Diane's overnight bag.

Cool evening wind blew through the screen door, bringing the scent of the lake into the brightly lit kitchen. Rita sat at the table, staring at the phone. Who could she call to help her? Carolyn Larchmont? Cassie seemed pretty thick with Nicole. She walked to the phone and dialed their number, but when no one answered she remembered that they had planned to attend Lisa's wake tonight. No doubt many people on the lake were at the funeral home.

Rita began to dial Robert Landers's number. The detective would certainly be interested in this new development. After he'd talked to Diane after Lisa's death, he'd left his home phone number, urging the Montanas to call with whatever news they might have.

Behind her, a loud banging rattled the screen door in its frame. Rita turned around to see a faint silhouette, but couldn't quite make out who it was. She hung up the unanswered phone. "Yes?"

"Hello, Mrs. Montana," she heard a little girl say. "I've come to see Diane."

Rita squinted at the door. "Who is that?"

"Why, it's Nicole Morgan," the child replied. "Is Diane home?"

Rita walked toward the door. "You should know she isn't," she said. "Come inside, Nicole. I want to talk to you."

"And I want to talk to *you*, Mrs. Montana." She spoke with careful enunciation, in a voice far beyond a child's years. When Rita opened the door to let her in, she was surprised by Nicole's appearance. She was tiny, and most of her weight seemed to be in her waist-length curls. Her skin was pale, almost sickly, and her eyes were as round as a doll's. She smiled.

"Nicole," Rita said, for the moment so taken aback by the girl's waiflike looks that she forgot her anger. "Please sit down."

"I'd like to stand, Mrs. Montana," Nicole said, folding a pair of doll-like hands against the apron of her brown flowered dress.

No wonder the kids say she's strange, Rita thought. *What kind of mother makes a child dress like that in the middle of summer?*

Nicole's stare was making the woman nervous. She turned to the refrigerator and opened it.

"Would you like some lemonade?"

"No, thank you."

Rita took out a jug of wine and poured herself a glass, needing it to steady her nerves. Why was she so edgy? She was the adult here, and she had every right to reprimand Nicole for her behavior!

"Nicole, Diane is in the hospital."

No reaction.

"She says . . ." Rita stopped to take a sip of the rosy liquid ". . . she says that you tried to hurt her."

Now Nicole was grinning. "Of course I did," she said. "She's in my way, and I have to get rid of her."

"What . . . what do you mean, she's in your way?" Rita demanded, annoyed by the break in her voice. She had to be firm! This was only a little girl she was dealing with!

"I don't want her here," Nicole said.

Rita put her glass down, some of the wine sloshing over onto her shaking hand. It seemed as if Nicole's staring eyes were sucking every ounce of strength from her. She felt her knees weaken and grasped the side of the table. "The same way you didn't want Lisa here?" she whispered.

"You're very smart," Nicole said. "You're so smart I'm going to show you what's at the house. Then you'll know what scared David."

"I—I can't leave him."

"He's asleep," Nicole said. "He'll never know. And once you find out what scared him, you can make him talk again. You want that, don't you? You want to know so you can help him."

"Of course." Rita's voice was a whisper now.

The room was deathly still—even the wind seemed to have stopped blowing. Everything around Rita grew blurry, until only Nicole was clearly visible.

"Come to the house with me, Rita," Nicole said.

"I can't . . ."

"You can," Nicole said firmly. "You will come to the house. You have to listen to me!"

The last sentence was spoken with such force that Rita jumped. She felt a tiny hand slip into her own, cold as ice. Nicole began to pull her toward the door, and Rita did not protest.

She did not know that David had awakened and was standing in the kitchen doorway rubbing his eyes.

"Mommy?"

Rita turned to her son. He looked so helpless, but she had no desire to go to him. She had to see what was in that house.

"Where are you going?" He was talking for the first time in days, but she hardly took notice, just kept walking.

"To the house," she said. "Nicole is taking me to the house to see what scared you."

David began to scream. When the back door slammed shut behind his mother, he raced toward it, but it refused to open. He began banging so hard on the screen that it started to work loose.

"Mommy! Mommy, *noooo!*"

His desperate cries went unheeded. Rita followed Nicole to the bridge, crossing it on legs she could not feel. She was beyond fear, beyond wondering what this was all about. They walked into Myrtle's kitchen without being seen. Nicole led

Rita through the darkness, up the back staircase. The woman stopped short at the door to the toy room, unable to understand what she was seeing.

"Just toys," Rita whispered. "Nothing bad."

Suddenly, she spotted a doll she was certain belonged to her daughter. Had Diane left the toy behind while playing here? Slowly, Rita knelt to pick it up.

She didn't see Nicole lift the large wooden block.

"There's nothing here but—"

She turned as the block came sailing toward her head, smashing so hard and fast against her skull that there was no time to scream.

TWENTY-SEVEN

THE STREET IN front of the Westin house was almost completely deserted when Robert parked behind Susan's car. He'd called her from the rest home in Zanesville, bursting to tell her his news, but she'd cut him off.

"Meet me at the Westins' stables," she'd said. "If you come after eight, no one will be there. We have to look at something."

Now Robert turned off the engine and got out of the car. Night had fallen completely, and in their grief and confusion the Westins had not left any lights on. Robert searched through the darkness for the stables, following the scent of horses that hung on the night air. He could see a crack of light under the door; he swung the door open silently, and entered, closing it behind him.

"Oh, Robert," Susan said, coming out from behind a large black horse. "I'm glad you're here. There's something you should see."

She opened the manila envelope she held and handed him a series of photographs. Blown up larger than life, they at first didn't seem to be what

261

they really were. When Robert realized what the pictures showed, he felt his stomach turn.

"Lisa's wounds," he said, handing them back to Susan. "I don't understand."

"You didn't look closely enough," Susan said. "Those enlargements clearly show the name and emblem engraved on the horseshoe. It's a staff of wheat, see? And I'm pretty sure this word is 'Farms.' Do you see these letters, too? T-R-E-L-something." She pointed to various parts of the photograph as she spoke.

"Does it match any of the shoes in here?" Robert asked, finally understanding what she was getting at.

"That's why I called you here," Susan said. "I asked the chief about looking the horses over, but he wouldn't hear of it. The Westins are important people in the summer community here, and they could cause a lot of trouble if they knew I was here. I need to check each one of these horses, but it's too much for one person to do alone. Especially on the sly like this!"

She turned to the handbag she had laid atop a bale of hay. Opening it, Susan removed a magnifying glass and walked to the first stall.

"If you'll hold up his hoof," she said, "I can get a look at the shoe."

The horse snorted, protesting their unfamiliar scent. For a few moments, Susan rubbed its side and talked soothingly to it, until it was calm enough to allow Robert to pick up its leg. Susan checked each hoof carefully, finally shaking her head.

"Not this one," she said. "But there's four more to go."

When they had finished the last of the horses, Susan leaned against the stall door and shook her head. "Maybe we'll never find it," she said wearily.

"Is it possible that the shoes were changed this quickly?" Robert asked.

"I don't think so," Susan said. "None of these horses looks freshly shod."

"There are other horses, across the lake," Robert suggested.

"Well, I tell you what," Susan said, walking across the stable to return the magnifying glass to her bag, "I'm still going to try to find out where this emblem came from. It's the only lead we have at the moment."

"Maybe not," Robert said. "My talk with Cyril Hollenbeck this afternoon resulted in more information."

"What happened down in Zanesville?" Susan asked.

"I talked for quite a while with Cyril," Robert said, stroking a horse's nose. "He told me that Myrtle was into the occult. She believed it was her means of getting back her children. I think she must have conjured up a malevolence that's still here."

"But we're getting closer to finding out what it is," Susan said. "And I know we can fight it."

Robert looked at her, his face yellowish in the reflection of light against hay.

"I'm not certain we can," he said. "It plays tricks with people's minds. You know what Cyril said? He told me his children were fantasizing a toy room in the upstairs of their house, just before they disappeared."

Susan shrugged. "I don't know, Robert. Mass hypnosis isn't unheard of."

"With willing subjects," Robert pointed out. "I'd like to think my mind is too strong to be impressionable. No, there's got to be something more. I know Diane Montana must have seen that toy room, because she was coming out of it one night when I went to the house. Of course, I didn't see it then—but I wasn't meant to see it. I'm going to talk to Diane, and to Cassie Larchmont and that kid named Nicole Morgan. Now, there's something else that's strange—Ellen Hollenbeck had an imaginary playmate, and she called Nicole Morgan!"

"This Nicole's mother?" Susan suggested. "Maybe she wasn't really imaginary."

"Well, finding the Morgan house is a priority," Robert said.

"In the meantime," Susan said, leading him toward the door, "I'll try to find out about this emblem."

She snapped off the barn light, encasing them in darkness. As they walked along the shadowed driveway, Susan kept a hand on Robert's arm to steady herself.

"This has got to come to an end soon," she said when they reached their cars.

"I think we're the only ones who can stop it," Robert answered. "No one else believes us."

He got into his car and started the engine, making a three-point turn to head around the lake to the Larchmont house. He saw Carolyn's car pulling into the driveway just as he turned the corner. The dresses she and her daughter wore indicated that they'd just returned from the funeral home. He doubted they'd be in any mood to talk to him, but there were too many questions to be answered. Robert pulled in behind Carolyn's car and got out.

"Oh, it's you," Carolyn mumbled as she answered the door.

"I'm sorry," Robert said, "I know you must be sick of me."

He followed her down the hall into the kitchen, where Cassie stood guard over a pot of milk.

"We're making cocoa," Carolyn said. "I know it's too hot for it, but Cassie needs something to calm her nerves. You can't imagine what it's been like for her tonight." Her tone implied that Robert shouldn't push the child.

"I understand," Robert answered. "Hello, Cassie."

"Hello," the little girl said. "Mommy, the edges are starting to bubble."

"Turn off the heat then," Carolyn said, walking to the stove. She carried the pot to the table, where two mugs waited. "Do you want some, Robert?"

"No, thanks," the detective said. "I have a lot to do tonight. Cassie, I know you think I'm a real pest, but there are some important questions I have to ask you."

Cassie watched her mother pour the hot milk into her mug, then picked up a spoon to stir it. "You always ask questions," she griped.

"And you've been really good at answering them," Robert said. "When this is all over, I'll make it up to you. You're really helping me to solve this mystery."

Cassie gazed at him over the rim of her cup, blue eyes solemn.

"Have you learned anything more?" Carolyn asked.

"As a matter of fact," Robert said, "I talked to Myrtle's ex-husband this afternoon. He mentioned a few things I think Cassie might be able to clarify."

Carolyn frowned. "What would my little girl have to do with an old man?"

"We'll let Cassie answer that," Robert said, looking directly into the child's eyes. "Cassie, what can you tell me about Nicole Morgan?"

"She's nice," Cassie said, "but a little weird. Why?"

"Does she ask you to do bad things?"

Cassie's head swept back and forth vigorously. "Oh, no!" she cried. "She's very sweet."

"She never asked you to do something that was against your mother's wishes?" Robert pressed. "Like going into Myrtle's house?"

"My daughter would never—"

Robert held up his hand, cutting her off. "Cassie?" he asked. "What do you know about a roomful of toys upstairs in Myrtle's house? I know you've been in there, because you were seen coming out the door. Diane and Lisa, too. In fact, I almost shot Diane one night because I thought she was an intruder."

Carolyn gasped.

"I didn't want to!" Cassie wailed, realizing that her secret had been discovered and knowing there was no sense in denying it. "I didn't want to go in that house! But they talked me into it, and then the toys were so great and it was so much fun I couldn't stop going there!"

"Cassie Larchmont," Carolyn exclaimed, "what am I going to do with you? How could you have disobeyed me when you know how dangerous I feel that house is!"

"I'm sorry, Mommy," Cassie mumbled, pushing her cup away. The chocolate had lost its appeal. "I just wanted to be with my friends. We formed a secret club. It was really fun at first, but then bad things started to happen."

Carolyn started to speak again, but Robert touched her arm to silence her. "What bad things, Cassie?" he asked.

"Well . . . well . . ." Cassie stumbled over her words. "We found David hiding in the closet, all scared-like. And then Lisa disappeared, and we found her in the—" She stopped, her mouth open.

"You found Lisa?" Carolyn cried. "You were there when she died? Oh, dear Lord, Cassie!"

"Did you see anything, Cassie?" Robert asked. "Was anyone with Lisa before she died?"

Nicole was with her, I think. I know she was! But the words wouldn't come out.

"No!" she cried, tears spilling from her eyes. "Nobody was with her!"

"What about Nicole?"

"She—she wasn't there," Cassie said.

"You aren't trying to protect her, are you?"

Robert asked. "I'd never hurt a little girl, Cassie. If Nicole knows something, I'll be as nice to her as I am to you. You do think I'm nice, don't you, Cassie?"

Cassie nodded, crying softly.

"Then you can trust me," Robert said. "Please, honey, tell me anything you can."

"Answer the detective, Cassie," Carolyn ordered, her voice stern. She was shaking inside to think that her daughter had been in that house.

"That's all I know!" Cassie cried out. "I'm sorry!"

"All right, I believe you," Robert said, standing up. "But if you remember anything else, any little thing, you let me know."

"Oh, she will," Carolyn said. "Thank you, Robert. I'm glad not to be in the dark anymore."

"We aren't exactly in the light yet, either," Robert said, walking down the hall with her to the front door. "I'm sorry if I caused any trouble. But Cassie seems to be an important part of this."

He looked toward the kitchen, hearing Cassie sobbing. "She's a great kid," he said. "Don't be hard on her, okay? You know how easily kids are tempted by things they aren't supposed to have."

"Good night, Robert," was all Carolyn said.

After he'd left, she stood for a few moments with her back to the door, breathing heavily. Every ounce of her mothering instinct wanted to punish Cassie severely for disobeying and endangering herself in this way, and she knew if she went into the kitchen right now she'd do something she'd regret later. She'd never laid a hand on her daughter, but tonight she wanted to thrash her, to shake her, to make her understand just how horrible that house was.

"M-Mommy?"

Cassie looked so small, so helpless, silhouetted in the kitchen doorway. Carolyn lowered her head and rubbed her eyes. She loved her daughter so much, perhaps more at this moment than ever before. Her daughter needed protection.

"Come here, Cassie," she said, opening her arms.

The little girl moved forward hesitantly, then broke into a run to embrace her mother. "I'm sorry, Mommy!" she said. "I'm so sorry!"

"I know you are," Carolyn said. "But still, you'll have to be punished. You can't begin to realize what dangers lie in that house. Just think, it might have been you instead of Lisa!"

"Oh, Mommy!"

"Cassie, I just want you to know how angry and disappointed I am," Carolyn said. "There are only a few weeks left of summer, but you won't be enjoying them. You're grounded until school starts."

Cassie looked up at her, ready to protest.

"Don't argue," Carolyn said. "I believe that's an appropriate punishment. Now, go upstairs and take your bath. Call me when you're ready to go to bed and I'll come kiss you good-night."

"Okay," Cassie said softly. She turned toward the stairs.

"Cassie, I love you," Carolyn said.

"I know," Cassie mumbled as she went upstairs. She felt numb all over, as if she were walking in a dream. She'd never seen her mother so angry! But now she realized what her mother had been talking about all these years when she referred to Myrtle's house as evil. Ever since Cassie had found that toy room with her friends, bad things had happened.

Cassie undressed as the water ran in the tub, carefully hanging up her good dress. She paused in front of the mirror, looking down at her chest and trying to decide if her small breasts had grown any bigger. She touched them, and they felt sore.

"Yecch," Cassie growled. "I don't want to be so grown up yet!"

When she looked up again, there was another face reflected in the mirror, just to the left of her own. Cassie turned abruptly, crossing her arms over her chest.

"Nicole!" she cried. "How did you get in here?"

Her friend smiled. "I just walked in the back door," she said.

"Didn't my mother see you?" Cassie demanded, looking out the bathroom door to the staircase.

"Nobody saw me," Nicole said. "Get dressed, Cassie. We're going to the house tonight."

Cassie reached for the water faucet and turned it off. "Are you crazy?" she whispered, grabbing a towel to wrap around herself. "I'm already in trouble! My mother found out I was there, and I'm grounded for the rest of the summer!"

"She'll never know," Nicole said. "It's really important, Cassie. I need your help with something now that Lisa's gone, and Diane is in the hospital."

Cassie's mouth dropped open as she sat down hard on the edge of the tub. The porcelain felt icy under her bare thighs, but she couldn't move. "Di-Diane's in the hospital?" she asked. "Why?"

"Because she was bad," Nicole seethed, her eyes narrowing. 'She disobeyed, and she had to be punished."

"Who did she disobey?" Cassie demanded. "What're you talking about? What happened to Diane?"

A slight smile formed on Nicole's lips. She bent toward the water in the tub, touching it gingerly with a diminutive finger. "She almost drowned," she said. "She fell off the bridge, and she was under water for, oh, such a long, long time. Her brother interfered and saved her, but she'll be dealt with in time. They'll all be dealt with—everyone who's trying to keep us apart!"

"I don't understand you," Cassie said. "Diane almost drowned, and you're mad because Bill saved her? What kind of friend are you?"

Nicole took Cassie by the shoulders. A shiver ran through the little girl in spite of the warm mist rising from the tub. She locked eyes with Nicole, suddenly afraid of her but unable to get away.

"I'm more than a friend to you, Cassie," Nicole said. "You don't know who I am yet, but you will—tonight. There's something I want you to do for me, Cassie. And I know you'll do it, because you love me."

"I love you," Cassie heard someone say. She wasn't certain if the words had come from her own mouth. She was getting cold.

"Put some clothes on," Nicole said. "We'll go to the house together, you and I. No one will know.

Your mother will not know. And when she finds out you've gone, it will be too late. We can fight them this time, Adele! I know we can!"

Slowly, Cassie stood up. Adele? Why had Nicole called her Adele?

"My name is Cassie," she whispered, bending to pick up the underpants she'd dropped to the floor. She slipped them on, then took her dress down from its hanger.

"Good," Nicole said. "Everything's going to be all right, Adele. From now on, we'll be together, and no one will tear us apart!"

Silently, obediently, Cassie followed her downstairs. Carolyn did not turn when they passed her study, and Solo did not bark when they opened the back door.

TWENTY-EIGHT

ROBERT RANG THE Montanas' bell repeatedly, certain that someone was home because the inner door was open and the screen door slightly ajar. But he couldn't hear anyone inside, not even voices from a radio or television. The house was eerily silent.

All of the instincts that had been sharpened through his years as a detective told him something was terribly wrong. Carefully, with one hand poised to grab his gun, he pushed the screen door open and entered the kitchen. Nothing looked out of the ordinary here, or in the adjacent living room.

Then he heard the mewling noises. Robert looked toward one of the three doors to the side of the room. He walked to it and touched the knob with his fingers. It was an odd kind of cry, sort of like a cat's and yet not like any cat he'd ever heard.

Someone's hurt. There's more horror waiting to be found.

Robert wouldn't let the thought turn to paralyzing fear. Firmly, he gripped the doorknob and pushed the door open. He entered a brightly lit room with a pair of green-blanketed twin beds. The shadeless lamp drew a large, bright circle on a seashell print curtain. Slowly, Robert stepped farther into the room, taking in the boys' playthings that ran from toy trucks to fishing equipment. A poster of Bruce Springsteen covered the closet door, and rock albums had been scattered around a small stereo system.

The mewling sounded again.

"Hey, there," Robert said softly. "Is someone in here?"

It was coming from under the bed. Robert's hand was on his gun as he crouched close to the floor, tightening around the grip as he lifted a corner of the bedspread.

David was crammed in a dark corner, rolled up in a tight little ball. His head was tucked into his knees, protected by his small arms. Robert lifted the covers completely.

"David?" he called. "What's wrong, kid? Want to come out and tell me?"

David kept whimpering.

"Where arc your mom and dad?"

Dead, Robert. Everyone's dead. They're all dying on Lake Solaria. He shook his head a bit to clear away the voices he heard.

"David, come out of there," Robert said. "Come on, I won't hurt you."

David didn't respond.

"If you come out," Robert coaxed, "we can find your mother, and she'll help you."

The little boy looked up abruptly, and in the light that managed to creep under the bed Robert could see two glowing points where his eyes should have been. David started screaming, an ear-shattering sound that made Robert leap to his feet. Quickly he pulled the bed away from the wall, removing David's shelter. Hurrying around it, he bent down and lifted the shrieking child into his arms.

"David!"

It was as if the little boy couldn't hear him. He became a stiff doll in Robert's arms, his muscles locked so tight it took all of Robert's strength to carry him into the kitchen.

"Where the hell are your parents?" Robert asked, turning his head away as the child's screams pierced into his eardrums.

Still holding David, he reached for the telephone and dialed 911. Whatever was wrong with David was more than he could handle. He heard someone speak, but David's screams were so loud he couldn't understand the words. Putting the child down on the floor, he turned away and covered one ear.

"Operator?" he called. "Operator, this is Detective Robert Landers. I'm calling from—"

"I'm sorry, but the number you have dialed is no longer in service."

"What the hell's that supposed to mean?" Robert demanded. "How could 911 be out of service?"

". . . or ask your operator for assistance."

Robert slammed the receiver down. Moments later, he lifted it again and redialed the three simple numbers.

"I'm sorry, but the number you have dialed is no longer . . ."

Robert hung up, rubbing his eyes. Why did he expect anything to make sense these days? He turned toward David, who had lapsed into making those catlike noises again. This time when he lifted the child, David was limp in his arms. Robert decided to take him to Carolyn's house, hoping she might know where his parents had gone. Maybe if he dialed Emergency from her phone he'd be able to get help.

Robert carried David out the back door, not bothering to shut it behind him. As he walked toward Carolyn's place, he thought he heard David mumbling something. He stopped and listened, looking down at the small boy cradled in his arms. David's eyes were shut, and his head was flopped away from Robert's chest. Even with the wind blowing, the word was very clear.

"House . . . house . . . house . . . house . . ."

Robert looked across the lake at the old Victorian, wishing David could tell him what had happened there. Anxious to get help for the child, he hurried on to Carolyn's, knocking hard at her back door when he arrived. Solo appeared from beneath the kitchen table, barking loudly.

"Solo, be quiet!" Carolyn ordered, appearing in the hallway that stretched between the kitchen and the front door. Robert saw her squinting to make out who stood in her doorway.

"It's me, Carolyn," he called. "Robert Landers. I need help."

She quickened her pace, shooing Solo out of the way as she opened the back door.

"Oh, dear!" she cried, seeing David. "What happened to him? Where are his parents?"

"That's what I'd like to know," Robert said.

"Can you lay him down somewhere while I call for help?"

Carolyn took David in her arms. He was sleeping now, but the tearstains on his strained face and his disheveled hair told her it was not a peaceful slumber.

"What happened?" she asked.

"I found him cowering under his bed and no one else was there," Robert said, reaching for the telephone. "He was acting as if he were in absolute terror of something. I want to get him to a hospital, but I'll need to find his parents."

He dialed 911, and to his relief was able to get through. Apparently, whatever powers had blocked him at the Montana house were not present here. Tonight's dispatcher was a good friend of Robert's, and Tom surprised the detective with more information.

"This is something," Robert said as he hung up. "The Montanas are already at the hospital. Their little girl nearly drowned this afternoon!"

Carolyn put a hand to her mouth, her eyes full of worry. "Another accident?" she said.

"I'm not sure accident is the word for it, at this point," Robert answered grimly.

They heard the ambulance siren. Lake Solaria was such a small town that it didn't take long for the emergency crew to respond to a call.

"I can't understand why Rita left David home alone," Carolyn said. "I mean, why wasn't Bill there? Or even Andy? They could have taken turns with Diane at the hospital!"

"That's a question I'll have to ask them when I

get there," Robert said. "Meantime, keep Cassie in the house. I don't know what the hell is going on here, and I don't want her hurt before I have the chance to find out."

He followed the paramedics out of the house.

"You don't have to worry about Cassie," Carolyn called after him. "She's safe upstairs, and she won't be leaving this house."

Across Lake Solaria, in the toy room of Myrtle's house, Cassie gazed in terror at Rita Montana's mutilated body. Rita's blood had formed a sticky puddle beneath her crushed skull. Cassie wanted to run, but her body was no longer in her control. She stared down at Diane's mother, silently begging her to get up, to be alive.

She's dead, Cassie. Dead like Lisa, like Myrtle, like Georgie. Dead like you're gonna be, soon. Nicole's gonna kill you!

"You don't need to be afraid," Nicole said, standing at her side. "I would never hurt you, Adele."

My name isn't Adele.

Cassie couldn't find her voice.

"All these people I killed," Nicole said, speaking in an icy, matter-of-fact tone, "deserved to die. They tried to interfere with my plans for us. Lisa hated me, and she didn't want me to be with you. She tried to drive me away, but I won in the end!"

Now Cassie looked up abruptly, tears suddenly welling in her eyes. Nicole was a blur.

"Why?" she demanded. "Why do you hurt people? Who are you?"

"You'll learn that in time," Nicole said. "You

don't know who you really are, Cassie. I mean, Adele."

"Stop calling me that!"

Nicole smiled, the placating smile of an adult dealing with a mischievous child. "You'll understand," she said again. "But now, we have to move this. If anyone found her, they'd spoil our plans for certain."

"M-move it?" Cassie whispered. "I'm not touching that thing!"

She tried to run from the room, but felt Nicole grab her tightly around her upper arm. Cassie struggled to pull away, looking over her shoulder.

Nicole was clear across the room. Cassie stood alone at the door, held fast by unseen hands.

"I can make you do anything I want," Nicole said, still smiling. "When this is all made clear to you, you'll forgive me. But for now, I must be stern with you. We have to hide this body, quickly!"

"No!"

But Cassie was being pulled toward Rita's prone form, invisible forces dragging her legs.

She's going to grab me. I know she isn't really dead and she's going to grab me and hurt me and kill me and—

"Pick up her ankles," Nicole ordered, taking a position at Rita's head. She lifted Rita's shoulders without effort, seemingly unaware of the blood that sloughed over her apron.

"She's—she's too big," Cassie mumbled. "We can't carry her!"

"We will," Nicole said. "And we can. Pick her up!"

Slowly, Cassie lifted Rita's ankles. Even through

the stockings the woman wore, she could feel the iciness of her flesh.

"We'll take her to the bridge," Nicole said. "When they find her, they'll think she drowned."

The two girls walked carefully to the back staircase, Rita swinging like a hassock between them. Strangely, she was light as a feather pillow, as easy to carry as a rag doll. Cassie began to hope that this wasn't real, just part of another bad dream. Soon she'd see the child in the lake full of blood, and she'd scream and she'd wake up in her bed. And her mother would come running to comfort her . . .

Rita's arm flopped away from her chest as they crossed the laundry room, knocking one of the pictures from the wall. Cassie jumped, but Nicole kept on moving.

I want to wake up! Wake me up!

"My—my mother will be looking for me," Cassie said.

"She doesn't know you've gone," Nicole said.

They stepped out the back door, into the cool, dark summer night. Cassie sensed that there was something more wrong here than her carrying Rita's body. It was too dark, too cold on Lake Solaria. She realized there were no lights on anywhere. The usual sounds of the lake—birds, radios, people—were nonexistent.

Nicole made her way through the darkness without faltering, leading them to the bridge.

"Here," she said. "We'll push her over the edge, right here. Then we'll go back to the house and I'll explain everything to you."

I don't want to go back to the house.

Cassie couldn't speak. Rita had grown suddenly heavy, and the girl felt every ounce of the woman's hundred thirty-two pounds. Cassie dropped her ankles, and the backs of Rita's shoes sent thudding echoes down the bridge.

"Kick her over," Nicole ordered.

Cassie merely stared at the girl.

"I said, kick her over," Nicole repeated, her voice stern.

Cassie felt her gorge rise, and fought to control her terror. She had to be strong, or she'd never escape. Nicole was crazy!

She gave Rita a hard shove with the toe of her sneaker, sending the woman crashing into the dark water below. To Cassie's relief, Rita fell face down.

"We're finished," Nicole said. "Come, let's go back to the house."

"I don't want to—"

Cassie's words were severed by her own screams. She fell against the bridge railing, holding fast to it to keep from collapsing.

Rita had flipped over in the water, and she stared up at Cassie with wide, dead eyes, pointing an accusing finger at the wailing child.

TWENTY-NINE

Carolyn stood in her foyer after Robert left, watching the flashing red lights of the ambulance until it disappeared around the corner. Feeling drained after all that had happened, she wearily closed the door and headed for the stairs. She stopped suddenly, and turned back.

For the first time in years, she threw the dead bolt.

Won't do any good against what's out there, Carolyn.

Carolyn started upstairs, hoping that a long talk with Cassie would set things right between them. The bathroom door was ajar, soft light flowing into the hallway. Carolyn could see one corner of the steam-covered vanity mirror. She couldn't hear any sounds of rippling water.

"Cassie?"

Her daughter didn't answer. Carolyn felt panic rise, but fought it as she quickened her pace up the stairs. Cassie was mad at her, of course. She just wasn't answering.

"Cassie, it's time to get out of the—"

Carolyn stopped in the doorway, confusion crossing her face as she looked at the still-full tub. The water was innocent of soapsuds, its clarity telling her that Cassie had never gotten in. The child's robe hung on the back of the door, her slippers tucked neatly beneath.

"She changed her mind," Carolyn said out loud, a breathless edge to her voice. "She went straight to bed without waiting for me."

But the child's bed was still perfectly made, unslept in. Her little girl was gone.

"She can't be!" Carolyn insisted. "She must be here!"

She ran out into the hallway.

"Cassie? Cassie Larchmont, you answer me this minute!"

There was no reply except for the voices in her head.

The house. She's gone to the house. It's got her like it got Lisa and Diane and Norman and Ellen.

Carolyn hurried back into Cassie's room, nearly tripping over a doll left on the floor. From the window seat she could see Myrtle's house, terrifying in its blackness. Cassie couldn't be there, lost in all that darkness! She couldn't have gotten out of this house without Carolyn knowing!

She's there. You know she's there.

Icy fear crawled over Carolyn's skin, eating into her bones. She began to tremble violently. Carolyn didn't want to go near that house. She rested her arm against the window, leaning her head into it as tears began to fall down her cheeks. She couldn't let her own apprehensions keep her from rescuing

Cassie! She had to be strong, to fight whatever it was that had taken her child away.

Resolutely, Carolyn raised her head. Instead of leaving Cassie's room, though, she froze. For a few seconds, she couldn't hear anything, couldn't feel the window seat beneath her. She could only look straight ahead, out the window.

Mysteriously, the night sky had brightened to daylight. Carolyn pressed her hands against the window and stared out over a sun-drenched lake. Not a thought of Cassie crossed her mind as she gazed at Myrtle's house. It was as if she'd fallen asleep and was in the midst of a dream.

Myrtle's house was in perfect shape. The paint was fresh-looking, the shutters tacked up neatly, the grass trimmed. Beautiful roses clustered under the back windows, trailing toward the kitchen door. Carolyn watched numbly as the door opened and two children emerged. There were a dark-haired little girl and a small boy, holding hands.

Carolyn knelt on the window seat, hard wood pressing into her knees. She glanced down. The cushion she'd made for Cassie was gone. Cassie's dolls were gone.

"Stop it! *Stop!*"

The scream jerked Carolyn's head up in time to see the boy running toward the bridge. She could see his face more clearly now, even as the little girl grabbed the back of his striped shirt. They stumbled ankle-deep into the water.

Norman Hollenbeck.

Like a woman made of stone, Carolyn watched without moving as the girl picked up a rock and smashed it into Norman's head. Again and again she hit him, blood spurting everywhere, coloring the water around their ankles.

With a scream of her own, Carolyn fell away from the window, her body crashing to the floor.

The impact woke her from her dizzy spell immediately, but for a few moments he could only lie on the floor. It was again dark outside, and the window seat was crammed with Cassie's dolls. Then she remembered: what had just happened wasn't a hallucination. It was a powerful memory, suppressed for three decades by terror. She had just gone back in time to when she was just eight years old, forced by Cassie's predicament to face the terror she had denied all these years.

Carolyn had seen Norman's murder, had watched in shock as that dark-haired child pummeled him to death, then dragged his body deep into the center of the lake. The little girl had dived under the water, tugging Norman's bloody corpse with her. Carolyn had wanted to run and tell her mother, but she was paralyzed. She had waited for the girl to resurface.

The girl never did, a fact so horrible and unbelievable that eight-year-old Carolyn had pushed the whole scene to the back of her mind, only to have it return in vague memories and nightmares. But now the child was back. She had returned to claim more of the children of Lake Solaria.

"I don't know who you are," Carolyn said, surprised at the force of her own voice. "But I'm not afraid of you anymore! I won't let you have my little girl!"

She turned and ran from the room, barely feeling the steps beneath her feet as she sped down the stairs and out of her house.

At last, Carolyn reached the back door of Myrtle's house. The place was pitch-black, not a light on anywhere. A small part of Carolyn still hoped that she was mistaken, that Cassie had gone off to tell one of her friends how angry her mother had been earlier.

But who would she visit? Carolyn wondered as she reached for the back door. Not Lisa. Not Diane.

"Nicole," Carolyn whispered. "Nicole Morgan."

Realization crept over her as she pushed into the kitchen. She had never seen Nicole, the child Cassie claimed had convinced the others to explore the house in the first place. Robert had tried to find Nicole's parents during his investigation, but couldn't.

Carolyn switched on the kitchen light, the sudden brightness making her squint. The kitchen looked so innocent, simply furnished with decades-old appliances. But when Carolyn looked more closely, she saw the rotted plants in the window, the peeling and faded wallpaper, the curled corners of the linoleum floor. The clock on the wall had stopped long since.

"Oh, God," she prayed, feeling very cold, "get me through this place!"

She entered the laundry room, trying not to look at the hundreds of pictures of the Hollenbeck children lining the walls. The hallway was like a long, dark tunnel, and Carolyn felt her chest constrict as she imagined what might be at the other end.

"Nothing, Carolyn," she murmured out loud. "It's just a house! There's nothing here!"

It's not just a house, Carolyn, and you know it.

The door to the back staircase was open. Carolyn reached for the light switch on the wall inside, her hand shaking so much that she had to make three tries before it finally snapped on. The tight, upward-curving passageway smelled of old linoleum and mildew. Carolyn made her way up the stairs, suddenly wishing she had brought some kind of weapon.

You can't fight what's here.

"I *can* fight it," Carolyn whispered, "and I will!"

She reached the top of the stairs. Summoning her courage, she called, "Cassie! Cassie, are you here?"

Dead silence.

"Please let me find her," Carolyn whispered, entering one of the rooms.

It was a simply furnished bedroom, with only a cot and a dresser. The closet door was open, revealing two metal hangers on the wooden rod. Carolyn moved on to the next room, and guessed at once it had been Myrtle's. There was a huge oak four-poster with a candlewick spread, flanked by two matching nighttables. The dresser wasn't laden with perfume bottles or jewelry or cosmetics, but with various sizes of framed pictures. Carolyn made no attempt to look closer, as if she feared that looking at Norman and Ellen's faces would conjure up their ghosts.

She turned off the light and continued down the

hall, checking each room carefully, finding nothing.

And then she came to a room with a glass doorknob. When she entered, it seemed perfectly empty. Cassie was not here. Carolyn was about to leave when something shiny caught her eye. She gasped, bending to the floor to pick up Cassie's hairclip.

"Cassie? Caaaaasssiiiiie!"

Her screams echoed through the empty house, beyond the dimension of time where Carolyn stood.

Cassie jerked away from Nicole, turning around to look along the dirt road that stretched behind them.

"I heard my mother!" she cried. "My mother's calling me!"

"She isn't calling you!" Nicole insisted. "Our mother's dead!"

"I know I heard her," Cassie whimpered, and she turned and ran from Nicole.

This wasn't happening! A few minutes ago, she'd been standing on the bridge, looking down at Rita's body. But Nicole had taken her hand and stared into her eyes, and suddenly she was in this strange place. And it was daylight! How could it be daylight?

"Adele, come back with me," Nicole said.

Cassie swung around. "Stop playing tricks!" she screamed. "Take me back to Lake Solaria!"

"This *is* Lake Solaria," Nicole said.

"It isn't!" Cassie wailed. "There aren't any big dirt roads near my house! You're making me have a bad dream, Nicole. And I want to wake up!"

Nicole opened her mouth to say something, but instead of words a gasp came out. Her brown eyes went round, and she looked up at something just beyond Cassie's head. Cassie glanced over her shoulder to see a stern-looking man, his hands on his hips, glaring at the two girls.

"Trying to run away?" he growled.

"No," Nicole said quickly. "My sister—my sister had to . . . well, you know . . ."

The man looked at Cassie, then jerked his head to one side. Nicole took Cassie's hand, pulling her along as she followed the man. Now Cassie saw a red brick building nearby, the roof painted with a sign that said "Lake Solaria." She recognized the train station.

But it didn't look right. The bricks weren't all chipped and faded, the roof wasn't in need of repair. There was no newspaper stand, no vending machines.

"What is this?" she whispered, too frightened by the strange man to continue arguing with Nicole.

"You'll understand soon, Adele," Nicole assured her.

The man prodded Cassie with his cane, pushing it into her upper thigh. Cassie jumped away from him.

"Don't you touch me like that!" she cried. "My mother says no one's ever to touch me that way!"

Wide-eyed, the man drew back his hand. "Why you foulmouthed, evil-minded little . . ."

Cassie cringed, expecting to be slapped. But she felt Nicole's arms go around her and let herself be led away. Cautiously, she sneaked a look back to see a woman holding the man's hand, arguing with him. The woman was dressed in a sunbonnet and a long, old-fashioned dress, a lace-trimmed parasol shading her from the sun.

Walking backward as she gazed, Cassie bumped into someone.

"Why don'tcha watch where yer goin', girlie?"

She had stumbled into a boy who stood a head taller than she did, a freckle-faced lad with fat red curls. Cassie looked him up and down, taking in his calf-length pants, baggy shirt, and torn leather shoes. Now she saw other children around her, some crying, some looking defiant, some holding each other close. The girls were dressed like Nicole, the boys like this red-haired kid.

"What—what is this place?" she asked, her voice small.

The red-haired boy sneered at her, then turned his head to spit. "You funnin' me?" he asked. He jerked a thumb at her. "Hey, this girlie don't know what this place is!"

"You been sleeping?"

"What a silly thing!"

"Maybe she just got on the train," a girl suggested.

"Wh-what train?" Cassie asked, folding her arms tightly.

More laughter raced through the crowd of ragged children.

"The orphan train, of course!"

Cassie shook her head, confused. Orphan train? What did that mean? She turned to Nicole, who stood smiling.

Orphan train?

"Oh, that can't be!" Cassie cried as she began to understand. "There aren't any orphan trains!"

"She's crazy," someone said.

"I am not!" Cassie screamed, the children's faces becoming a blur through her tears. "We studied about orphan trains in school! They ran across the country a hundred years ago, but there aren't any more! This is a dream, just a dream. You aren't real! Go away! Go away!"

Someone yanked at her arm. It was the mean-looking man, his eyes flashing as he held Cassie close. He pinned Cassie to him, holding his cane across her chest.

"I don't take kindly to troublemakers," he snarled. "You say another word, and I don't care if Mrs. Guffey says I'm not supposed to mark the merchandise, I'll tan you!"

He gave Cassie a squeeze that pushed the wind from her lungs, knocking the little girl into blackness.

Carolyn felt a sudden rush of ice course through her veins. She knew in her heart that Cassie was in danger, but she didn't know how to save her. Confused, weary, she dropped to her knees on the bare wooden floor and began to cry.

THIRTY

ROBERT WAS ON his way out the front doors of the hospital when Susan came rushing up to him, waving a manila envelope. Her cheeks were reddened with excitement, her auburn hair askew from her rush to get here.

"I thought I'd never find you!" she cried. "Wait until you hear what I've learned!"

"How did you know I was here?" Robert asked, leading her back into the waiting room so they could sit together.

"The dispatcher told Chris about your call," Susan explained, "and he tracked me down at the library. I went there right after leaving you, to check out some information."

They found an empty pair of seats and turned them closer to each other as they sat down. Susan pulled her notes from the envelope.

"This is the first time we've been lucky on this case," she said. "The library did a history of farming display about two years ago, and the woman there knew exactly where to find everything. That 'T-R-E-L' I found stands for Trellis Farms. A wheat staff was its insignia. How it got onto a modern-day horse is beyond me—the shoes haven't been made for ninety-five years."

"Antiques?"

"Not in this condition," Susan said. "The impressions that showed up on Lisa Westin's skin were too well defined. But there's more, Robert, and I think you'd better brace yourself."

Susan handed him a photocopy of a newspaper clipping. Dated in the early 1870s, it showed a picture of a little girl with long, dark curls staring solemnly forward. Beneath her was the caption "Have You Seen This Child?" It was eerily like the pleas found on the sides of milk cartons and in grocery store windows. Robert scanned the lead, but looked up suddenly when he read the little girl's name.

"Nicole Morgan."

"Right," Susan said. "Trellis Farms took up most of the land around that side of Lake Solaria in those days, the same side as the Hollenbeck mansion. I think Myrtle's house used to belong to a man named Karl Trellis."

"Who disappeared a century ago," Robert said, his eyes still fixed on the piece of paper in his hands, "after being accused of murder."

"Of Nicole Morgan's murder," Susan said. "And I don't believe it was this Nicole's ancestor that was killed. That child is still here, Robert!"

Robert handed the paper back to her. "What happened to the woman of science?" he asked.

"The woman of science doesn't wear blinders," Susan said. "I accept the obvious, and right now the obvious tells me that Myrtle's house is haunted by the ghost of a child who was murdered there!"

She handed him more articles. "Look, here's the continuation of her story," she said.

Robert read the clippings, then stood up.

"I've got to get back there," he said. "I have to find out what she wants."

"In the meantime," Susan said, "I'll see what else I can learn. Call me at the lab when you get home, okay?"

Robert promised he would, then left the hospital. As he drove toward Myrtle's house, Robert ran the stories Susan had found through his mind. Nicole Morgan had originally been from New York, but her poverty-stricken father had sent her to the farmlands of the Midwest on an orphan train.

"Great way to deal with hungry kids," he muttered, driving down Moxahala Street. "Just get rid of them."

A hundred years ago, families who could not care for their children had sometimes put them aboard trains headed west, hoping someone along the way would take them in. Many of the children were taken in by decent families, and were well cared for in exchange for doing chores. But sometimes a child would fall into the hands of a cruel person who would mistreat him, regarding him as little better than a slave.

Robert grimaced. Had that been Nicole's fate?

Cassie felt as if she were in the midst of a slave auction. She watched as all around her grim-faced strangers pulled the children away from the platform, one by one, until only a few were left. Nicole had an arm around her, and though Cassie wanted to get away from her, she found herself unable to move. Her mind still begged for her to wake up, but more and more she began to accept the horrifying fact that this was really happening. Somehow, she had become one of the orphans she'd read about in school!

"Don't worry," Nicole whispered. "This time, we'll be together. They won't separate us again!"

A man pointed one finger at Cassie, and the man with the cane prodded her. Even as Nicole clutched her arm, she felt herself being yanked off the platform.

"No!" Nicole screamed. "You can't take her! She stays with me this time! She stays with me!"

"Be silent, girl!"

Cassie gaped at the man who was pulling her arm. He looked mean, his face reddened by an afternoon in the sun, shaded by the start of a new beard. His eyes were like blue ice cubes, cold and hateful.

"Let me go," Cassie whispered.

The man ignored her.

"Let me go!" Cassie screamed. "I don't want to go with you. I want to go home! I want my mother! *I want my mother!*"

Carolyn turned a full circle in Myrtle's living room. Could that have been Cassie's voice she'd just heard? It seemed to come from all directions, as if carried on the summer wind. She hurried to the window to look out, seeing nothing but shadows of trees.

"Cassie?"

Frustrated, she shook her fist in the air. Which way should she go? Where was Cassie now?

"Caaassssiiiiie!"

Back in time, Cassie jerked her head up. She'd been sobbing uncontrollably; then she had heard her mother's voice again! But how? There were no buildings here, only vast stretches of open farmland.

Cassie buried her face in her arms again. Maybe it was only the squeaking of the wagon wheels that made her think her mother was nearby.

"Adele!"

Cassie peeked over her arm to see Nicole running after the wagon.

"It wasn't supposed to happen again!" Nicole cried, her hair flying in all directions. "It was supposed to be different this time! They weren't supposed to take you, and I want to change this!"

For a split second, Cassie felt as if someone were trying to pull her out of her own skin. She collapsed to the floor of the wagon . . .

. . . and suddenly she was standing in an open field with Nicole. The other girl threw her arms around her, laughing.

"We tricked them!" she said. "I brought you back to me, Adele."

"Stop calling me Adele!" Cassie cried, pushing Nicole away. "My name is Cassie Larchmont!"

"You're my sister, Adele!" Nicole said. "I knew someday you'd come back to me, so I waited and waited. And now we're together again, and you have to be happy because you know you're my sister and we're together!"

"I am not! You're crazy and I hate you. I hate you!"

Nicole covered her ears. "You beast," she said. "You really aren't my sister, are you? Dear Adele would never hurt me so! You tricked me, and now you're going to pay!"

Cassie's terrified screams traveled through time, to the room where Carolyn stood. She traced her daughter's voice to the front of the house. Heart pounding, Carolyn raced to the hall and fumbled with the latches of the front door. She finally jerked it open, and froze, unable to comprehend what she was seeing.

There was no stretch of blacktopped road, no street lamps, no houses in the distance. There were only acres and acres of farmland, as far as Carolyn could see. It couldn't be real . . .

Like the memory of Norman's death wasn't real?

She tried to convince herself she was dreaming again. Nothing looked real! The sky was an odd yellow color, blending into the vast stretch of soil to make a blurry horizon. The trees were leafless and black. Only the wind was tangible, blowing hard against her face, hot as the draft from an oven.

In the distance, Carolyn spotted a galloping horse, still too far away for her to make out the two figures on it.

Cassie was being held on the horse. The little girl turned to see a stern-faced man behind her, the very man who had yanked her from the train station platform. But how had she gotten here? How could Nicole move her from place to place so fast?

"Let me go!" she screamed.

"Keep silent," the man said, his voice deep and threatening. "I will not tolerate insolence from my workers."

"I'm not your worker!" Cassie whined. "You let me go!"

The man only held her tighter. Cassie struggled and screamed in protest, and suddenly felt a slap so hard across the back of her head that she went flying off the horse. Soil and sky whirled around her, still spinning madly when she hit the ground. Stunned, she lay frozen, pain shooting up her back and through her legs.

The horse circled her, closer and closer . . .

"Nnnnnooooo!"

Cassie couldn't move.

Carolyn heard the scream and knew the child who had hit the distant ground was her daughter. She yelled for her, lunging forward to run to her little girl's aid. But as she tried to pass through the front door, a hot, powerful force struck her, knocking her back to the staircase. Driven by fierce determination, Carolyn pulled herself to her feet and struggled through the impossible wind back to the front door.

"Cassie!"

She tried again to get through the doorway, but was held back by the invisible barrier. The more she strained against it, the more it pushed back against her. It was like walking through a hurricane.

She saw another child appear in the distance, and was sickened to realize it was the same little girl who had lured Norman Hollenbeck to his death. Now this monster had her own child, and Carolyn was helpless to stop her!

"I thought you were my sister," Nicole said, staring down at Cassie, even as the horse thundered around them. "You were so nice to me, and I thought you'd come back so we could be together again. But you tricked me! You aren't my sister at all! Now you'll die instead of me, and I'll be free to find the real Adele!"

The horse tightened its circle around Cassie, who lay paralyzed by fear, or by Nicole's powers. Cassie looked up at the driver with pleading eyes, trying to find the strength to get up and run. He only laughed at her, a demonic, maniacal laugh like the stuff of nightmares.

Carolyn screamed for her daughter.

"You can't save her," Nicole said, suddenly appearing on the front steps. "She's going to pay for lying to me!"

"Let her go, please!" Carolyn begged.

Nicole turned to watch the scene in the distance, her eyes wild. "You watch!" she cried. "Watch your daughter die!"

"Monster!" Carolyn shouted. "You horrible, wicked—"

A hand on her shoulder silenced her. Carolyn gasped and spun around to see Robert behind her.

He stared at the scene before them, his eyes full of awe.

"My God, that's what happened to Nicole," he whispered.

He pulled Carolyn back a little, then stepped forward and shouted to the ghostly child, who had now materialized just outside the horse's range. "Nicole Morgan, *let that child go!*"

The sound of a man's voice seemed to startle the child, because she jerked around to face the house.

"No!" she yelled. "She pretended to be my sister and now she's going to die!"

Robert shook his head. "No, your sister is waiting for you," he said as Carolyn watched him in amazement. "She's in the churchyard, where she was buried. She spent her life trying to find you, Nicole!"

"You're lying!" Nicole called back. "Adele would have found me!"

"She couldn't!" Robert said. "She suspected that Karl Trellis had done something bad to you, and when she married a rich man years later she used his money to seek justice. She believed you had been murdered, Nicole, right up until her death as an old woman!"

Nicole shook her head vigorously. "She's not an old woman!" she cried. "She's a little girl like me! You're just trying to keep me from my sister!"

She turned back to the horse and rider and pointed a finger, making them move closer to Cassie. The little girl watched them in terror, frozen.

"Nobody's trying to keep you from Adele," Robert said. "But I can bring you to her. I promise! Please, tell me what happened to you, Nicole."

Only the rush of the wind and the pounding of hooves answered him.

"Nicole, please tell me what Karl Trellis did to you!"

Slowly, Nicole turned to face him. It was the first time anyone had ever shown interest in the horrors she had faced. Captured by her past, the ghost child crumpled to the ground. She began to shiver violently and to cough and gasp as if she couldn't get air.

"The water! I can't—can't b-breathe!"

"What's happening?" Robert yelled.

Nicole's voice was tiny when she answered, not the powerful, demonic sound Carolyn had heard just moments earlier.

"He pushed me off the horse," she whispered, her eyes closed. "It ran me down—oh, I could see its hooves right over my head! And then everything went black."

She moaned and rolled onto her back, pulling her knees up to her chest.

"I woke up and he was carrying me into the lake," she went on, sobbing. "He was going to hide me there, but when he saw I was still alive he picked up a rock and hit me. He hit me again and again! Everything was bloody and black and . . . and . . . *I want my sister!*"

"We'll bring you to Adele!" Robert shouted. "But you have to tell us where you are now. What did you see when you woke up again?"

Nicole thought for a while, even as the horse

spun around Cassie, inching closer. Carolyn knew that the beast should have trampled her daughter long ago. Obviously, Nicole was in control of the whole scene.

"Everything was different," Nicole said at last. "There were houses on the farmland. And a bridge, over my head. I could see people walking on it."

Robert took Carolyn's hand. "Trellis must have buried her under the bridge," he said. "We have to find her, or she'll never let Cassie go!"

"I'm not leaving my daughter!"

"You can't help her now!" Robert insisted. "You have to give Nicole what she wants!"

Cassie screamed again, jolting Carolyn. What could she do, standing here? She had to help Robert find Nicole's remains!

"Come on," Robert said, hurrying back down the hall. "There's a toolshed in the backyard—there must be shovels we can use!"

Carolyn looked back over her shoulder at the surrealistic images outside the front door, afraid that taking her eyes from them would make them go away.

Would make Cassie go away.

"Carolyn, hurry!"

Robert pulled her into the kitchen and out the back door. They stumbled through the tall grass to an old, broken-down metal shed. The rusted lock broke easily with one blow of Robert's fist, letting the door fall open at an angle. Robert inched his way inside the black cavern, feeling the walls. An axe, an old lawnmower, something made of net. . . .

"Here!" he shouted, pulling a shovel from the wall. He felt in the darkness, and found another right next to the first.

Because of the late hour, there were no people on the bridge, but this fact didn't even register with them. They stopped at its edge, staring at the vast stretch of land and water below the bridge.

"Where do we start?" Carolyn asked, discouraged.

Robert thought hard.

"No one found her remains when this bridge was built," he said, "so she can't be buried near the supports. And I don't think anyone in those days had the equipment for an underwater burial. She has to be under or close to these rocks."

Without another word, Carolyn hurried onto the slippery, lake-grass-covered slabs. She poked her shovel between them, trying to find some clue that would lead her to Nicole Morgan's grave. Robert worked a short distance away, throwing shovelfuls of sand into the water.

Carolyn began to cry. She'd never see her daughter again! There was nothing here!

"If she's underneath the rocks," Robert said, "it'll take heavy machinery to find her!"

"We don't have time for that!"

Robert shook his head. "I just don't know what else to do, Carolyn!"

"I won't let that monster have my baby!" She began to stab the shovel into the sand, tears blinding her. It seemed so hopeless, so useless.

And then, a miracle.

The moonlight caught something in the hole.

Carolyn bent to retrieve it, then waved it over her head with a triumphant cry.

"She *is* here!" she yelled. "She's here!"

Robert took the scrap of rotted fabric from her and looked at the silver button that had been sewn to it. He didn't know about antiques, but he guessed that this button hadn't decorated any modern garment. Quickly, he retrieved his shovel and began to dig.

The tiny skeleton was so close to the surface that it seemed impossible no one had discovered it before.

"The rocks must have formed a barrier," Robert said, digging away at the sand, "keeping the wind from unearthing her."

She was dressed in the same pinafore frock that the ghost Nicole wore, only this one had rotted to shreds.

"That's her," Carolyn whispered.

"Look at her skull," Robert said. "Trellis must have hit her over and over, just like she said."

Half the small skull was caved in, evidence of the murder that had been committed here so long ago. Carolyn was reminded of Norman Hollenbeck.

"We have to go back to Cassie," she said, her fear rising again as she realized how much time they'd taken.

She picked up the skeleton and ran into the house with it. The front door was still open wide, but the bizarre scene of a short while ago was gone. Beyond the door was only the street, and the street lamps, and the houses. There was no sign of Nicole —or of Cassie.

"Oh, my God," Carolyn said. "She's killed my little girl!"

"No!" Robert cried. "It can't be too late! Give her to me!"

He took the skeleton from Carolyn and sat with it on the bottom steps, rocking it as he would rock a living child.

"Nicole, Nicole," he whispered. "We know what that beast Trellis did to you. We know the truth now! You don't need to hurt anyone. Just let Cassie go, and we'll take you to your sister!"

Understanding what Robert was doing, Carolyn sat down next to him. She reached toward the skeleton with a trembling hand, thinking how insane this must look, not thinking that there was no one to see.

"Nicole, I know you love Adele," she said, her voice tremulous. "She was all you had in the world. Well, Cassie's all I have. Please don't take her from me!"

The house was deathly still, the two adults making a bizarre family portrait with the skeletal child. Carolyn stood up, her fists clenched.

"Give my daughter back to me, Nicole! Give her to me, and you'll see Adele again. Please!"

Robert cried out, and Carolyn looked down to see that he was holding Nicole, the semblance of a living child. Nicole looked up at him with wide, innocent eyes, blood trickling from the wound on her head.

"I just want to see Adele again," she said, softly.

She closed her eyes, and faded away to the skeleton once more.

The sound of screeching brakes made Carolyn leap for the front door. A car had stopped just in time to miss hitting Cassie's unconscious body in the middle of the street. The driver jumped out, yelling, as Carolyn ran to take her daughter in her arms.

"What's she doing in the street?" the driver demanded.

Cassie opened her eyes, but threw her hands up to shield her face and began to scream. "The horse! The horse!"

"What horse?" the driver asked, confused. "Is she okay?"

Carolyn pulled her daughter close, hugging her tightly.

"She's fine," she said, a strange smile spreading over her face. It faded away, and tears of relief began to fall. "Oh, thank God, she's just fine!"

EPILOGUE

CASSIE SAT IN the living room at her mother's feet, dangling a piece of yarn over a tiny, tabby-striped kitten. She was pretending not to be interested in the conversation of the adults around her, but was in fact listening very carefully. Her mother had taken the armchair, while Robert and Susan shared the plaid couch. Susan had brought the kitten to the hospital this morning as a coming-home gift for Cassie after the night she had spent there for observation. A lot of people had looked at her, but no one had found anything to worry about. That's what they had told her mother. But Cassie was still worried, because she wasn't one hundred percent sure Nicole was really gone.

"Think of a name for your kitty yet?" Susan asked.

Cassie shook her head.

"It was sweet of you to bring it," Carolyn said. She lowered her voice, although Cassie was too near to make whispering worth the effort. "It'll give her something else to think about."

The kitten got up and ran out of the room. Cassie

stood up and followed it.

"Finally," Carolyn said. "I've been wanting to talk to you, but things were so hectic last night there was no chance. Now that Cassie's home and safe, I'd like to know what made you come back to the house last night, Robert."

"It was Susan's detective work, really," Robert said. "She was the one who learned what had happened all those years ago at the Hollenbeck mansion."

Susan picked up a copy of a magazine and began to fan herself with it. Reaching for the pitcher on the end table between her chair and the couch, Carolyn refilled everyone's iced-tea glasses.

"It was the Trellis home when this story began," Susan said. "I did some research, and I learned that the original owner of Myrtle's house, a man named Karl Trellis, had been accused of murdering a little girl named Nicole Morgan. It was her sister, Adele, who pointed a finger at him."

"Both little girls had been passengers on an orphan train," Robert put in. Seeing the look of confusion on Carolyn's face, he explained, "A century ago, when there were no public funds for caring for unwanted children, the orphan trains were offered as one solution. Parents with too many mouths to feed would pack off a few of their kids to the Midwest, hoping farmers would take them in and care for them, in exchange for work."

Carolyn thought about what had happened last night, how Nicole had referred to Cassie as Adele.

"She saw my daughter as her sister," she said.

"It seems that way," Susan answered. "The two

girls were separated at the train station, and Nicole was never seen again. Adele was convinced that something bad had happened, but because she was so young she couldn't do anything about it. As time went on, she improved her station in life and married one of the town's richest, most influential men. He helped her pursue her quest for the truth, and demanded that Trellis explain what had happened to the little girl. Instead, Karl Trellis disappeared, never to be seen again."

Robert put his empty tea glass on the table. "Adele never gave up the fight to prove that something had happened to her sister," he said. "She claimed to the day she died that Nicole had been murdered."

"But what brought Nicole out?" Carolyn asked. "Why, after all those years?"

"There were no children in the house until the Hollenbecks came along," Robert explained. "She must have seen Ellen as her sister, just like Cassie."

Carolyn thought for a moment, leaning back in the chair. "Norman must have tried to protect Ellen," she said. "That's why she killed him, as well as her. But why did she choose Cassie? My daughter never went to that house until this Nicole talked her into it. She knew it wasn't allowed."

"Myrtle might have been a protective influence in the house," Susan said, "whether she knew it or not. It was shortly after her death that Nicole came out again. In fact, I believe Nicole was the one who forced the old woman to suicide."

"That child was evil," Carolyn said. "In spite of the reasons for her actions, you'll forgive me if I can't feel sorry for her. When I think of the people she hurt . . ."

No one knew what to say now. The image of Rita Montana's body being dragged from the lake early that morning was fixed in all three of their minds. Andy Montana had packed his car, collected his children from the hospital, and left Lake Solaria without saying good-bye to anyone. There was talk that the Westins were planning to sell their house, and other people on the lake were considering doing the same.

"I won't leave," Carolyn said abruptly.

"What was that, Carolyn?" Susan asked.

"I was just thinking of all the people who are leaving Lake Solaria," Carolyn said. "I'm not going to be one of them. Even with all the things that have happened here, I love this place, and I don't want to raise my daughter anywhere else."

Robert smiled. "I'm glad to hear that," he said. "Now I'll know where to find you."

Carolyn looked up at him. "Why would you want to do that?" I thought this was over."

"Our business together is over," Robert said. "That's why I'm hoping you'll say yes to dinner some night."

Before Carolyn could answer, he held up his hands. "I know you can't leave Cassie right now," he said. "But in a few weeks, when this has blown over and she's back into the routine of school and other friends, maybe you'd like to go to Nick and Herb's, for dinner."

"Oh, I've always wanted to try that place," Carolyn said, smiling a little, but with hesitation in her tone. She'd only known Robert through this case, and though she found him very nice she wasn't certain about dating him. It was so hard, even this long after Paul's death, to accept another man in her life.

"We could double-date," Susan said, coming to the rescue. "You and Robert and me and Chris. It'll be great, Carolyn."

Carolyn's smile broadened, and she nodded vigorously. Why shouldn't she enjoy herself, after all that had happened? She would give Cassie and herself time to put their lives back together. But not too much time. It had been dark on Lake Solaria for too many years, and it was time for the sun to shine again.

SPINE-TINGLING
HORROR FROM TOR